VALE BORN

Lorin Petrazilka

FATEBOUND BOOKS
A WOMEN-OWNED IMPRINT

The content of this book is protected under Federal Copyright Laws. Any unauthorized use of this material is prohibited. No portion of this book may be reproduced in any form without express written permission from the author.

Vale Born
First Edition
Copyright 2020 Lorin Z Pillai

All Rights Reserved. Printed in the United States of America.

Published by Fatebound Books
For rights inquires, please contact rights@fateboundbooks.com

FATEBOUND BOOKS

ISBN 978-1-7360622-4-1 (hardcover)
ISBN 978-1-7360622-0-3 (paperback)
ISBN 978-1-7360622-1-0(e-book)
Cover design by Alberto Carranza and Lorin Z Pillai

This is a work of fiction. Names, characters, places, and incidents either are the products of the author's imagination or are used fictitiously. Any resemblance to actual persons, living or dead, businesses, events, companies or locales are entirely coincidence.

Dedicated to anyone who faltered in their path finding their way. The most interesting people in the world are forever becoming who they are.

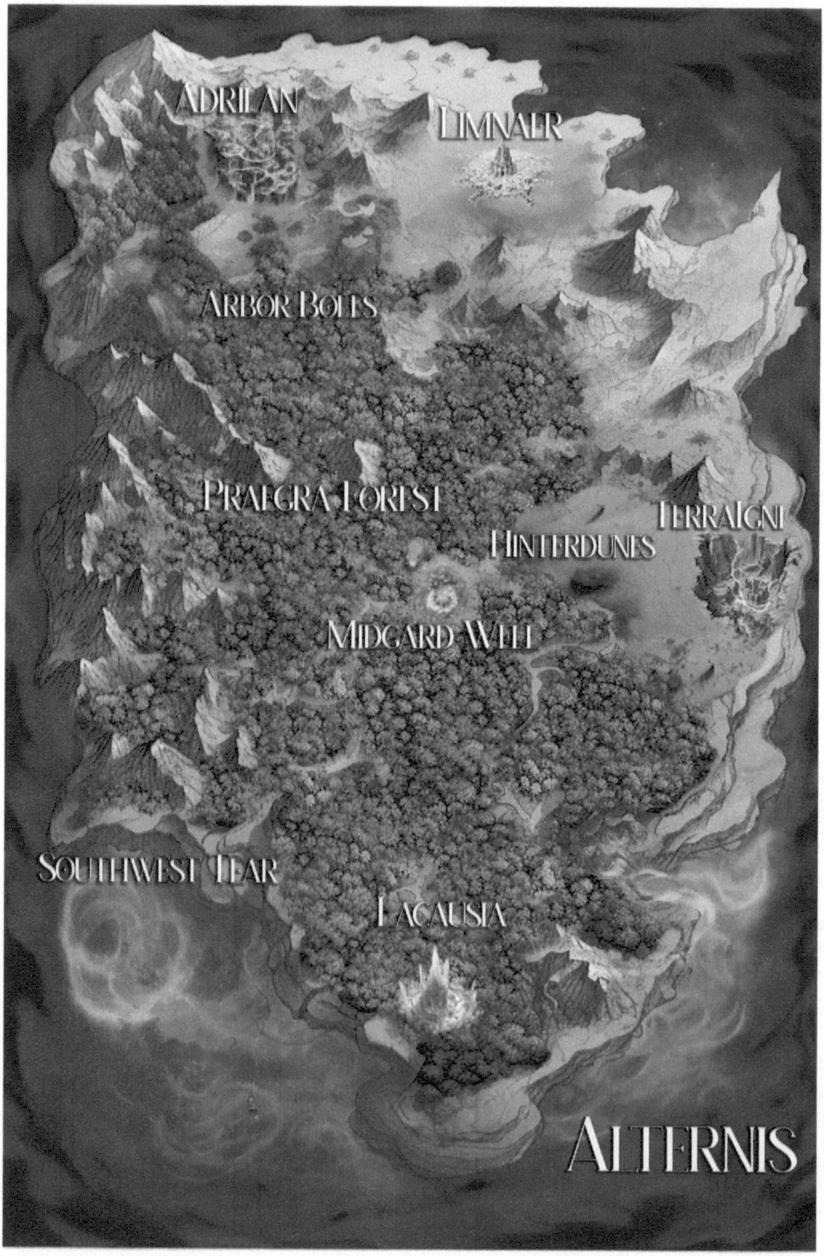

Adrilan
Limnalr
Arbor Boles
Praegra Forest
Hinterdunes
TerraIgni
Midgard Welt
Southwest Tear
Lacausia
Alternis

TABLE OF CONTENTS

CHAPTER 1

I stumbled and crawled on my knees, clawing the fine, foreign dirt now thankfully beneath my hands. Moments before there had been nothing to hold to. Sucked into a chaotic passage and dragged through it like a twig in a thundering river, my fingers had raked at walls that weren't there. I had struggled to find purchase with flailing limbs, to pull myself back to the glen—the one I never should have gone to in the first place, at the farthest edge of my rural California town. The glimmer of light I had seen in the trees lied to me, it conveyed longing, yearning. It told me I wanted to come closer, so I did. Foolish, Lily, so foolish. Though I suppose it gave me exactly what I asked for, what I'd galloped my horse out into the hills for—a way out. A reprieve from my failures, my static life, my lack-luster college career. And more. Searching the hills for Josie Brooks had become an obsession, my only friend vanishing had left me single-minded.

Ragged breaths shuddered through me, my chest constricted and hands balled into involuntary fists, as I finally gave way and crumpled to the ground.

Debris stuck to my tear-streaked face and hair from my braid clung to my neck. I cradled my legs with teeth clenched and eyes squeezed shut, my brows formed a knot. The inevitable digression that always followed a trigger event had started. Bad memories that waited to edge out my logical, steady self finally elbowed their way to the surface. Coiled around my mind like dark demons squatting inside me, they tightened—getting more of a foothold as they re-played yet again; a firestorm, unchecked and rolling across the land like an angry god intent on destruction. Embers rained, singeing my skin as I struggled to kick my immovable rock of a horse on-ward, with the flames fast approaching.

Not again, count, just count. I moved my lips, but no words came out. Pulling my knees tighter to my chest, I forced a slow breath. That was always the hardest part, the first measured inhale when all my body wanted to do was to hyperventilate.

The second breath came easier, but as I exhaled the vision of what had brought on this current episode flashed in my mind: plagued by indecision on whether covering my ears or my eyes would be more effective. Loud, electrified cracks had zipped through the air, as multicolor lights strobes and flashed. I slid through the vortex, unprotected from the chaos, to where I now lay panting. Both terrifying darkness and impossible brightness had saturated the tunnel, the memory of the stark contrast made me cringe. And the pain, the horrible pain that scorched through my body, with the sensation of being stretched and pulled beyond my physical limits.

No. I forced another slow breath through my nose as I tried to quiet my mind. I opened my eyes and shook out my hands, my fingers still curled and locked as I struggled onto my shins. *Three, two, one, you are safe.*

But was I? I hadn't even looked around, I couldn't. The transition through the passage was like what I imagined birth must be like, so turbulent that babies can't remember it, pushed from everything they knew into a loud, harsh world.

I placed my hands under my shoulders, into the ground, and struggled to get up.

I blinked several times to force my vision to adjust, when blinding pain shot through the arches of my feet. I squinted and cringed at my paddock boots, scuffed and worn with years of use. They were farther away than I would expect, like looking at them through a wide angle lens. The leather domed on top, distending from my feet inside. I bent over to unlace them, forcing them open so I could wriggle my feet free.

As I wrenched out the first foot, I did a double take. My feet were larger, longer, and stronger. I worked off my other boot and sock, both feet had grown at least two sizes. I traced the red marks left by the stitched toe piece, normally not even in contact with my foot.

My eyes shifted up to the hem of my riding breeches, now good eight inches higher up my calf, the seams shrieked with stress and constricted my skin. My shin bones ached like a ten year old's in the midst of a massive growth spurt.

The distraction of my painful feet passed, and the memory of where I was struck me. Or rather, the fact that I didn't know where I was. I shot up and looked around. My jaw dropped and eyes rounded as I took in my surroundings.

I stood on a smooth rocky landing, at the peak of a huge precipice. Edging toward the drop off, I peered over the descent.

Thick, woody vines grew across the vertical surface, down into a forested area far below. Gone was the glen of Black Oak Grove, there was nothing recognizable about the landscape I now gazed toward. Trees so tall they loomed higher than the cliff I was perched on, bigger by far than the great sequoias I had visited when my family was still whole.

I spun around to face where I had come from, if I could see the tunnel by which I traversed here, or the circle of oaks that marked the entrance to the hidden passage, or my horse Apollo beyond that.

None of those things were there.

CHAPTER 2

There was no trace of the riotous tunnel, all I was greeted by were multitudes of curving brambles. I reached a hand forward to touch the mass of vines, twisted in a radiating fan from a central point. The tight knot they formed felt impenetrable as I probed it. I pushed harder, wriggling my fingers in trying to see if it would open for me. Broken nails and scratches across my knuckles was all I got for the effort.

I pushed more insistently, but the branches did not give way. The woody overgrowth didn't seem like it had ever been anything other than a tangled mess. I realized, as I clawed the vines, that the dense border of trees surrounding the trails of Black Oak Grove was there for a reason. I should have stayed away, and listened to the old lore about people who disappeared after wandering too far. Whispers echoed in my mind about how the forest swallowed them, never to be seen again. Was this how Josie had disappeared? But then there were the other whispers, the little voices that had told me since I was young to make my way out into the hills. The same whispers that Josie had heard, she had confided in me before she wandered off. Years of hearing their quiet songs, of promise and magic, of what waited beyond. The warnings of the townspeople lasted only so long. I had followed that beckoning call eventually, riding Apollo all the way out to the forbidden hillside stream to try and escape, with the faint hope I would find my best friend in the process. Just a few weeks my junior and my lifelong friend, she had disappeared two days before her twenty-first birthday. I shook my head and pursed my lips at the idea we had hatched for our party: camping out in the desert and drinking around a campfire, blasting our music under the stars. Even though it was just going to be us and my brother Felix, they were plans we never got to fulfill. Maybe there was a chance she had slipped through the passage, just as I had.

I turned back to the lush landscape, beyond the impossibly high drop. With no path down, and nothing up at the top of the spire I stood upon, I had few options. Less than few.

I looked out at the huge trees that sprang up intermittently from the ground far below, which rose to dizzying heights. Tiny lights illuminated the wide trunks in spiral paths up the bark. A large, glowing patch nestled far off in the forest floor snared my attention, the ethereal light it emitted was like a luminous gem cradled in a soft moss.

I should have been terrified, cut off from my family, my horse, my life. But I wasn't. Calmness washed over me. Euphoria. Belonging. My usual reaction to panic or gasp in rapid, shallow breaths hung back in the recesses of my consciousness, like it was someone else entirely that endured those effects in the past. I watched intently as the glowing center pulsed little flits of light. The droplets of energy floated outward from the source, some blinking out of existence, some venturing farther. Their mesmerizing colors shifted between every hue.

One increased in brightness, and followed a meandering path toward me. I gaped at it as it drew nearer. A high-pitched sound vibrated from it as it approached. My ears tingled and twitched in response, sending a delighted shiver down my spine. I laughed at the feeling, and raised my hands to feel my ears.

Shock and wonder filled me as I brushed them with my fingertips. Gone were my small, softly rounded ears. My human ears. In their place were pointed, stiff extremities that swooped up, a good two inches taller than what was there before.

I dropped my hands as the orb floated closer, the sensations I felt from it now a clash of overjoyed excitement and unbearable stimuli. I followed the fleck and raised my hand to touch it, but the little ball was already out of reach. The center of the knotted vines uncoiled slightly, allowing it to slip through, into the hidden passage beyond.

I scrabbled at the opening, which had promptly shut itself again. I puffed my lips as I turned back around, then resolved to find a way down off the ledge.

My stomach dropped as I peered over the edge, the vines twisted haphazardly down the whole way. The bottom loomed—hazy and indistinct—far below the vertical drop. My nerves flurried at the thought of climbing down.

I knelt down and pulled the closest strand, averting my eyes from the terrifying abyss. The thick branch was solid and mostly stable, but shifted a little. I closed my eyes and took a steadying breath. *I can do this.*

I swung my legs over the edge and began to lower myself. I

grasped the mass of natural ropes as I eased my weight onto them. I looked at my grip and almost let go in surprise, my hands were bigger, and longer too.

If only Felix could see me now, he would for once be jealous of me—rather than the other way around. As I grabbed back onto the vine I sucked in a breath, when realization dawned. It wasn't just a physical change. I felt empowered. Alive.

Something surged below my skin as I began my descent, hand over hand, lowering myself faster and faster. Each swing down was liberating, though my body felt new and strange, I had a surety of movement I had never known before.

The fear completely vanished, whisked away by the rapid, confident traverse downward. I reached the bottom and settled my feet into place on the ground.

"Well that was easy!" I exclaimed aloud with my fists on my hips, as I looked with pride at the enormous drop I had just mastered.

"I would expect nothing less from a Vale Born," a melodic, deep voice announced from behind.

CHAPTER 3

I snapped my head in the direction the voice had come from, my fight-or-flight instincts surged. I shifted my weight back on one foot ready to run, as my heart thundered in my chest.

I froze, not even a breath escaped when I saw him.

He stood like a stag on an outcropping of rocks, without a doubt he was the most beautiful being I had ever seen. My new-found confidence shattered as I lost my ability to speak at the sight of him.

"Being" was the closest thing I could think to call him. He twitched his tall, piked ears, and stared—unblinking. His subtle movements and long muscular legs gave me the distinct impression that he was built for speed and agility. The talons, which extended out from his strong, unshoed feet, told me immediately that he was a predator.

But his face.

His perfect face like chiseled marble was what I could not stop staring at. He looked at me from under opal white eyebrows, arched like the wings of a bird of prey.

I was still sizing him up from a distance when he asked, "May I approach you? I promise I will not bite." His nearly white, braided hair fell over his shoulder as he moved, the opalescent sheen shifted colors with the slightest movement.

When I hesitated, a smile spread on his face that all but disarmed me. Sensuous lips revealed perfect, gleaming white teeth with elongated canines. The approving look he gave as he passed his brilliant teal eyes over my curves made my core tremble.

I finally nodded, my words could not escape my mouth.

He strode over in long strides, stopping just in front of me, then went completely still. Humans could never be that still, it was unnerving to see a humanoid creature cease motion. I flinched at his size, with him perched over me I realized how imposing he was. His substantial, honed muscles and complete lack of covering besides his teal calf-length breeches was a lot to take in—which I did without hiding my sweeping glance well. *Um, why am I still standing like this?* I moved my feet into a more relaxed stance with as much grace as I could manage—which was none.

When I still didn't speak he asked, "Have you ventured into the Vale before?"

"The Vale? I ended up here by accident just awhile ago, I didn't know it was here," I mustered a response at last.

He regarded me for a moment. "Surely as Vale Born, you must have sensed it was here."

Standing so close to him, his features were even more distracting. The luminous glow his silvery skin gave off made me want to reach up and touch it. *Stop staring, Lily! Get a hold of yourself!*

My mind cleared finally. "Well, I had always felt a pull to... what is Vale Born? I've never heard the term. Where exactly am I?

And who are you?"

He smiled again and replied, "Let us take a walk as I answer you. I can show you my realm and explain as best I can. I could take you to Lacausia Palace, where my kind live."

He offered his arm, though I didn't take it. I still didn't know what to make of this charming being and the new reality I had entered. "I should probably try to get back home. I don't want to make my family worry." I shifted away from him and flashed a glance up at the vines. I should have tried harder to get back into the bramble. If I were just to vanish—even just for a little while—it might send my mom and Felix into a panic. After Josie's disappearance six months ago, I just couldn't do that to them, vanish without a trace. Six months I had gone without her, the sister void she filled vacant again as I once more closed myself off from all others.

He lifted a hand toward me and said, "I will tell you that although our realm occupies much of the same space as the human realm, we are out of temporal sync. We exist in a different matter resonance. For every twenty eight rotations here there is only one rotation in the human world. You have some time before it will even be noticed that you are not there. Perhaps, it is acceptable to venture a little further? At least let me show you the castle."

"So...same place, different time?"

"Same place, different frequency. The offset inherently changes the time."

I furrowed my brows. *Ridiculous.* I mulled it over for a few moments. Apollo had appeared nearly frozen in time when I entered the perfect circle of trees, right before the vortex started. It did seem to add up that time could be different here. Most likely it was a dream, it was all too fantastical.

At last I nodded. The dashing male smiled again and gestured with his palm, toward the path ahead. He strolled by my side, with his hands respectfully clasped behind his back.

We crested the rocks I had first seen him standing on, then walked down a gentle descent to the mossy forest floor. I stopped in my tracks to gaze at the foliage. Greens and blues that cast a soft glow surrounded every unusual leaf, and luminescent lavender flowers sprouted up from the moss in silky blankets. My guide turned to me, urging me forward with an angled nod of his head. As I moved I realized every step I took caused a phosphorescent reaction in the lush ground.

"That is the energy of the moss interacting with your own, lovely is it not?" He mentioned. I nodded in amazement as we continued to walk. It took significant effort not to stop and absorb every ounce of the wondrous view, to touch the velvety leaves or to nuzzle my toes into the pillowy softness of the ground.

"I am called Opius, I am an Umorfae," he said as he gestured yet again to move along.

I half-halted and glanced at him sidelong, I had almost forgotten I still didn't know his name. I was still doubting him, all of it. I could just be at the creekside napping, while Apollo played in the water. Maybe I drifted off then. *Wake up, Alice!* I joked to myself. I frankly didn't want to wake up yet, if it was a dream, going back to my reality did not sound appealing.

He huffed a laugh at the skeptical look I gave him. "I realize this must be a bit overwhelming. Shall I continue?"

"Yes, I'm sorry. It's just...I was trying to decide if I might be dreaming. All of this sounds like what we call a fairy tale. Not real."

"Well, you are here, which tells me you are Vale Born. You would not be able to venture here otherwise. Vale Born are Fae hybrids and the only humans that can enter our realm by way of a tear."

I blinked, still processing the absurdity of it all. "Are others like me...common here? Has another come here recently? Light brown hair, named Josie. Tall, thin, pretty. Did you see her?"

"No, not common at all. We haven't had a Vale Born visit in some time, I forget when." He waved a hand dismissively and looked away. "There are very few tears in the Vale that connect to the human realm, and those tears are only in mostly uninhabited areas. You are a rarity."

My face fell as I mulled over his response regarding Josie, or lack thereof. "What is an Umorfae?"

"You will have many more questions I believe, I will answer them for you as best I can, but for now,"-he bent down and scooped up several of the glowing flowers. Opius deftly braided their stems together with inhuman speed, then leaned toward me, tucking the bundle behind my pointed ear-"there, just beautiful." His dashing smile nearly made me swoon. He motioned to proceed down the path with his palm outstretched.

The ambient sound of the jungle was like a melody I couldn't place, vague and soothing, as we trekked deeper into the majestic forest. Flickers of light intermittently rained down from above. They faded in and out as they fell to the ground, akin to miniature falling stars giving their last light before they burned up in the atmosphere. Opius cocked a sideways smile as I marvelled at my surroundings. I gave him a sheepish grin in return. I was starting to feel more comfortable around him, though I wasn't sure if he was to be trusted completely. Like a feral animal, even if they seem docile, they may not always be safe. The edge of danger made him even more attractive, and so far he hadn't given me any reason not to trust him.

"How is it that you found me at the cliffside?" I asked. "When someone comes through the Vale, do you hear or sense it?" Maybe if he hadn't seen her, someone else might have. Perhaps I could finally find my surrogate sister and bring her to safety.

Opius narrowed his eyes at the question, then flashed a wolfish smile. "I was fortunate to be nearby when I saw you descending the vines…very fortunate."

I blushed at his husky tone, then looked down as my mouth twitched up at the corners. He still smiled at me when I looked back up through my eyelashes. We held our gaze just for a moment. My heart leaped and breath caught, the connection between us went taut with electrified tension. I cast aside my previous hesitation about him. As if he read my mind, he offered me his arm again. A coy smile crept up my face as I slid my hand against the interior of his muscled bicep, both cool and warm at the same time. He smelled of rain and waterfalls on a misty morning. I had to resist the urge to lean closer and breathe in his essence.

"What are you called?" he asked.

The question surprised me, I realized I was caught up attempting to drink him in. "My name is Lily."

He raised his chin in measured appreciation. "It is a beautiful name. What does it mean?"

It hadn't occurred to me that names and things would be different here, that there was no such thing as a lily in this world. But then, there were no Umorfae or forests that looked like this in the human world, so it made sense the reverse could be true. "It's a flower from my home, fragrant and beautiful."

He nodded his head and replied, "A perfect name for you."

I nearly giggled with glee, but managed a more confident, "Thank you."

I traversed with him for what must have been several hours, though the passage of time felt static, I couldn't see even a hint of the sun. The unusual sky gradually shifted from purple to a cobalt blue as we crossed the terrain, darker in color than the daytime skies I was familiar with, however all the surroundings were well lit. With no cast shadows and only diffused umbrages that gave no indication of light source, the lack of direct sunlight did little to help indicate time of day.

The forest thinned and the landscape transformed into a rocky terrain, with veins of sparkling ore growing within the crust. Great pools of vivid water illuminated from below appeared along our path, some flowed into each other with gently cascading waterfalls and streams. My bare feet began to ache, the mossy forest floor had given way to a harder rock base.

Opius flashed a broad smile and announced, "We are almost to my home, it is just a bit farther."

CHAPTER 4

We rounded a bend, which revealed a massive castle in the distance, composed completely of crystal. "It's like the Fortress of..." I trailed off as I beheld the impossibly beautiful structure. My words failed me, I couldn't tear my eyes from the refracted light, and the spectral colors displayed within the walls.

"Fortress of what?" Opius twitched an eyebrow up.

I was busy wondering how the walls could even refract the light, if it were not directly hitting the surface, when I heard his question. "Oh, uh, it's a human thing. Well...actually not really even a human thing but it reminded me of a story," I babbled. I couldn't think of a fair comparison.

I walked behind him onto a sweeping bridge, suspended over a brilliant river. I wanted to stop and stare at the huge quartz monoliths which rose up for the towers, and the enormous swaths of translucent azure stone that made up the sides of the palace.

Two guards flanked either side of the imposing doors, past a stone arch. Their white hair and gleaming skin were similar to Opius, and their physiques just as honed. They rapped a fist on embossed metal chest plates, which rang as it struck their armored gauntlets. I glanced at Opius, who stared straight ahead without giving the guards so much as a nod. I mused as to who he might be, if he could so easily enter the castle with an unknown individual. Or maybe they were relaxed with security. But if they were, why have guards at all?

My mental wanderings were halted by the details on the doors, metallurgic fittings for the hinges and oversized handles formed in dark silver masses. They looked like they could interlock in a complicated jigsaw if moved closer together. I ran my hand over them as we passed, the cool metal had a polished, geometric quality, but the slightly rounded edges made it smooth to the touch. *Weirdest door handles ever.*

Light filtered in from everywhere as we entered—even the floor. A double staircase climbed up past the grand foyer, composed of cubic green and lavender transparent crystal. It rose up from millions of minuscule white mineral points and billowed in mounds beneath the risers like sparkling clouds. I could smell and feel the water before I saw it, streams of it washed down along the pale stone into luminous pools, which collected between the two sides of the crystalline stairs.

From the large towers, to the battlements, to the perfectly placed moat and the precise portcullis all made of seemingly unhewn mineral, I realized the whole castle had been grown, rather than built. Not only were the formations incredible crystal specimens, they had been grown with intent and purpose, rather than haphazardly as they do in the human world. Their value must have been immeasurable.

Opius took my hand as we approached the stairs. "Come, I

have quarters here, allow me to show you to your room that you may freshen up."

Without waiting for my acceptance he drew me up the stairs, then through a long corridor. An inlet off the hall housed several translucent doors arranged in a large half circle. He pushed open the first one, which swung silently inward. The expansive room was nothing short of breathtaking. The cool smoothness of the gleaming white quartz floors was soft on my aching feet. Dark, glittery veins laced the precision laid tiles.

A tub made entirely of polished amethyst practically called my name. It took up a large portion of one side of the room, and a massive bed made of the same sleek mineral was on the opposite side. I wanted to run across the spotless floor and flop down in the regal-looking bed, and feel the gossamer curtains that hung down on all sides of it.

"Everything you might need is near the bath for you, I will have fresh clothing sent up shortly. My room is just across the hall whenever you are done. But please, take your time and enjoy." He turned, then shut the door as he left before I thought to thank him.

I was speechless, I had never been so pampered. I was used to life on a ranch, having to shower quickly and spend little time on primping.

I found the bath was already prepared and dipped my hand in. The warm, silky water comforted my mud-crusted fingers. I patted my tangled braid, which was a mess with flyaways. Most of my hair was not even in the plait anymore, little strands stuck to my face. I undid the tie, then shook it out. *This bitch needs soap*, I sneered at my now loose, wild mane. The forgotten flowers he had placed behind my ear fell on the floor, right next to the dirt that had flaked onto it. I picked them up, turning over the soft petals which still glowed with a faint pulse. I smirked, it was probably the only clean, lovely thing that had been on me.

I set them down then started to undress, finding my impossibly tight clothes problematic to take off. I grunted with difficulty as I tugged at them ungracefully, eventually freeing myself from their unbearable compression.

At last I slipped into the luxurious tub. I sighed with relief as I sunk lower in, then ducked my head under, my hair fanned out in floating tendrils. After a few moments of soaking, I crested the water to reach for whatever was available to wash with. I experimented with the various soaps and oils while I lounged. Hints of lemon verbena mixed with a scent that reminded me of a bountiful garden on a late spring day wafted out of the faceted bottles. The amount of dirt that washed off of me was cringeworthy. I must have looked a mess to Opius, just a muddy ranch girl that stumbled into his perfect world.

When I finally emerged and reached for a towel, my eyes fell on clothes that had been dropped off, on the corner of the entryway table. I hadn't seen or heard someone bring them in. My old clothes had been removed from where I left them crumpled on the floor, as well as the dirt and dust that had shaken onto the tiles in the process.

I finished toweling off my hair and sat down at the vanity to investigate the drawers contents. A gorgeous heavy hairbrush, its metal handle inlaid with abalone shells, rested on a mirrored tray in one drawer. I wrinkled my nose at a small makeup set in another drawer, I was never good at applying it. Unused eye shadows made from shimmering ore, lip color and a fine, anemone-like brush were neatly arranged in the palette. I set them out, selected the most neutral color for my lips, then raised my hand to my face to apply some.

I practically dropped the brush when I finally looked at myself in the mirror, my face was not my own. Slowly, I turned my head, more angular in the jaw and cheekbones, my eyes bigger with irises that were a more intense shade of gold, flecked with bright green. As I studied my face, my pupils dilated and contracted quicker. My sight scanned in almost a mechanical fashion, picking up the most minute details and mentally noting with speed the changes reflected.

I stood up from the chair, the body I had known for years being altered was a shock to say the least. I was always confident in my own skin—even with my human imperfections—and didn't feel the need to change myself. As I stared, I remembered the pain as I had come through the Vale. The horrible ache that had surged through me must have been my body elongating.

Why did I change? Longer legs meant I'd be faster, planed facial features would mean better draft and less drag. The science geek in me tried to parse out and rationalize why the passage had affected me. And how, for that matter.

I shrugged and stepped over to the clothes that had been left for me, then grimaced as I held them up. Short-cropped and sleeveless, the blouse would barely cover me. A sheer fluttering swag hung from the back. *Oh man, when have I ever worn anything like this.* I looked around for my riding clothes. Dirty though they were—not to mention painfully small—at least I'd feel like myself. It didn't take long to confirm they weren't there, and this was all I had to wear.

I ran my hand over the whisper-light material, then slipped them on. They settled with a nearly imperceptible kiss against my skin. The skirt—fitted at the top—transitioned down to a high hem in the front that swept to a long sheer train in the back. The uniquely thin fabric, like lavender-white chiffon, gradually shifted from opaque in the bust and hip area down to nearly transparent at the hemlines with no visible stitching.

Feeling exposed as I looked at myself in the mirror. I had to stave off the instinct to cover my bare abdomen with crossed arms. *This is what they gave you, Lily, so you might as well own it!* I glanced at the makeup, debating if I should bother an attempt. I leaned into the mirror and tried to apply the unusual lipstick, it was awkward to maneuver the strange brush. After five attempts I puckered my lips at my reflection, mildly presentable at least. I swept some of the darkest blue crushed ore on my eyelids. Swiveling from side to side, the colors shifted from blue-black to purple. Not quite a straight line on the eyeshadow, and the lipstick definitely needed help, but hopefully passable. I squared my shoulders and lifted my chin, then turned to step out into the hallway to look for Opius.

CHAPTER 5

Startled by a knock on the door as I reached for it, I opened it to see Opius standing there, hands clasped behind his back.

Even more magnificent than before, his waistcoat and calf-length pants made of pale blue silk shimmered, as his muscles shifted below the fabric. He glanced down as he ran his hand across the side of his silvery opal hair, half back in a low braid. As he met my eyes again, the subtle arch he quirked his brow into made my breath hitch.

"You look beautiful, I hope you enjoyed the bath."

I blushed, the butterflies flurried in my stomach as I responded, "It was most refreshing." Truth be told, I was trying to speak more eloquently. His formal manner made me self-conscious of the way I spoke.

He smiled that devilish grin of his. "I am glad to hear that. I imagine you are hungry. We have nocte fare waiting for us in the dining room." He turned, offering his substantial arm.

The drape of my garment fluttered as we turned right out of the ring of doors. Corridors and staircases opened to either side intermittently as he guided me further into the palace. I lost count of how many we passed by the time we descended a set of stairs, framed by twin, structured waterfalls that cascaded down in precise frequency. Perfect in its design, fifteen steps down and five equal falls bubbled as we swished past. I wondered as I gazed at the impressive structure, if this castle was grown, who grew it?

I was still lost in thought when we reached the bottom of the stairs, then entered a wide dining room. My eyes adjusted to the low light of the room, darker by far than the rest of the palace. To offset the darkness, mineral sconces dotted the walls, emitting a soft glow.

"Will anyone else be joining us?" I asked my solitary host as I looked around, the entire palace felt devoid of life. He moved to pull out a chair at the solid onyx table, large enough to seat at least twenty and took up most of the room.

"No one will join us for this meal. However, our arrival was not announced. I thought we could enjoy this nocte together, then tomorrow I can introduce you to Empress Celestine. Someone should be along soon, to serve us," he said as he motioned for me to take the seat.

I stared at him wide-eyed. The thought of meeting an empress gave me instant panic, I had never met anyone of real status before. Would I even know how to act? My mind started to race before I managed to grab hold of the mental reins, *fake it till you make it, Lily.* I finally moved my feet to sit when his face darkened at my hesitation.

I forced a smile at him, trying not to think about what it might be like to meet an empress. Some might think it exciting. To me, it sounded terrifying.

I took a steadying breath and lined up my place setting to keep my hands busy, adjusting the gleaming stone plate that was in front of me. A waterfall centerpiece burbled on the table, offering a soothing sound to my noisy mind and otherwise quiet room.

I sat watching it, when Opius asked, "Would you like a glass of water while we wait for our first course?"

I nodded, becoming instantly parched once he offered. I hadn't had any since I downed a tall glass in my family kitchen before heading down to the barn, which felt like an eternity ago.

He held out his hand toward the fountain, then rolled his fingers inward and flicked his wrist. Water began drawing off the fountain in a steady, midair runnel. My jaw dropped as he directed it to my glass, and filled it while I gaped. He shifted the stream and moved it to his. Once it neared the brim he sent the stream back to the fountain. My mouth hung open as he took a sip.

"My kind have superior powers over water, we are able to survive under it for long periods, and control it to our will."

"Well that was something!..Show off," I finally said with a chiding smile as I raised my glass to my lips.

He snapped his head at me and shot his eyebrows up. After a heartbeat he threw back his head and laughed heartily.

I giggled and added, "That's what humans call an ice breaker."

He laughed a little more, beaming as he leaned closer. "I quite enjoyed it," he said as he reached his hand forward to cover mine.

Smiling at each other, the air charged with attraction. My chest heated and breath quickened. We were still studying each other, when a form appeared in my peripheral vision.

I tore my eyes away to see a lithe, small creature, beautiful and graceful, with her heart-shaped face lowered in deference. She kept her extremely large, black eyes averted downward as she set a tray on the table. I spied gills below her jaw, and webbed hands and feet, as well as a delicate dorsal fin which peeked out from underneath her waist-length black hair. I had initially mistaken the fin for a part of her garment, which looked similar to the blue green iridescent membrane. Clearly an aquatic being, though not an Umorfae. Opius didn't glance away from me as she finished setting the plates in place.

She startled when I thanked her, but didn't look up, and instead turned to leave the room without a word.

The trays she brought were laden with food and decanters; strange oysters, steamed crustaceans with tiny ramekins of a cream sauce, and bowls of dark green noodles. Opius reached for one of the two crystal carafes, filled with a pale pink liquid.

"This is a special vintage called vinisomn, made here. Would you like to try some?" He asked as he was already pouring. I nodded and accepted it.

"May your rotation be as sweet as the vinisomn, may your nocte be sweeter." He gave me a mischievous grin that made me nervously giggle, then intently watched as I raised the glass to my lips.

We eyed each other as we sipped, the moment I tasted it I flashed my eyes to my glass. An explosion of flavors danced on my tongue, familiar ones like strawberry and rose combined with memories of feelings: mist on my face and mouth in the early morning, or being momentarily sun-warmed on a brisk spring day.

"I don't know if we have anything like this in the human world. It's wonderful."

He laughed lightly. "Even here in Alternis it is unique. Not many others compare."

"Alternis?" I asked as I finished my first glass, I could easily overindulge with the exceptional wine.

"The name of our realm as a whole. There are many territories within. It used to be called T'al Belgranrael. But, our former ruler chose to rename it as he saw fit," he answered and began serving the artfully arranged food. I wasn't normally one for seafood, but I wasn't surprised that was the fare given the fact they were a water-centric people. *Just smile and be nice even if you don't like it.* He poured us each a glass from the smaller bottle, and a refill of the wine.

"This drink is meant to be had with the shell meats. It is strong, so take small sips. It is called vocafortis." He demonstrated, taking the oyster all in one bite off the shell, then drank a sip and swallowed.

I stifled a groan. I had oysters once, I didn't like the experience. The person I had them with had described them as a "meaty slurp", there's probably not a more horrible sounding description than that. I pushed the image from my mind, as well as the face that popped up with the memory. Just another guy that tried to use tricks to get my affection, before I was ready to give it.

I tentatively slid it off the shell with my teeth and swallowed, following with the vocafortis. The shot complimented the crisp saltiness and started to warm my stomach right away. I smiled, then took another bite and sip. *Okay, not so terrible after all.*

I copied him as he moved around his plate, eating some of the other offerings. Periodically taking a sip of the wine, or vocafortis if I had another oyster-thing. My blood warmed and cheeks flushed as we ate and drank more.

I leaned back in my chair when the petite server came back in bearing another tray. She lowered it gently and removed the used plates. I tried to smile at her, but she kept her almond-shaped eyes down and rushed out of the dining room. He poured more wine, then placed one of the dishes in front of me; white fish steaks plated with steamed leafy greens.

"What is your role here at the castle? Are you...someone of importance?" I asked.

He lifted his glass and eyed me for a moment, before leaning back in his seat to respond. "I am the Generalis of the Guard, I lead the Praetors for the Empress, and I am her cousin. I carry out her orders."

That explains the easy entrance and why he has his own set of rooms. "Is that a position you chose for yourself, or enjoy?"

His raised eyebrows made me realize I may have gone too far with my question. I backpedaled. "In the human...realm, there is a lot of pressure placed on young people to choose their career early and many people end up not being happy in their career pursuit, or they feel forced into it. I myself have struggled with that."

He sighed. "Well, as cousin to the Empress, there is an expectation for me to serve in some way. I had few options and was eventually picked for this role because of my skills with weaponry and strategy—particularly strategy. It is a great honor to be named Generalis."

I nodded, going back to my food as a distraction, when the server came with a tray of desserts. I wanted to know more about her; what species she was. Her quiet, reserved way piqued my interest, was she expected to act that way? After my last questions I decided to leave the pondering for another time and ate a berry-like sorbet in silence instead.

Opius held up the wine bottle to me with an inquiring look. I smiled and nodded. He poured for both of us and mentioned, "There is a sitting room nearby, where we can drink and talk, if you like."

The corner of my mouth curved up and I motioned with my glass for him to lead the way.

Where one might expect a hearth and fireplace there was yet another fountain, this one different from the others. It ran down the wall in a wide sheet and made a melodic sound where it collected at the base, the pool sang as the falling water returned to it. Opius glided over to an ornate loveseat shaped like an open clamshell, flanked by two overstuffed chairs. Upholstered in a pale silk embroidered with interlocking fish, I ran my hand over the delicate stitching as I settled in. We sat, knees angled toward each other, on the cloud-like couch.

My clothing felt like a breeze on my skin, it swished and sighed as I shifted in my seat. His eyes roved over me, causing my skin to tingle and my body to warm.

"I want to know more about you, beautiful Lily. How did you spend your time in the human realm?"

I took a sip of wine and tried to ignore my creeping self-consciousness. "Well,"-another sip-"I was going to school to become a horse veterinarian, but...that didn't work out. Instead I attend junior college now, studying a lot of different subjects. I ride my horse, Apollo, every day training for competitions, and help my mother take care of the animals on our land. Those aspects of my life consume most of my time." I was getting to the point where it was a struggle to keep my words clear.

"Do you have an affinity for lesser beings?" he asked.

Lesser beings, that's a funny way to put it. "I do, my mother and the people we live near all say I have a gift for helping and healing them. I've healed most everyone's animals in the area from one thing or another. I enjoy caretaking for them."

"You know, you being Vale Born means that you possess abilities, some manner of control over elements—perhaps even multiple."

"Me? I don't know. There were times where I healed and calmed animals that should have been far worse off and terrified of what I was doing. Yet somehow, they always knew to trust me. I certainly studied veterinary medicine a lot, but there were instances that my knowledge was not enough and-"

"I said control over *elements,* such as water. We will have to find out," he said as he lounged and drank.

He asked more questions about growing up near the Vale, if there were other children like me, and if I manifested any other special abilities. His curiosity increased as we talked about my life growing up there. He wanted to know more about Black Oak Grove, my family home of Brennanfalk Ranch, and other things I didn't want to think about.

"Do you have siblings? Are there any other filias or filios in your familial structure?"

"What are filias?" I asked.

"I apologize, that is our term for females, or males. I was asking if there are any that are related to you. Sired by your faeder."

I gulped as I looked back to my hands. "Ah, um, yes. I did. I mean, I do, I have a brother. His name is Felix. However my sister, well, she passed away. With my father—faeder—two years ago.

Life has been...hard since."

I struggled to contain the tears that threatened to spill out. Crying in front of him was not how I wanted to spend my evening.

"Passed away? I do not know that term."

"...Died."

"I am very sorry," Opius said soothingly as he slid closer to me. He put his arm around my shoulders, and gently caressed down my arm in a rhythmic motion.

"It's okay. I try not to think about it most days."

"Were you or...Felix is his name? Close by when they passed away?"

I dropped my mouth at the question, as the horrible memory of that day started to quicken my breath.

"Let us have a drink, to happier moments." He reached for the carafe and filled our glasses again.

I took a deep breath, then let it out slowly. "To happier moments," I said with a sigh and clinked his glass.

The wine had dwindled and conversation became more intermittent. I was just about to move closer to him when he asked, "Would you like to take a swim?"

"Swim?"

"Yes,"-he cracked a smile that crinkled the corners of his eyes-"we spend a good part of our time in the water, we like to go for a relaxing swim after nocte fare."

"That sounds nice, I'm not accustomed to swimming after dinner. Sorry, nocte fare. It seems like an...interesting thing to do."

He took my hand and led me out a door at the back of the sitting room, onto a veranda. He pulled me closer as we approached a set of stairs that descended into a serene pool of aqualine water. I gazed across at the waterfalls bordering the pool. Their height hemmed in the entire far edge in privacy, and created secluded grottos behind some of the falls.

He took off his jacket and waded in. As I debated if I should get undressed, he looked at me and assured, "Do not worry, your clothes are made for it, they will dry quickly afterward." He stepped in and held out his hand for me, then gave me a beckoning smile that I couldn't resist.

I descended the smooth stone steps until I was freely floating. The water slipped along my skin, more viscous than a swimming pool. I tingled from the warm, comforting cocoon. My thin, diaphanous clothing did little to hide any of my body, it billowed and floated like expressive fins. He circled underwater like a predatory shark, then came up, sliding his arm around my waist.

"Come, there is a spot I want to show you. Under the waterfall is a beautiful place to rest."

His fingers along my side made my heart race, as he guided me to the largest waterfall. We passed through to sit at the underwater seat, completely enclosed by the cascade. The rocky wall that curved out over us was embedded with sparkling crystals, illuminating the small space and casting a glimmer over us.

The soft light of the cave reflected in his eyes, the desire I saw there was unmistakable. He looked at my curves appreciatively, pulling me closer. His proximity was even more intoxicating than the wine. Feeling emboldened, I traced the curve of his jaw with my fingers and down to his smooth, hardened chest with my hand.

We studied each other as the air charged with anticipation. He leaned in as I parted my lips, my body going pliant as I ached for him.

At first his kiss was gentle, caressing my lips against his while he ran his hand down my back and cradled my head with the other. The heat rose as the kiss became more insistent, growing into a deep, feral need.

More, more, more. His hands roved over me, I arched my back and pressed myself against him. Gradually the fervor tempered and the kiss lessened. He pulled back to study me again with savage want.

I panted as his chest heaved, I realized it was not just with the heat of the moment, but also the heat of the water. "Did the pool get hotter?" I asked, as the steam rose from the surface surrounding us.

With a big grin he said, "I think you may have caused that, I do not have that ability."

Stunned, I looked around. It wasn't unbearably hot fortunately, but how could I have done that?

Opius smiled as he took my face in his hands, pecking me on the lips. "I think you have many things to discover about yourself. I, for one, am *very* interested to see what you can do."

I laughed and shook my head, it was all too much to fathom. I readjusted myself and nestled into his side. We lounged with our arms wrapped around each other, my head on his shoulder for some time before the water started to cool off.

"You're right," I commented, "this was a beautiful place to *rest.*"

He looked at me with a sideways grin and arched an eyebrow.

"Can you blame me? You look so beautiful, and in the water you are especially irresistible. Though I think perhaps it is time to return you to your room, I am sure you could use some actual rest after your journey here."

Was it only just today that I had stepped through the tear to come to this magical place and met this amazing male? I nodded to him, a bit reluctantly as we departed the glorious, private cove.

I looked back at it once more as we exited the pool, and frowned as we left the wondrous little nook where an unfathomably beautiful creature had kissed me. Though tired, and a little drunk, I would have been content to stay there all night.

"Do not worry," he whispered in my ear, "we will have more opportunities later."

I batted my eyelashes and had to stifle a flirtatious giggle from leaping out.

Opius walked me back to my room, holding my hand the whole way. I felt like I was floating on air. As we arrived at my door, he turned me around and leaned in for another kiss. The intensity rose, he pushed me up against the solid stone and kissed me so intently that I almost begged for him to go further. His strong hands gripped my lower back as I began to warm again. He pushed into my hips, pressing his body into mine. I was tempted to fling my door open and drag him into my room, and into my bed.

I hesitated, recognizing that I was still feeling the effects of the alcohol and was definitely feeling uninhibited by it. *Chill out, you just met him.*

He pulled back to study my face. "Rest well, Lily."

"Sweet dreams," I responded with a seductive smile. I opened my door and slipped inside.

After closing the massive block I leaned against it, wishing I had brought him in. Though I knew I would have gone too far if I did. I took a deep breath trying to calm myself. I spied a fresh set of clothing on the sideboard; a light, short chemise. *I think someone is trying to barely dress me on purpose.* I slipped off my clothes, then into the nightdress.

I made my way over to the bed, then slid into the cool sheets. Thoughts about the events of the day flitted through my mind, and I smiled as I drifted off.

CHAPTER 6

I woke up and forgot for a moment where I was. Memories of the day before filtered in as I stared up at the lavender canopy. I rolled up to sitting and looked around the pristine room. More clothes sat on the sideboard near the door, the outfit from the night before had been collected and whisked off to who knew where. A yawn fought its way out as I stretched, *I may be in a magical land and part magical being here, but some coffee right about now sounds amazing.* I tossed my lengthened legs over the edge of the bed, then padded to the vanity.

After I washed up, I sat down and applied some quick make-up, and looked in the drawer for a clip or tie for my hair. A set of delicate hair combs sat in a box, embellished with pale pink rose quartz. I brushed out my ash blond hair, then tried pinning it back a few different ways. Apparently even as a Fae hybrid I still couldn't style my hair. I managed to get a decent look when I twisted each front side up and back, and slid the combs in to secure it. Simple, but it worked.

I stepped over to the sideboard, and held up today's outfit. A pale orchid pink dress, made from the same gauzy fabric. I slid the chemise off my shoulders, letting it puddle to the floor, then put on the fresh clothes. I was so used to wearing utilitarian clothes back home, always either jeans or riding breeches. Or leggings and a cozy sweater. It was kind of nice to wear something so feminine for once—however awkward. Pink was never a go-to color for me. Earth tones, warm hues, rich golds that matched my eyes. That was what I gravitated towards, clothes I could move in, work in. My current outfit felt like it would disintegrate if I did even one chore on the ranch. Good thing I wasn't home to test it.

I walked out the door to find Opius.

"Bonum mane, you look lovely, Lily. I thought we could enjoy mane fare in my private dining area." He held his arm out to guide me.

"Um…bonum mane, that sounds great."

I followed him to his room; masculine, clean and cool with varied blue tones. In the closest corner was a white stone dining table large enough to seat six, with a covered tray. I hoped mane fare equated to breakfast.

He lifted the lids and began to part out the plates. The single, large poached fish egg gave me pause, while a roll made of rough grain assured of something familiar. Steamed crustacean-like legs with a cream dipping sauce sat in the corner, waiting. I nearly groaned at having to eat seafood for breakfast. *So not my style.* He turned over two delicate teacups and poured…*coffee!* I wriggled a little cheer as I reached forward to take it. I cradled my cup and sniffed ceremoniously, as I did every morning. Floral and fragrant, I took a cautious sip. Different from coffee for sure, it lacked the dark nuttiness I was used to. Still, it woke up my senses just the same. I wrinkled my nose at the absence of cream and sugar. I also didn't want to be impolite and mention that I would need about three more of these cups, as they were so miniature.

I inspected the egg, and cringed at the greenish, off-putting color. I cut a piece of the roe, then cautiously took a bite. I wondered what creature the egg had come from, it must have been big. I did my best to eat more, but it turned my stomach. I grimaced as I watched Opius devour his completely. Little bits of egg were dotted around his chin as he finished inhaling it. I looked away as I tried to brush aside the image.

He poured us each another cup and mentioned, "I have sent word along to the Empress for an audience today, we should know soon when she can see us."

My stomach dropped and I froze mid-sip. What would she think of me? Was she a kind ruler or a ruthless one? *I suppose I'll find out one way or another soon enough.* I swallowed, then drank my second cup in silence as I mulled over the possible ramifications of meeting an empress.

Opius let out a small laugh. "You have little to worry about, Lily. She is a passive leader," he sneered. "We can go for a walk around the castle while we wait for a response."

Feigning reassurance, I smiled and nodded.

He guided me around like a perfect gentleman, showing me all kinds of sights; more fountains, pools and stunning rooms. My jaw dropped when we entered an ornate, huge library, filled with levels upon levels of books. I ran my finger over the spine of a volume, shelved within a crystal enclosure. Were there fantastical stories written in some of these books? Histories of their people, maybe even tales of other Vale Born that might have come here? I wanted to end our tour and spend the rest of the day reading what Umorfae novels were like—if I could even read their language.

The mineral formations that rose up to serve as the library walls made me wonder again about the castle, how did it come into being?

"I'm curious about your magnificent palace. I know your race has powers over water, but what about stone? The castle seems like it was grown into creation. Did your people create it?"

Opius stiffened and looked at me sidelong. After a brief pause he said, "Another race of Fae built it, that have powers over earth."

"Was it built long ago?" I sensed he was holding something back.

"Yes, a long time, before I was born."

"How old are you?"

"Quite old compared to you, we can be nearly immortal. Our bodies are much stronger and more resilient than humans, though we are not infallible. I myself am almost three hundred cycles old. The magic in our land is regenerative, continually replenishing those that live here."

Three hundred years! My twenty one years seemed so small and insignificant by comparison. *What the hell does someone do with all that time? Deciding a future must be so much easier.*

A knock at the open library door startled me out of my thoughts. A distinguished-looking Umorfae waited there, Opius motioned him over and they spoke to each other out of earshot. Opius set his jaw and clenched his fist, as the newcomer bowed before excusing himself.

"It seems the Empress has no time currently, however we have an appointment with her two rotations from now." His mood had visibly soured. I was relieved to have a small extension, I would rather adjust more before meeting her. Resigned, he continued, "I suppose this will give us more time to spend together." He attempted a smile as we left the library.

We spent the next two days eating, lounging, and talking. I wanted to know him more in every way, he wanted to know more about my town and other young people born there. It was the last thing I wanted to think about.

Unease settled in my stomach as soon as I woke up on the third day. I lay there, thinking, worrying. I'd have to start getting ready to be introduced to Empress Celestine soon. The anticipation and thought of the unknown spiked my anxiety. I shut my eyes and took a breath. *Three, two, one, get your ass out of bed.*

After a quick bath I sat down at the vanity, staring at myself trying to decide how to prepare myself to meet an empress. Lacking skills in makeup and hairstyling, I was ill-equipped to even begin. Stitch up an injured horse? No problem. Haul hay bales? Easy. Put on makeup? Nearly worthless.

I looked blankly at my reflection, Josie was the one that was good at hair and makeup, try as I might I just never had the knack for it. She always said I had a great "canvas", though I never could make much use of painting it. I frowned as I thought about her again. It had already been three days here, since she clearly wasn't in the castle I needed to move on. Either go home soon, or press on and look elsewhere for her. A tap on the door tore me away from thoughts of my friend.

"Yes?" I called, thinking it was Opius.

The door slid open to reveal our dinner server, her long hair partially obscuring her face in black-silver slivers. "I have come to help you dress, my Lady."

"Oh thank god, come in!" I was beyond relieved she had shown up before I made an egregious error with the makeup that I would be stuck with. I shuddered, as I pictured myself with wobbly lipstick attempting to smile at a larger-than-life queen.

The female slipped in and closed the door behind her. As she stepped over to me she kept her eyes averted, picked up the hair brush and got to work.

"What is your name?" I asked, watching her in the mirror.

"Naiya, my Lady," she whispered.

"That's lovely, what does it mean?"

She stopped for a moment, and finally looked at me as she responded, "It means fast moving water, a common name among my people."

"Are there many others of your kind here in the castle?" I probed, hoping to garner a bit more of a response. She hesitated and lowered the brush a moment.

"Yes, there are quite a few of us here. Many of us work in the kitchen, laundry, or other areas of housekeeping." By her tone and weighted subservience, there was more to the story than her words conveyed.

"What are your people called?" I could tell I was asking too many questions for comfort.

"We are called the Syrenni."

She pressed her lips together and got back to work, twisting and braiding my hair into lovely shapes and coils. I marvelled at the way she could form a design with a larger braid and have other smaller roped braids flow with it. They had a fluidity that was reminiscent of a roiling river. They looped up around the crown of my head and snaked their way down my back.

"That looks pretty, you're very skilled."

Naiya's eyes widened slightly, and there was a sudden horizontal movement across them. I realized she had a nictitating membrane. *What an interesting creature!* She twitched up the corners of her mouth and looked down again as she finished my hair.

She pulled the makeup out of the drawer and opened it, arranging it into a work area. Naiya dipped the anemone brush in each eye pigment, layering the colors together. She swept in a single line across my lids, then pivoted the brush to coat my lashes. She spread a pink color on my lips, then dotted each cheek with it and blended. "I figured I was missing a few steps when I tried using it before," I commented while I grinned at her. She cracked a small smile as she closed the kit.

She held up an aqua blue gown of incredible beauty, and intense impracticality. I gasped at the thousands of minuscule diamonds that adorned the neckline, which scattered bands of color on the whisper-thin fabric. Naiya eased it over me, carefully avoiding my sculptural hair and pristine makeup. As it settled over my curves with a swish, she was already fastening the sheer scarf sewn into the vertical length of the side waist seam. It draped asymmetrically to the opposite hip, the tail cascaded down the tulip-shaped skirt. *Well I suppose I look the part now.*

She turned to leave, bowing as she did. I bent down and caught her webbed hand. "Thank you, Naiya, you did a beautiful job. I appreciate it." I realized how much taller I was as I towered over the thin wisp of a female.

"You are welcome," she answered quietly as she bowed again, then backed out the door.

"Well, here goes nothing," I said, as I sucked in a breath and squared my shoulders.

CHAPTER 7

Opius waited in the hall, looking like someone had spent even more time preparing him than Naiya had spent on me. His hair, sophisticatedly braided and potentially the envy of anyone that did Celtic knots, shimmered as he turned towards me. His embellished short coat and matching breeches were pristine in their silken weave, polished and perfect, not a thread out of place. He offered his arm as he smiled. "You look stunning. Mane fare is waiting downstairs in the dining room. After that, Empress Celestine will see us."

I nodded and took a deep breath. "You look stunning as well." I instantly wished I hadn't said that. Anything but that. Why didn't I just say thank you? He twitched a corner of his mouth and patted my hand as we walked down to the dining room to have our usual breakfast.

My nerves made it difficult to eat much, though I certainly had my fill of the coffee beverage, which I learned was called capuli. We left our plates and began our walk to meet her. I looked back at the mess on the table and frowned. Surely Naiya would be the one to have to clean up after us. Opius ignored my glance and angled his chin a little higher as we proceeded.

"Is there anything I need to know? I wouldn't want to say the wrong thing to the Empress," I asked.

"I am sure you will do fine, simple rules such as speak when spoken to, and, though I know you are a curious being, you should attempt to keep your questions to a minimum. I find with her that silence can be useful, eventually she will tell you all you want to know—if you are listening," he answered as we began climbing wide circular stairs, ascending into what must have been the largest tower I had seen from the bridge.

The nearly clear, faceted walls let light in from every direction, making it impossibly bright. I stepped onto a wide landing before a massive arched doorway, and held my breath as I walked into the expansive throne room.

Congregations of Umorfae murmured amongst themselves, they sat on either side of a wide aisle, and hushed as we entered. Up until now the entire castle had been almost completely empty. My heart thundered as I took in the well-dressed and stunning crowd. The males—all of them handsome and groomed—varied only slightly in bone structure and garment color. And the females. I had to stop my jaw from hanging and pretend I didn't want to stare. They were the most beautiful creatures, with their pastel dresses lightly covering their perfect frames and supple curves. I gulped as an occasional curled lip marred their otherwise pristine faces, when their gazes passed over me. They sat facing a large raised dais, on which the Empress perched with attendants to either side.

I tried not to falter as I beheld her, and her exceptional beauty. Long opal hair cascaded in rivulets down past her waist. She raised her manicured, arched eyebrows ever so slightly as we approached, framing her ice blue eyes. The glittering silver gown she wore flowed out over the base of the high backed throne, carefully arranged. Her serene expression portraying a magnanimous ruler did not waver in the slightest as we neared. We walked straight up the center, then stopped at a marked hemisphere below the dais. The line in the floor sent a clear message to not pass it.

"Greetings, Empress Celestine, thank you for granting us an audience. I would like to introduce you to Lady Lily, a Vale Born that has come to visit us," Opius professed with a saccharin edge to his voice and flourished a bow.

"Greetings, Opius...and Lily," she articulated slowly with a honeyed tone as she drifted her gaze over me, "welcome to our realm."

I curtsied as best I could. Imposter syndrome threatened to buckle my knees, my blocks-for-feet faltered as I awkwardly bent forward. "I have enjoyed my time in your beautiful castle." Every word was laborious and slow, like molasses unwilling to come out.

Her mouth curved up at the edges at my words, her stone face did little to convey her thoughts; was she pleased, annoyed, perhaps amused by my obvious lack of understanding court intrigue? After a moment she nodded once, then shifted her glance back to Opius. "Generalis, I have need of your services past our borders. There has been a disturbance at the Well. I order you to investigate with a small contingent of Praetors. You are to leave at once."

His eyes flashed, and his face darkened at the command. He recovered just as fast as he conceded, "Yes, of course, Your Majesty. What information do we have at this point?"

"Our flow of power has been interrupted. Our outermost

villages are now without power and we have had to send aid. As to why, I can only surmise a guess. Perhaps it is as simple as damage to the Imperiductus. What damaged it, I cannot say, naturally caused or otherwise. But if it was sabotage, we need to investigate. You may take your guest, or leave her here." She dismissively waved her hand in my direction, without bothering to look at me.

He paused, then affirmed, "Yes, Your Majesty, I will leave at once and investigate this issue. Water for life."

"Water for life," crowed the crowd of watching Umorfae.

He bowed, then turned to leave the throne room. I curtsied, then spun to trail him, catching up to his side after a few paces.

I resisted the urge to duck my head after being so quickly disregarded by Empress Celestine, to be discussed as if I wasn't standing right there was disheartening. Part of me wanted to excuse myself from the whole situation and go my own way, but I didn't know where I would go. Out of my element—even out of my own space and time—being alone in a strange castle did not sound appealing.

I descended the stairs silently beside Opius, waiting until we reached the bottom of the spire before I hazarded a comment. "I would like to join you." I was not a girl afraid of a little adventure, and though I had enjoyed milling about the palace and seeing the sights, I would not enjoy it without Opius. Plus, it offered the perfect chance to poke around for clues about Josie. I had stayed too long, much too long.

"It will be a journey of several rotations, four or five at the least. It is more than two rotations march to reach the Well," he said, as he flashed a skeptical eye at me.

"That's fine, I'm an experienced outdoors person. I have done my share of camping and hiking," I declared proudly. That *was* my element, in any realm.

He chortled and replied, "Very well then. We shall prepare to leave within an eighth rotation."

"Is a rotation like...a day? Or what? I'm not quite grasping what that means."

He looked at me from the corner of his eye as we made the long walk back from the tower. "I suppose. A rotation is what we call a single sleep-wake cycle. Is that what a day is?"

I sensed a twinge of annoyance in his response, so I shrugged and nodded. "Yep, I guess that's one way to describe it." I could see that wrapping my head around this whole days-to-rotations thing would be difficult, without the sun to guide me.

"What do you think might have caused the damage to the... ductus?"

"Imperiductus. Do not concern yourself. I am sure my Praetors and I will discover the problem and correct it. I would be glad for you to join me as my companion. Here, I forgot to give you this earlier. As you are always marvelling at the stones in the castle." Without stopping he whipped something out of his hip pocket, then closed my hand around an egg sized mass before I had glimpsed what it was. I uncurled my fingers to reveal a diamond that glittered with unparalleled fire.

I dropped my jaw as I raised it closer to my eyes, the weight of it suddenly leaden as I realized how much it might be worth. I tripped as we continued walking, distracted by the extravagant gift. *This would make everything on the ranch so much easier, no more scraping by.*

Rendered nearly speechless, I gasped a thank you as he quirked the corner of his mouth upward.

I was still stunned when we returned to our rooms.

He dropped me off at my door and said, "I suggest you take a short rest while I attend to preparations. Someone will be along to deliver clothing. I am pleased that you are coming." He leaned forward and intended to kiss just my cheek, but I turned and caught his mouth with mine, enticing a longer, deeper kiss. He slipped his arms along the small of my back and drew me in against himself. I stifled a moan as I felt his solid body up against mine. Slowly he released me, giving me a rakish grin and turned to head back out on his errands.

I opened the door to my room, and made my way to the fluffy bed. There were no other clothes for me in the room yet, but I struggled out of the fussy gown anyway. It took effort not to rip it, and messed up my hair in the process. *Well that was short-lived.* I gave up trying to save my hairstyle, then climbed into the sheets to rest my eyes for a few minutes.

CHAPTER 8

A faint noise woke me up some time later. I must have napped for at least an hour, *or...one twenty eighth rotation?* Naiya stood just inside my doorway with clothing for me as I was still sorting out how long I had been asleep for.

"I am sorry to disturb you, my Lady. I was sent up with clothing for you," she said in a hushed tone.

I yawned through my words. "Not to worry, Naiya, thank you. I actually didn't have anything to change into so I slept...uh... without," I said as I pulled the sheets closer.

She hastened to say, "That is fine, I can come and assist you." Her fine fins dragged as she crossed the floor in slow steps to me. The way they usually floated slightly appeared absent, they had reminded me of a fancy goldfish's tail before, trailing every move in graceful, fluid lines. Now they hung limp. Naiya set a pile of neatly folded clothes on the corner of the bed, then unfurled a pair of leather pants from the top, along with a pair of undergarments.

Yes! Pants! The dresses had been fun, but I was ready for something with more mobility. She held them up, waiting for me.

"Actually, I can put on my own clothes, thanks though."

Nodding, she set them down before turning to the vanity to pull items out of the drawers. I slipped on the underwear and pants, then put the white cotton-like top that was laid out. Soft in its texture, and the coverage better than what I had been given previously, though the sleeves that flared at the elbow and peplum waist were a little flouncy for my taste. *Still, not constricting and feels natural, I'd call it a win.* I put on the last item, a fitted suede vest. I pulled it closed, but there were only hooks and no clasps. Fumbling with it for a moment, I finally gave up and left it hanging open. I stretched, testing the pants, then ran my hands over the thin teal leather. *Better than any chaps I've worn!* Even my custom fitted, black butter-leather chaps back home couldn't compare.

I stepped over to her at the vanity, she cracked the faintest smile as she looked up. "It needs the torque," she said, as she removed a delicate chain draped around her neck.

Naiya attached the glinting chain to the bottom hook of the vest, then cinched the front closed, zigzagging back and forth to catch it on the hooks. She made one final adjustment to pull the low-scooped front properly into place. The finely stitched leather stretched to just below my waist, the peplum of the cotton blouse flared out slightly underneath.

"Guess I did need some help." I grinned.

Her face didn't so much as flicker as she motioned for me to sit, then began fixing my hair into a simpler braid. As she wiped my smudged makeup, I could see her exhaustion. Sense it, even.

"Are you all right, Naiya? You seem...tired."

"Oh. Yes, my Lady. I am fine."

I narrowed my eyes at her. *Doubtful.*

Finished with her work, I turned to face her. "Thank you again, Naiya. You've been very kind and helpful to me." As I passed my glance over her, I noticed some scrapes and missing scales marred her shoulder. She realized what I was looking at, then covered herself as she bowed slightly.

She blanched and held her breath. After a moment she looked back up to me and responded, "You are welcome as always, Lady Lily. Here is a pack of extra clothing for your trip. I hope you will be safe."

She hesitated a moment, her expression unreadable, as she handed me the pack.

I waited to take it, her hesitation gave me pause. "Do you know something, Naiya?"

Her eyes flashed, and her gills puffed a breath. "There was another, another Vale Born. I do not know what happened to her."

My eyes flew open. "Josie?! Did you see her?" Finally, *finally* I had a lead. An answer to where she might be.

She retreated a step after she forced the bag into my hands. "Yes, I did. She was here, long ago and only for a short while. I cannot say more, just be safe. Keep your wits about you." With that, she slipped out the door, leaving me grasping the pack as I stared after her.

I released a breath as I took one last glance in the mirror and searched my reflection. I looked more like myself than I had the whole time here; hair braided and wearing clothing more conducive to being outdoors. Armed with the knowledge Josie had been here and ready for my adventure with Opius, I stepped out through the thick crystal door, ready to turn over any stone along the way to find my lost friend.

I could hear movement and low voices from Opius's room as I approached. As I stood in the doorway, he looked up and stated, "Magna, Lily, we are just now ready to set out. I have all provisions set and the Praetors who will join us. This is Connyk, my Praetor Legatus." Their matching leathers creaked under various sheaths and scabbards, packed with an assortment of weapons. Knives were strapped across their chests and thighs, and swords secured to their backs. *That's a ridiculous number of blades.* I felt like I was looking at overburdened characters from a tabletop game.

Connyk stood a few inches taller than Opius, even more muscled and defined. His chest flexed as he saluted me with a fist to his heart. Clearly he was built for fighting and most likely spent a good deal of time training for it.

I had to resist the urge to interrogate them if they had seen my friend, I had already asked Opius before and he had sidestepped the question. Instead I dipped my head in acknowledgement to the lead guard. "Is there anything I can help with or carry?" I asked.

"No. We have all packs prepared and gear ready to be carried by the Praetors. I would not have you carry a heavy pack."

I frowned, after all I was strong—even stronger now since my shift—and preferred to be useful. It was ingrained in me that everyone should pull their weight on an expedition, it was foreign to me to just go along and not help. I slung my clothing bundle from Naiya across my body, and didn't look at either of them, in the off chance catching their glance might be an invitation for them to insist they carry that as well.

Opius led the way out of the castle, over to three warriors who stood on the bridge talking with the door guards. Any words spoken to each other were washed away by the rushing current underneath the structure. As we approached, they gave a wordless greeting, and nodded silent goodbyes to their companions.

"These are some of my trusted Praetors; Jhaeral, Locrien, and Aidroth," Opius stated as he motioned with a chop in their direction.

I nodded my greeting, then marched with Opius over the bridge; Connyk and Aidroth armed to the teeth in front, Locrien and Jhaeral hauling the supplies at the rear.

I looked over my shoulder to catch one last glimpse of the pristine castle, before we rounded the bend and it would drop out of sight. *Goodbye beautiful! It was an amazing couple of days!* I never was one for being indoors for too long, and the prospect of a chance to look for Josie had my heart skipping.

CHAPTER 9

The brisk pace challenged my stamina, as we headed back the way we had come several days before. We trekked for some time until we reached a juncture, then veered a different direction. To the left would have been the trail back to the cliffside forest, though that was some distance from the fork we were currently at. I glanced down the path, my mom and Felix flashed in my mind. How long had it been? Opius motioned toward the other direction, away from the tear I had entered.

"We need to press on, Lily."

I caught my breath. "Do you think I have more time before my family notices I'm not there?"

"Yes, yes. Plenty of time. Several rotations at least. Come, we should keep moving."

I nodded, I didn't want to leave. But I didn't want to make them worry either. Hopefully a little more time would go unnoticed. And maybe a little more time would mean I could find Josie and bring her back with me. My heart fluttered with hope at the thought.

The chosen path must have skirted the Umorfae territory, the beginnings of the rocky landscape mixed with pools of water on the right, bordered by the edges of the luminescent forest to the other side.

We headed north or northeast for several more hours. *I wonder if this could drive a human mad after a time, since we are so accustomed to the sun telling us when to work and when to sleep. Maybe it's like how astronauts need to prepare for that change when they are in space.* My brain rambled in concert with my strides as I tromped along following Opius's commands.

My legs ached and feet were tender, but I said nothing as we pressed on. I could smell the water before I could see it, I inhaled the fresh, damp air as we came upon a clearing near several bodies of water. My escorts knew without needing to ask that this was our first camp spot. They dropped their packs and unloaded their contents as they prepared the campsite, completing the tents with blinding speed. The guard's tents were simpler and smaller, only what they would need to crawl inside and have sufficient room to sleep. Set up in a small perimeter, two larger tents were nestled next to each other and flanked by two smaller tents to either side. The ample size of mine made me feel more guilty that they had carried all our things without my assistance, the generous size of my tent compared to the meager utilitarian shelters for the guards made me feel conspicuously over-pampered.

"Come, let us go down to the waterside and refresh ourselves," Opius said to me as the Praetors started parceling out food. I looked to where he motioned and hesitated. It felt unnatural to leave others working while I went to play in the water with him. He motioned insistently, curling his hand toward himself to call me to his side—like I could be commanded the same way he controlled water.

I shrugged and nodded, and took his outstretched hand. We walked over a small rise, then down along the bank of one of the small lakes. The secluded water glimmered, as he stripped down to just an undergarment and waded partway in. I stood awkwardly for a moment. "The Praetors will stay at camp, I assure you," he commented with a sly look over his shoulder. "Or if you prefer, you can just put your feet in the water, you do not have to join me in here if you are uncomfortable."

My momentary shyness abated, and I disrobed, leaving only my thin blouse and undergarments on, while Opius submerged himself. As I stepped into the cool pond, a rush surged through my body. He emerged in front of me and wrapped his arms around my waist, and dragged me in with a gentle tug. I giggled as he brought me further out, looping my arms around his neck as he nuzzled his face in my breasts.

I twirled with him, delighting in the invigorating coolness against my skin. He gripped me and angled his face up to my lips. Every kiss made my heart race and body heat. I played coy, released my embrace then ducked under the water. His upper hand was obvious as he gave chase. He swam around me, taunting me with his skill and speed. Underwater by several feet, we faced each other when he reached his hand to the surface and pulled toward himself. He brought a large air bubble down through the water and fitted it over his nose and mouth.

My eyes widened, *I want to try that! I wonder if I can do it?* I made the same motion, with no effect. Again, and again. I surfaced as I started to run out of air.

He came up and laughed. "Determined to try it yourself?"

"I thought I might be able to do the same, if I happen to have power over water as well."

"Here, try this." He pushed the water with his hand, just as I would if I was swimming.

"Well that's simple, that's using my actual hand!" I blurted as I splashed him. He flicked his hand, redirecting the water about to hit him away.

"It is the same, imagine just the motion of your hand will do that, without the need to physically touch the water. Push or pull it with your mind's eye. See the water moving and it will move for you." He coached and demonstrated.

I tried again, focused on my hand, I thought of it being an extension of a power that welled inside me. Taking a breath, I pushed my hand in midair, the water responded in a soft current away from me.

"It worked!!" I exclaimed, astonished.

He beamed. "You see? It is not so hard if you have the ability. Try more."

I tried several more in different directions, then pulled my hands together in a clap to make two small waves come crashing together. Gradually they increased in strength as I became more confident. Becoming more courageous, I tried pulling a stream of water off the surface, as I had seen Opius do at our first dinner. My first attempt pulled the beginnings of a rivulet, but it dropped back into the water and left a small ripple in its place. I frowned, then mustered more concentration to try again. Opius watched me in silence as I tried once more. This time I flicked my hand a little more forcefully and spoke in my mind to the water. *Come to me!* The water rumbled in response and a bead funneled out toward me, and wound its way through the air.

"I did it!" I shouted, just as it hit me in the chest. I laughed as I realized I should have kept my mind focused and told the stream where to go.

Opius chuckled and was in front of me in half a beat, then lifted me up from my hips as he spun me around. "I knew you had it in you!"

I radiated, every part of me was alight with energy and exhilaration. I wrapped my legs around his waist and kissed him. He kissed me deeply, and gripped the back of my thighs. Opius gradually moved us over to a grouping of large rocks at the water's edge. He pushed me up against them and pressed his body hard into mine, letting out a low groan as the friction increased.

My breath caught in anticipation as he deftly unbuttoned my blouse. He pushed the collar back over one shoulder and cupped my breast, thumbing the sensitive tip and making me ache even more. He swept his tongue against mine and hooked a thumb at the hip of my undergarments to pull them down, when a clatter sounded from over the rise—back at camp.

We both stilled at the sound, breathing heavily against each other. When another clash of metal rang out, followed by shouts, he snapped his head in their direction. He was out of the water before I could blink, then snatched up his sword. I followed in a rush and left my leathers where they were, as I ran back along the shore. I buttoned my shirt up while I scurried toward camp, nearly tripping in the process.

I crested the rise and saw the tail end of a skirmish, two assailants ran off into the jungle after they narrowly escaped Opius's blade. There was little more than a streak of color that I noticed of the attackers, pale tan against dark skin and a trailing black smear, hair perhaps. I waited for a moment and held my breath, while Opius surveyed the damage and his guards. One of them moaned on the ground, shot with an arrow through the interior shoulder, the other three were unharmed.

"Should we follow, Generalis?" Connyk shouted, ready to race after the bandits.

"No, this may be a trick to split us up. Locrien needs mending, we need to assess the situation before we make any decisions," Opius ordered.

I didn't wait for an invitation and made my way down to them. Opius looked warily at me. I was barely clothed, in now transparent, wet garments, but I didn't care. I went straight over to Locrien and inspected the arrow wound.

"Do we have any wound dressings or some sort of medical pack?" I questioned anyone who would respond.

Connyk answered, "No, we have nothing like that."

I steeled myself, and tried to think of what I could do. "Grab me a spare cloth," I demanded as I studied the injury. The arrow was clean through, the large, finely detailed metal head protruded out the front along his upper pectoral muscle, blue blood leaked down around the wound. The wide shaft would undoubtedly cause intense pain if I tried to break it. "Who has the sharpest blade? We need to cut this off from behind with minimal pressure, so we can pull it through." I placed my hand on his chest to try and comfort him as Connyk handed me the cloth.

Opius positioned himself behind Locrien, then took one adept swing, effectively slicing the arrow off in front of the red fletching. Locrien winced, however it was as gentle as it could have been. I placed my hand close to the shaft and used it as leverage while I pulled the arrow free. I focused on my hand, and willed it to emit comforting white light. His face softened slightly until the arrow was released, at which point he grimaced in pain. A gush of bright blue blood rushed out. I pressed the cloth on both sides of his shoulder to try and slow the hemorrhage. I kept the compression on for a few minutes before I checked it. It surged again once I lifted the cloth. *This isn't good, that must mean an artery was nicked. Shit, I should have left the shaft in place!* I glanced at Locrien, his color changing from exsanguination.

My thoughts raced for a solution, but our options were limited. We were a day's hike from the castle, and had no medical provisions. Even clean cloths were probably in short supply. *Think, Lily!*

Opius and the other three guards spoke to each other, while I tried to work out what I should do. *Maybe...I can do more than just comfort if I focus, like with the water. If I see myself being able to heal him...*

I took a few breaths, and looked him in the eyes. He was brave, stoic, but his round eyes darted back and forth. Helpless. And that meant possibly unpredictable. I closed my eyes and centered myself, and looked deep inside to conjure up whatever was within me. I pictured a power that welled inside not just as comforting light, but a light that could mend flesh from the inside out. Just like I had visualized when I healed animals back home. All of that light radiated from my heart, down my arms and out of my hands where it met in the middle, right where I imagined the tear in the artery was. I visualized it as it closed, and carefully attempted to seal the rupture. *Knit, knit, knit.* It was all I could see, all I was. Everything else disappeared from existence. My whole being was centered around the injury. I could see inside the wound, and moved out with it as it stitched together with a white gold thread, that worked simultaneously to suture and repair the trauma. Piece by piece, I envisioned it all back into place until I was at the outermost borders of the epidermal layers.

I felt the final stitches pull into place, both the front and the back closed off from further hemorrhage. I blinked back into my surroundings, once again on my knees with hands on either side of Locrien's shoulder. I dropped my arms and only saw the wound a moment, now closed like it had healed a few weeks prior. My vision faded as I fell to the ground and retreated into a dark, dreamless sleep.

CHAPTER 10

The light filtered back into my consciousness one pin prick at a time, a static sound buzzed in my head as I sat up. I winced and rubbed my temples as I looked around at my surroundings; Muffled murmuring came from outside my tent, so I smoothed my hair and crawled out. My cotton pants billowed as I stepped onto the dry ground, wriggling my toes in an attempt to keep the dirt from going between them.

They stopped speaking by the time I emerged, and waited for me to walk over. They cast tentative glances as I approached.

"How do you feel?" Opius asked.

"I'm okay, I guess when I healed Locrien it drained me. But after some rest I feel much better," I reported. "How long was I asleep? And you, Locrien, are you okay?"

"Just over one rotation," Opius confessed. "We were concerned you might have needed to sleep even longer than that. Locrien is fine, your healing powers are quite impressive, he has nearly full use of his arm. Here, food for you."

Locrien smiled a big, toothy grin and nodded, then gave a

quick demonstration with the injured arm to show his progress. "Those filthy rebels cannot pull that faex on us!" He exclaimed.

Opius flashed him a glare. "Watch your mouth around my guest."

The corners of my mouth twitched up, I appreciated someone who swears once in awhile, even if the word was foreign to me. He pursed his lips in a sheepish pout after being admonished by Opius.

I pushed around the unremarkable food as I replayed the events in my head, how it had actually worked, really worked. It was certainly better than thinking about the Umorfae camp rations; a kelp-like dehydrated brick, some fish packed in oil, and a crusty bread roll. It was not tasty in the least, but it was enough. *In fact it tastes like faex.* I sat at the makeshift eating area and silently attempted to eat.

Opius sat down with me and threw me a questioning glance as I worked a bite of the lackluster food. "I didn't know if I could actually heal that way, I thought we didn't have any other options, so I had to try. I saw the wound close up with my mind's eye, just like with the water," I answered his unasked question. "I'm not even sure how I was able to do it. I wonder if I can learn to do it without draining myself so much. Do you know about healing that way?"

"No, I do not," he answered before changing the subject. "We have but two options, unfortunately. I can send two Praetors back with you to the castle so that you may rest there, but it is a rotation to travel back. Or we can all continue on together to the Well. My orders still stand, I must proceed to the Well to investigate. Two Praetors would be acceptable to join me if you would prefer to turn back," he laid out as I continued to pick at my algae cake.

This is like a bale of fish food compressed by an angry foot, I decided woefully.

I considered for a moment, but I knew I did not want to separate from him. "I'm fine to continue on to the Well. I don't want to split the group up, and I would rather stay with you. Plus, safety in numbers right? We would be better off if we all stayed together," I suggested. I didn't want to slink back to the castle and be coddled—or forgotten. The chances of finding Josie would most likely diminish if I didn't press on with them. "Do you know anything about who attacked? Has there been any more activity since I healed Locrien?"

He shook his head. "No, nothing further and we do not know who it was. It could have been one of the rebel factions that we thought were much farther away. But, it looks like they may have ventured closer to Lacausia territory. I still have to investigate, because of this event I have surmised that the interruption of the Imperiductus was most likely sabotage."

"Sabotage! Why? Also, what is the Imperiductus, exactly?"

"It is the conduit of power from the Well which runs all the way to our stronghold. There are several Wells, they emit power locally and it is also transferred by way of the Imperiductuses to different areas of the realm. If someone is sabotaging our conduit, they mean to cripple us and possibly invade our territory," Opius explained, with an edge of impatience.

"Why are there rebel factions? What are they rebelling against? And why would they come so far this way?" I questioned, pretending I had some understanding of the distance they may have travelled. It seemed this beautiful realm was not as peaceful as I thought.

"Most of the issues are far from our borders. But perhaps, it has to do with the fact that the Fae have been in power for eons, sometimes there is in-fighting. It has been this way a long time, since a Vale Born ruled here long ago." He answered me slowly. It felt like he downplayed the situation. *But then...maybe he didn't know for sure.*

"You said Fae and not Umorfae. You had mentioned another kind before when I asked about the castle. How many races of Fae are there?"

"There are also Petrafae, Ignisfae, and Caelifae. They cannot control water like we can, but they can control other elements; earth, fire, and air." He listed them off with a slight sneer. "We should proceed. If we are all to go together to the Well, we need to leave soon."

I nodded in agreement as the other part of what he said struck me, a Vale Born had ruled here. I wanted more information, but he clearly didn't want more questions. The guards had already started to break down camp. I went back to my tent to change back into my leathers and repack my other clothing. I started to disassemble my own tent when Locrien ambled over.

"I will help you with the remainder of your tent, my Lady."

Pfft, my Lady, I scoffed to myself. *If Felix heard this he would literally laugh out loud.* I was about as far from a lady as one could get.

"Here, roll it like this to make it as small as possible," he instructed. I copied what he did on one side as we worked in tandem. "Thank you, for what you did. I have never seen healing like that. The closest I have seen is being submerged directly in the Well, or the use of the Well power through the Imperiductus, but even that takes much more time than what it took you."

I snapped my head up to him. "The Well? Healing like that comes from the Well only?" I blurted.

He glanced around cautiously. "Yes. Fae cannot heal others directly. We have to use the Well. You seemed to bring it out from inside yourself."

Maybe he's afraid he's saying too much? I thought in silence as we finished rolling up the tent. *Why hadn't Opius said this when I questioned him about it?* I began to feel like Opius was either hiding something from me, or it was an attempt to shield me for some reason.

I went down to the waterside to freshen up as I mulled everything over, while they continued packing. *Maybe he was just being protective. After all, there was an apparent threat now with these rebels.* I shook it off as I splashed water on my face. One thing that I couldn't shake was the rebels, maybe I needed to protect myself. I wasn't trained to fight—other than what Felix had taught me—but being completely unarmed didn't seem like a good idea.

When I returned to camp, they had completed and were ready to set out. I approached Opius, who was discussing in hushed tones with Connyk. "I gave it some thought, I'd like to have one of the knives or something, just in case. I feel uncomfortable not having any sort of weapon," I declared. He flashed a dubious look, for a moment I thought he would say no. Maybe it was silly, but what if it became necessary or needed in some way? Perhaps it would only serve as a comfort to me.

"Have you had any weapons training?"

"No, maybe you could teach me some things? I'm a fast learner."

After a few weighted moments, he unstrapped his thigh knife then turned to face me fully, getting down on one knee to cinch it on. "We cannot have you feeling uncomfortable, can we? I think you are right, I believe it is a good idea for you to have one of the blades, but I do not have time to train you," he said, as he touched my thigh gently and looked up at me with an eyebrow cocked. I was relieved he had agreed to give me the knife, but to not even offer a minute to show me how to protect myself left me dismayed.

After he finished the adjustments on the thigh strap—and made sure to touch me a bit more than necessary—he stood and with one curt nod commanded, "Let us be on our way."

"Sounds good, maybe with some luck I can find signs of my friend, Josie, as well. I believe she did come here."

His face darkened, as he motioned to the others and ignored my comment. "March, now."

I grabbed my bag, then slung it across my shoulder, while the others hoisted up their heavier packs. And with that, I set out with them to the Well. *Hopefully without any more arrows through our backs!*

CHAPTER 11

Opius's sour mood reflected in our pace, he pushed us harder over the increasingly difficult terrain. The short break he allotted was welcome, though not enough to rest my feet, and he hadn't said more than two words to me since we left camp. I tried to edge closer to him, when he ordered that it was time to head out. My face fell as he didn't even glance in my direction.

The rocks gradually changed in composition from crumbly sedimentary layers in swaths of ochre, to pale grey monoliths jutting out of the ground like dragon's teeth. They grew up haphazardly, intersecting the trail so that we periodically had to climb over them. The rough, glittery surface of the rocks scraped my hands as I scaled them.

The same phenomena that I had seen in the forest fell intermittently from the sky, fizzling out before they reached the ground, like thousands of minuscule falling stars making their way through the atmosphere. Their indistinct vibration called to me, a song that sent responding tremors through my skin. I wanted to be near them, to reach out and touch them if I could.

Opius glowered at me as I watched the flickering lights, a small reprimand for lollygagging to gaze at them. I winced, and brought my focus back to the trail as we pressed on.

A glowing spot appeared on the horizon, growing larger and brighter as our group travelled toward it. Opius at the lead halted with his fist raised, as we arrived at the luminous basin. I looked over his shoulder to peek at the mysterious lake. Out of the center of the pool, a strange tree wound its way out. Barkless and brilliant, it was composed of multitudes of luminescent cords twisted together that branched out in a huge splay, high over the Well. The tiny falling lights I had been watching throughout the journey emanated from the tips of the tree, and dispersed in a wide area. I walked to the edge to peer in, the reservoir had no bottom that I could see, and emitted so much light that it took a moment for my eyes to adjust. I was tempted to jump in and bask in the water. *I wonder how far down I can swim, if I figure out how to do an air bubble like Opius?*

"I am going to begin investigating the Imperiductus, just a preliminary look while the Praetors scout the area, would you like to join me? I think you will find the Well beyond replenishing," he proposed, finally breaking the silent treatment.

"I would love to!" I exclaimed, then immediately upbraided myself for being overly enthusiastic. But I couldn't help it, *Dive into a mysterious Well of magic? Yes please!* I halted, relieved his moodiness had lifted, though less eager to be near him after the way he held me at arm's distance and ignored me all day. "That sounds…enticing," I continued, making an effort to be more subdued. Though it was the mysterious tree that I found more alluring.

I stripped down to my undergarments and dove in. Instantly I was filled to the brim with…whatever it was that the Vale had gifted me with. *I guess that's my magic Well inside me.* Euphoria flooded as my skin tingled all over, and imagined I might be able to take flight directly out of the water.

"I am going to dive down and see what is going on down there. After I figure out what the issue is and how to resolve it, perhaps you and I can then…enjoy ourselves," Opius suggested with a feline grin.

I made an effort not to roll my eyes at the suggestion, after his indifferent treatment toward me. *It's going to take a little more than that.* He ducked under the water before I responded with a negative, and pulled a bubble with him to use for breathing. I watched him submerge, to one of the roots that funneled off of the great tree. The root was like a large fiber optic cable that pulsed with energy. The thrum it emanated synced with the sensation in my skin. Opius crawled along one of the many cords, checking it carefully. He surfaced after he reached the point where the cable tunneled into the rocky wall of the Well.

He emerged and announced to the Praetors, "It appears that someone has grown a rock vice around the Umorfae Imperiductus to pinch off our power, it has definitely been sabotaged. It is going to take some work to get it off, and will be difficult to remove without damaging the conduit."

I frowned at the news. "Someone grew a rock vice? Is that the same kind of power that grew your castle? Is there…maybe a Fae that does repairs on the stone in the castle that can help with this?"

I pondered aloud.

He rolled his eyes, shifting his gaze away as he scoffed, "No, there is no one at the castle we can call on with those skills. That would require a Petrafae. You can leave the problem solving to me."

I dropped my brows and my smile. I understood I was a young being in his realm with little knowledge of it. But having my suggestion disregarded and swept aside without consideration darkened my thoughts.

He proceeded, "I will go back and see if there is something I can do for now. Stay here while I return." Without giving me a second glance, he dove under the water and went back down. *Fine, I will stay up here and enjoy this magical paradise!* I shook my head and turned my face to the sky, even if I was annoyed by his dismissal.

Floating upward in the luminous volume, I watched the pulse of the ethereal tree emit the droplets of esoteric force. It reminded me of lying on my back on my parents land with Maris, watching the Perseid meteor shower on a warm summer night. Hundreds of beautiful streaks of light that had whizzed through the sky and waned out of existence. These streaks were much slower and gentler, they radiated peacefully from the source like a comet shower, and flitted along their merry way in the direction they were sent.

As I gazed I realized the surrounding area was getting darker, and a strange sound approached. A threatening wind rushed and grew. I righted myself and looked around, trying to discern its direction. Shouts echoed and light flashed from behind a rocky outcropping. The whole area darkened further, but the light from the Well persisted. The ambient light had been sucked from the sky. Jhaeral and Aidroth charged past the Well from another direction, into the path of the flashes. They disappeared behind the rocks as more yelling ensued. I waved my hands at Opius, still far down with the Imperiductus. He was hunched over, wrenching the vice off—without much luck—and took no notice of my attempts to get his attention.

I paddled for the edge where I had dropped my leathers, pack, and knife. I pulled myself out, crouched behind the rocks and struggled into my clothes, which clung to my wet skin. Finally I wriggled into them and cinched up my vest. I threw on my pack and strapped on my knife. Opius had surfaced and spotted me. In a flash, he was at the Well edge closest to me.

"Run and hide, Lily, something dangerous is nearby. Get as far away as you can. I will draw it off. If you see it, whatever you do, do not look into its face. It will consume you," he cautioned.

I opened my mouth to protest and ask questions, but he held up his hand to silence me and gave me a warning glance. The look on his face told me enough, no time for questions and no time to explain.

He swam lightning fast to the other side of the Well, closest to the path of the terror. Connyk barrelled in at that moment, the two of them met near the basin and charged ahead.

I sat stunned, staring after Opius and Connyk, just as the creature came into view.

CHAPTER 12

It was a woman. Or rather, it bore a resemblance to a woman. Her long, wispy black hair that floated out around her in angry, electrified whorls was not human-like at all. It carried on a life all its own as it sent shockwaves out from the frayed ends. The creature's slight, shapely build suspended unnaturally in the air, her toes dragged on the ground, leaving intermittent scrapes as her tracks. I shuddered as I peered over at her, nightmare incarnate.

Her araneous dress swirled in a toxic mist, webbed material laced her frame at odd angles, the tendrils of the tattered hem reached out like tiny fingers toward the remaining Umorfae. Opius and Connyk shielded their eyes, as they slashed blindly in her direction. The inky wisps of her deadly skirt came dangerously close to being able to take root and wrap around the Praetor's arms. A vortex of wind and light drew inward to her gaping mouth, her head slung back as she endeavored to suck in her prey. I opened my mouth in a silent scream, terrified that I would see her envelop them in her cavernous jaws. Her deathly white skin cracked and bunched around the corners of her lips as she opened her mouth wider, preparing to inhale.

I had to help them, she inched nearer and nearer, drawing them inexorably closer. My chest tightened and fists balled as I watched the event unfold. Opius was losing ground to her, and their weapons swinging wide were not effective in the least. I hid behind the rocks, paralyzed, and racking my mind to try and come up with a plan. Hopefully without becoming a meal myself. I was still uselessly spying and shook my hands, when I bumped a small rock. It toppled over and brought others with it, causing a cascading rockslide that clattered to the ground.

I cringed as she turned slowly—so slowly—at the sound, the vortex momentarily abated as she surveyed me, still a short distance away. My eyes fell on her face, and stilled as I finally saw her fully. She was not terrifying at all. In her place was a lovely young maiden, a gatekeeper of another realm.

"Well," she hissed, her voice an eerie, snake-like sound, "a Vale Born. How magna. I have not had one in ages."

She opened her great maw again and the siphon restarted. But it wasn't the scary, turbulent tunnel I had seen from the side. I was frozen in place as I beheld her, and heard the welcome she bade me into the realm she sentried. Me, she had picked me to join the selected few who were chosen to venture into the charmed and closely guarded dimension. Inside the funnel was a beautiful galaxy, awash with colors and blooming nebulae. Stars being born and life happening, but at a slow, stellar pace. Peace and serenity was the promise, all I had to do was to step in to be a part of the great existence. I could be anywhere and everywhere at once if I entered the expanse. Just a few steps and I could join.

A lulling call rippled out, offering sanctuary, insisting that I walk toward it. Everlasting dreams made real, only a couple short paces away. I lifted my hand to the entrance, toward the beckoning escape. The opening widened, showing more and more of the star-scape beyond, glittering jewels cast in a velvety field.

Opius slashed her from behind and knocked her off balance, as a spray of black blood splattered his face. She let out a shrill, angry scream that tormented my sensitive ears. It was enough for me to avert my eyes and to break the spell I had unwittingly fallen into.

I blinked as the amorous feeling vanished, and the current reality set back in. The monster that she was filtered into my vision. Gone was the lovely beauty beckoning me to a better place.

My mouth dropped at my foolishness. Even with Opius's warning, I had looked right at her. And I was ready to submit myself to her lie.

"Go!" He shouted as I was still berating myself.

She started to advance my position again, even as her blood dribbled onto the dirt below. I backed up a few feet reflexively, before I turned away from them, shaking.

And I ran.

CHAPTER 13

I ran and ran. To my shame, I ran. I propelled myself faster than I knew I could. I tore across the earth until I was out of breath and the terror had eased. My chest heaved as I slowed and looked around, I had no idea how far or long I had gone.

The light long since returned to the sky, the threat of the witch creature apparently passed. I doubled over, gasping for air as tears streamed down my face. Opius, what had happened to him? Was he able to fight her off? I hadn't seen Jhaeral, Aidroth, or Locrien. Were they her first victims? I choked back tears as I replayed the appreciative look Locrien had given me when he showed off his healed wound. I recalled the sense of relief that emanated from him after I had saved him, was that all for nothing? Just to live one more day. It was all so futile. Memories of past events started to infiltrate, times that I had tried to make a difference and failed. Loved ones lost, friends lost, animals lost. It all felt hopeless. Pointless. Everything dies anyway. I crumpled to the ground with my arms around my waist, and sobbed.

Stop. Stop it, Lily. Three, two, one. You might have a chance to find Josie. I took a breath as I closed my eyes and shook out my hands, to school myself out of despair. At least I could take away the fact the witch creature had said she hadn't devoured a Vale Born in ages, that would mean she didn't cross paths with Josie. Hopefully.

It set in how utterly alone I was. Worry for my Umorfae friends pecked at me, however, they were trained fighters. They stood more of a chance than I did. Opius was right to tell me to run and I was right to obey. At least that was what I could tell myself in my logical mind. But I couldn't help the gnawing guilt at escaping while they were attacked. And now, I was on my own, with no guide and no idea where I was. A sob worked its way out of me again. *Get up, Lily.* I pushed myself off the ground and wiped my nose with the back of my hand. *Breathe.*

My hands still shook as I took my thigh knife from its sheath and clutched it. It probably wouldn't do much good if I crossed paths with anything fearsome, but it at least made me feel better. I took a step, then another. I pushed myself to walk as I scanned my surroundings. The terrain transitioned to a desert-like landscape. I meandered through a craggy cliff lined area that bordered the great jungle, hard-packed dirt gave way to sandy ground. Sounds of various creatures filtered in from the trees, peaceful chirps and caws. Their twittering eased my concern, a deep breath and unclenched jaw helped me relax a bit more.

I didn't know where I was going, or if I should turn back to try and find Opius. But if I did, would the wraith-witch find me instead? I couldn't feel at ease knowing that she was out there somewhere, unless Opius had managed to kill her. The reality that this realm wasn't as safe as I had previously assumed disconcerted me.

There were also rebels to think about. Would they attack if I was on my own? Maybe I should find my way back to that vine-covered cliff wall and get myself home. To where Apollo still stood in the glen and waited for me. It had been five days here. He was probably right where I left him. If I tried to get to the wall that would be a problem though. I didn't know what direction I needed to go to reach it. If I went through the wrong Vale opening I could end up somewhere different entirely—if there even was another opening that I could find. And could I open it if I found it? Too many things could go astray trying to find my way to the exit, and too much I didn't know. Leaving would mean turning away from the chance to find my best friend. I couldn't go, *wouldn't* go back. Not yet. Not when there was a chance.

I resolved that I would proceed until there was reason to do otherwise. Going back would have the highest chance of running into that terrifying creature again. Maybe surroundings would look familiar at some point and give me an indication of what I should do. I spun, searching the area as it dawned on me that there may be other dangers that I didn't yet know about. I learned about deadly animals in the human world all my life, I had only just begun to learn about Alternis and the beings that inhabited it. I tightened my grip on the knife.

I wandered until my feet dragged and my stomach rumbled. *Great, I have no food with me.* I wasn't a hunter, and foraging for strange fruits or vegetables could be dangerous also. I had no idea what may be poisonous here. Water though, I did need water soon. I hadn't crossed a water source since I started running, *Great, I've run myself into an arid region without giving water a second thought.* I'd done weeks of survival training, I should have known better. *Survival training!* Remembering the risky situations I had gotten myself out of in the wilderness before eased the tightness in my gut. *I'm going to be okay, I just need to keep a clear head and tackle one problem at a time.*

With a renewed sense of purpose, and confidence bolstered, I resheathed my knife and set out to find water.

I adjusted my course to just clip into the tree line, zigzagging too much could disorient me. The humidity increased as I entered, a good sign I would find water at some point. The ambient hum of the forest soothed my nerves. I headed further in, and kept the cliff landmarks to my right. They popped into view when the trees intermittently opened up, useful to keep my bearings.

Some time later and still unable to find water, I hazarded moving further into the jungle. I rarely saw through the trees to the cliffs, but still caught sight of them every so often. Moss sprouted up in patchy clumps, a welcome sign of water not far off and soothing to my aching feet.

A crystal stream burbled over mossy rocks. I swiveled in place, searching the trees to be sure I wasn't being followed or watched, then plopped down and scooped up a sip. *Hopefully giardia is not an issue with water here in the Vale!* I didn't have much of a choice, I needed replenishment. Though I hadn't had fluids for a long time, I still wasn't uncomfortably thirsty. *I must be able to go longer without water.* If I had run that long and then walked so much further as a human, I would be going mad for water already.

I soaked my feet as I looked around the peaceful jungle, vines hung between the trees and swayed gently. I realized there wasn't much of a breeze, not enough to warrant how much they moved. I tilted my head as I noticed they drifted in different directions from each other. *They are moving on their own!*

I bent down to take another sip, and stopped. I realized I didn't have to use my hand to get water. I mustered a kernel of power from my inner reserve and drew a small stream in an arc, drinking from it like a water fountain. I let it collapse into the stream as I finished. A droplet that splashed off the surface sparked an idea. *I wonder if I can somehow take some water with me.* I had nothing to contain any liquid, but maybe I could form a ball of it. The ability to bring some would certainly help my situation. I practiced, pulling up a small amount and tried to maintain it. *Sheesh, this takes a lot of concentration!* I picked up progressively larger globes, challenging myself to hold them longer. I stood up and tried to walk with one, just a few steps at first.

My first attempts took both hands to maintain the shape of the sphere, after several failures and having to return to the stream, I was finally able to keep it steadily floating just above one hand while I walked.

I straightened my shoulders and faced the direction I decided to take. After siphoning another drink, I formed a water ball, and was on my way.

I angled back closer to the treeline again, walking along the border of the two regions. Having to look down frequently to maintain the reserve slowed the pace, but hopefully worth it.

The footing became more difficult, and my concentration was taxed further to deal with both; to keep everything balanced I occasionally had to shift my hand over to the side to keep the water afloat. Like a reverse magnet, moving my hand in just the right spot stabilized the sphere.

I was so focused I didn't notice the vines that had thickened around me. A tendril wrapped around the arm that was held out behind my body as a fulcrum. The world rushed downwards as it snatched me into the air. I watched the ball of water splash to the ground as I came to a stop, about twenty feet in the air. I gasped for breath, my anxiety skyrocketed as I swayed, restrained.

I swung for a few moments, angry with myself for not having paid closer attention to any possible threats surrounding me. *Dammit, Lily, you even noticed the vines earlier!* Labored deep breaths were all I could accomplish at first. Gradually I eased enough to think clearly. *Ok, what's my next step. I would probably be fine from a drop this high with my altered body, hopefully.* The vine tightened further. I realized it might not be long before another part of the vine wrapped itself around my neck or chest, if it did squeeze its victims like a python. I palmed my thigh knife with my free hand then slashed wildy, trying to slice across the woody surface. After a few misses, I adjusted the blade in my hand, then stabbed near the choke point three times as hard as I could. It uncoiled and my arm slipped straight down, dropping me to the ground far below. I shrieked as I fell, immediately regretting my poor planning. I could have tried to be ready to grab for another vine to swing myself. But it was too late for that. The terrain flew up to meet me. I tumbled as I landed to lessen the impact of the fall, though I got a pretty good scuff on my shoulder in the process. I wasted no time as I rolled back up to standing, then sprinted away from the possibly carnivorous plant.

I panted at the edge of the trees, and made sure I was not near any more vines as I steadied myself. I took a shaky breath and restarted my trek.

After I beat myself up over the near fatal error as I walked, it sunk in that I was drained, deep inside my magic well. It had cost some of my reserve to maintain the water ball. I frowned and sagged my head. *Another mistake.* I needed to let it go and chalk it up to a learning experience, I became better at controlling the water, so it wasn't a total loss. I lifted my chin and pressed on.

Weakness started to set in. I had no idea how long I had gone since escaping the witch, but I could assume it had been the better part of a rotation. My immediate need was shelter. I moved my trajectory further away from the forest, toward the craggy walls that formed the border of the desert region, hoping to find some sort of cave or crook to rest in.

I wandered until I was stumbling, exacerbated by the lack of food. My skin ached from exhaustion. At last I found a small tunnel in a crumbly cliff wall, just big enough to crawl into. It wouldn't be comfortable, but it was better than nothing and wasn't readily visible.

I crept in, tossed my clothing pack down as a pillow, and then the world went black.

CHAPTER 14

Opius's shoulder comforted my head as it lolled to the side, he caressed my back as I lounged against him with my eyes closed. *I could stay here all day,* I sighed to myself. He tickled my feet, I giggled and jerked them away. He tickled again, too forcefully, then whacked them.

"Ow! Why did you do that?" I sat up and blinked, and hit my head on the cave ceiling. Sand rained down, obscuring my vision.

For a moment I was disoriented, where was Opius? It all came back to me as I looked at two mostly covered faces, peering at me from beyond the entrance to my sleeping nook.

"Come out of there," a brusk, male voice ordered.

My heart sank, not only was this not Opius but by his tone I got the impression that he was not going to be gentle. I slid out with my pack in my lap. I stood up with my heart in my throat as I surveyed them, a male and a female, both armed with long spears, a multitude of knives. My eyes fell on a bow and quiver slung across his back over wide shoulders. He watched my face as I recognized the arrows, with intermittent wisps of red in the horsehair fletching. No doubt the etched metal arrowheads were on the other end.

My blood chilled. He had shot Locrien. These were the rebels that attacked us.

I caught my breath and held it a moment, not sure what to say. My heart raced, would they kill me now? They had the upper hand, I was completely at their mercy.

"She is dressed like an Umorfae, but she is not one of them, her color is not right," the female muttered to the male.

"She is Vale Born, see her ears? She is not Fae," he responded coldly. Only his piercing cognac eyes could be seen through the wrap covering his face.

I fidgeted, unsure of what I should do. *Should I try and negotiate?* Or would that just get me killed sooner.

"Maybe she would be willing," the female whispered to her companion, "she might be able to traverse the-"

The male snapped a fist in the air to silence her. He stood completely still while he stared into my eyes, boring deep into my soul.

"She is a collaborator, we cannot trust her." He spat as he stood defiantly with his spear anchored in the sand. He adjusted his shoulders and triangular torso as he pulled his head back, trying to get further away from me without moving his feet.

The sand-hued fabric that encircled his body stretched as he shifted back, allowing a single wisp of dark hair to escape near his eyes. I followed the continuous wrap down as it angled across his chest, then around his waist and legs.

The female peeked over his shoulder, appraising me with a curious glance. The tail of a long dark braid snaked out from under her matching wrap and fell over her shoulder as she looked at me. Her silky, beautiful curves were crafted from sculpted muscle beneath her skin. She was like a svelte cat, strong and had an easy grace about her. They were like two halves of the same coin. Both with the same striking bright eyes that stared me down with an unyielding gaze. And both with colorful tattoos covering their right arms: a large wing, some sort of curved sword, and other objects were inked into their dark skin with bright swirls and detailed linework.

After a few moments of evaluating me, he barked, "Bind her, we will bring her to camp and interrogate her." With a rapid motion he reached forward and snatched my thigh knife. "I will take that as well."

The female nodded, bound my hands and attached a rope to it, which she kept ahold of, then blindfolded me. *I'm really in trouble now, I guess I should have made my way to the wall to see if I could get home.* I dropped my chin to my chest, I had no idea what was going on here, I had become a pawn in whatever situation was brewing in this land.

"If you try to pull off the blindfold, I will kill you. I cannot risk you knowing the way to our camp," he taunted, his voice just over a whisper and dangerously close to my ear.

The rope jerked me forward, initiating the trek to their camp. I trudged, every so often getting a yank on the restraint; never strong enough to pull me off balance, just enough to remind me that I was tethered. The female led the way, and the male walked behind, no doubt with the spear angled at my back. Even blindfolded, I could feel his disdainful eyes boring through the back of my skull.

The trek lasted an eternity, a long, gruelling day with little reprieve given. The temperature increased after a few hours. I tried to use my senses for where we might be, the warmth indicated a desert region, heat emanated from surrounding rocks and ground. The sand became thicker underfoot. The depth of it was more work to walk through than the hard-packed dirt near the forest.

I was left to my wandering thoughts as I considered my circumstances. *Magic eight ball says: Outlook Not Good.* My weak jokes to myself weren't working. My situation was so bleak, my outlook could probably not be worse. Who knew what their camp would be like, or how they would interrogate me. *It's not like I have any information to give anyway, I don't even know what they are fighting about.*

With both a sense of dread and relief, sounds of what I assumed was their camp could be heard. Cheerful voices and a happy clamour echoed from nearby. Smells of cook fires drifted through the air. Before seeing anything, I started to get a little more optimistic, what I heard did not sound like hardened warriors sharpening blades.

She removed my blindfold, I squinted at the immediate brightness. As my eyes adjusted, I spotted families in the camp, a small handful of children running in the distance. Tents made of heavy canvas with colorful draped doorways were everywhere, with awnings out front that offered shaded entryways. Red clay chimneys dotted around, some puffed smoke and wafted tendrils of savory food being cooked within. My stomach gurgled as we passed the hearths. My bonds chaffed my wrists as I tried to adjust them, my skin had been rubbed raw with deep sores. I grimaced as I looked at the injuries, which were getting worse with each movement against the ropes. I had been such a fool to come here, to think that this realm was an escape. I had run away from the safety of the ranch, only to enter a treacherous world, and then I walked right into the middle of some conflict like an unaware doe. I chastised myself repeatedly, I didn't even deserve whatever delicious food was being cooked, it didn't seem that they were considering feeding me anyway as they dragged me past the various fire pits.

We approached a group of twenty warriors. My blood went cold as the male that had captured me halted, with his fist raised. She and I waited as he stomped off to confer with the other equally built fighters.

I did a double take when I looked back to her, she had unwrapped her mask. Indeed beautiful, tan skin glistened from the long hike, black hair glinted with golden and ruby highlights. She arched a thick, angled eyebrow at me, which framed her stunning cognac eyes.

"My name is Lily, what's yours?" I hazarded a conversation. *Maybe I'll get lucky and she'll be an ally to me, if I don't give her a reason not to be.*

She looked at me for a long moment before she finally responded, "Kerenza." Then looked away.

It was something.

"You mentioned before about traversing something. Maybe... there's some way I could help you." I needed to try to make myself more valuable alive than dead. At least until I could get away from them.

"It is not my place to discuss it with you, if my... leader decides to tell you, he will," Kerenza stated without glancing at me.

"What is your leader's name?" I coaxed.

"If he wishes to tell you his name, he will. That also is not up to me. I have given you my name, it will have to be enough for now. Hear this, do not press him too much, give him as much information as you can and do not fight back. Do not give him any reason to not trust you, and perhaps things might work out for you." She offered quietly without turning to face me.

I lowered my head in appreciation. "Thank you, Kerenza. I will try."

"Be sure that you do. I cannot protect you if he decides you are not worth the risk," she declared, giving me one hard look before tearing her eyes away, waiting for him to return.

"Meaning you might protect me, if it was your choice?" I pressed.

She didn't get to respond. Her leader turned to march over to us, arresting any further discussion.

My stomach dropped as he approached, he wordlessly held out his hand for the rope from Kerenza. Once she handed it over, he turned on his heel and began walking for a nearby tent. I trotted behind him so that the rope didn't become taut, and kept pace quietly. I took slowed breaths to prevent panic from gripping me as we neared a tent, what would be their method of interrogation? Torture? I gulped as we arrived at the hut. *Three, two, one. Take a breath.*

CHAPTER 15

He threw back the door flap to the large tent, then ducked inside without waiting to see if I followed. By the time I returned to a standing position, he was already seated on the ground and staring me down. The upper part of his face wrapping was now unwound, exposing his intense eyes framed by strong, discerning eyebrows.

I lowered myself to the floor without making a sound, and sat on the ground facing him. For a few minutes, we just looked at each other. Too scared to say anything and worried I would say the wrong thing, I waited for him to demand information or threaten me with bodily harm. I stole a glance around, the tent was devoid and dark, save for a shaft of light that shot down the middle from the support pole. It cast a bright slash on the ground and separated us.

"How long have you been a collaborator of the Umorfae?" He demanded.

I said nothing at first as my eyes settled back on him, hesitant that I would seem like I had selected a side for this conflict without even knowing what was going on. *The truth of what little I know is best I guess, which is probably nothing useful for him anyway.*

"I don't think I would call myself a collaborator, I've only been here in Alternis a few days—er, rotations. I accidentally slipped through a tear in the Vale, I had never been here before or heard of this realm. I met Opius right after coming through, he took me to his castle and treated me as a guest. That's the extent of me being a *collaborator*, as you called me." I tried to respond openly, but I couldn't help but have an edge to my voice. His accusatory tone seethed just in the first question.

"You expect me to believe you were only a guest when you accompanied him on a mission?" He snapped with venom.

"Yes, only a guest. He was kind to me and showed me around a little. He told me about your realm here, but never mentioned anything about any sort of unrest or issues here, not until we were going to inspect the Imperiductus anyway. Our connection was more...personal, and I was never introduced to anything beyond their food or the way they manipulated water." I snipped back.

"The Umorfae manipulate a lot more than water, and you must think me a fool if you expect me to believe that Opius had no further plans for you, other than feeding and bedding you," he sneered as he cast his eyes over me.

My face flushed. "What does it matter to you if we had a personal connection? I knew nothing of your conflict and frankly still don't!" My eyes flared as I practically shouted back at him. My temper had gotten the best of me, heat simmered under my skin.

He gaped at me. "You forget, *hybrid*, that your safety is not guaranteed here. And so far your answers are not proving useful." His voice was a threatening hiss.

Way to go Lily, you need to turn this around now or you're done for! I counselled myself, then summoned up as much humility as I could to try a different approach.

"Maybe I could recount the last few rotations, so you could see that I wasn't really given information. I was just...there," I offered.

He glared at me through lowered brows and made no comment one way or the other, so I proceeded to tell him the events of the days since my arrival. When I reached the part about meeting Empress Celestine he blurted, "You met the Empress?!"

"Well, yes I did. Briefly, and she wasn't too interested in me actually. She seemed a stately and benevolent ruler I guess—perhaps rude and indifferent to me, maybe even kind of boring aside from her looks—but she didn't talk about anything I think you would find useful in front of me."

"Benevolent! There is no amount of benevolence in any Umorfae. They are takers, slavers, and some of the most vile creatures in our realm," he scoffed. "Why would you think her benevolent? What, *exactly*, did she say."

"Well..."I pondered for a moment, "I suppose it was just my impression of her. But she did show concern for the outlying villages that lacked power due to the Imperiductus being cut off, and mentioned that aid had to be sent to them. She then ordered Opius to investigate why the Imperiductus had lost power, whether it was by sabotage or natural disaster. She gave me the option to accompany him or stay at the palace and wait for his return. I chose to go with him."

"Did she mention rebels, children, or something that could be used as leverage?"

"No, the first time I heard there were rebels was after the attack on us on our way to the Well, when Locrien was shot." I glared back at him, the heat rose in my tone again. "It was only after that when Opius said anything about it. And—wait, what do you mean children?" I squawked after I heard the second part of his question.

He ignored my query and continued with his own. "What did you find at the Well?"

"I'm guessing some rebel handiwork," I retorted. "The Imperiductus had some sort of a rock vice grown over it to choke it out, Opius tried to pry it free but I don't think he got it loose at all. Right when he was trying to free it this witch-like creature attacked us."

He straightened his back. "What witch creature?"

"I have no idea, it all happened so fast. There was this darkness that came over, and wind sounds. She...hovered and created some sort of wind tunnel that sucked living things toward her. I don't know who she got, I think she may have killed two of the guards first, Jhaeral and Aidroth, maybe Locrien too but I don't know. She sensed what I was before Opius ordered me to run while he and Connyk battled her. So, I ran. I didn't see how it ended. I ran for as long as I could and eventually found a hole to sleep in, where you found me." The guilt of running away crept back as I recounted the story.

"So, like a coward you ran," he jabbed with his eyes narrowed.

This guy has a knack for throwing verbal daggers. Heat flashed in me again momentarily, then I sagged and cast my eyes down in quiet agreement.

"However," he continued, "if you had not run she most likely would have consumed you, she is called the Pythonissamul. We do not know where she came from, she has been in Alternis for eons. She is a threat to any creature and has no allegiance to anyone but herself," he explained. I shuddered as I recalled her ghostly visage and the eerie, alluring vortex she attempted to call me into.

He regarded me for a short time, his expression softened slightly before he asked, "What skills have you discovered that you have as a Fae hybrid? I see you have fire, perhaps even Fire Bringing. Are there any other elements you can control or create?"

My jaw dropped as I stared at him. "What do you mean Fire Bringing? I don't know anything about that."

He scrunched his eyebrows. "You did not realize you have fire ability? Twice already I have seen your eyes flash and heat emanate from your body. It may happen when you get angry and you spout a little fire energy, that is a sign that you can Fire Bring. And since you are a Fae hybrid, you could have more than one element that you can control. I want to know what else you can do," he explained impatiently.

I winced at the thought of having fire within me, I remembered the night in the pool with Opius, how I had inadvertently heated the water. *Wouldn't that be sadly ironic, if I had power related to fire.* "Well, I was learning to control water. I can push it around and carry a ball of it with me. I don't know how much control I have over it, but I was getting better at it." I offered. Inwardly I hoped that I could learn to control water more, and not have this fire aspect that I seemed to have no control over.

"Anything else? Can you move rocks and earth or push air?" He probed insistently.

"Not that I've noticed, but like I said I've only been here a few days—I mean, rotations—and really the only one I was actively trying to use was water, I didn't know about fire, air or earth." But then I remembered Locrien, how I had healed him. I didn't know if that was the same as controlling an element but maybe it was somehow relevant. "I did do something else though. I healed the Umorfae guard you shot. I used my hand and focused energy from...inside me and pictured the injury stitching back together. I sealed up the wound from the inside out in a matter of minutes. I think it was minutes anyway. I used too much energy and passed out, but I was able to heal him completely first."

He stared at me wide-eyed. "I have never heard of someone having that skill. Only the Wells can heal like that," he remarked incredulously.

"Yes, I heard that from the guard I healed," I replied.

He was quiet for a few moments, then declared, "I have a proposition for you. We have a problem that we have not been able to solve, but I think you might be able to help us with it. If you do, I will not harm you." The hardened look on his upper face had turned to a more imploring, placid expression.

I sensed an opportunity to negotiate. I thought as fast as I could to try for a better bargain with this rebel. "I want more than a promise not to harm me. I want...I want your help in return. To help me find Opius, and to help me get back to the tear in the Vale where I had come through when I want to leave Alternis. Also, my friend went missing before I came here. I think she is here somewhere. I want help to find her. And no more wrist binding." I leveled my gaze at him in an attempt to stand my ground.

He narrowed his eyes and glared at me. "Fine," he muttered, "but you have to help me first. If you do not succeed I will not help you at all."

"Deal," I said flatly as I held up my wrist bindings to be cut. I realized that I didn't actually know what I had agreed to help him with. "But I won't hurt innocents or torture or anything like that." My mind raced to try and add anything else to amend this deal that I had promised to uphold. "And I'm not a thief or a terrorist. And I want your promise that helping me find Opius also means you will not harm him when and if we do find him. Also, I don't know how to leave this realm. When I came here I couldn't get back through the tear. I want you to tell me how to do it, how to travel back. And...I want to know your name."

"Is that all, or are there more stipulations I can expect you to add?"

"Well, obviously I want to know what it is you want me to help you with. Since you are a rebel I don't know what kinds of things you might want from me," I quipped and held my wrists up higher to wordlessly insist that he cut the ties off.

He rolled his eyes and whipped out a knife, then sliced them off. I watched them flutter to the ground, landing in the bright patch on the ground between us.

He looked at me intensely and stated, "You have the ability to control water, which my people do not have. You can also create and thereby control fire. My people can control fire—control it, but not create it. We have been trying to get back something very treasured that was taken from us. The only way we would be able to get to...this treasure, is if we could control water because we must traverse an underwater cave. Also, we found out that the grotto where...it is being held is guarded by a Daemalum. We could deal with the creature, but we would need to get there first by traversing the waterway."

My head buzzed with questions. *Daemalum does not sound good!* "What is this treasure? I told you, I'm not a thief. And what is a Daemalum?" I demanded, I was already regretting this bargain.

"Well, first off, it is not stealing as they were taken from us in the first place. And...well it is not treasure. It is to us..." he hesitated, and looked at me pensively. Finally, he continued, "It is our children. Most of our children were taken from us when we were near Umorfae territory. They are trying to use them as leverage against us. We had tried to fight back at the time, but they had the upper hand, the children were already captured. To fight at that time would have risked their lives even more so." He slumped as he explained, clearly in pain over this serious transgression.

I sat dumbfounded, I couldn't believe that the Umorfae would do that. I reeled at the thought of what those children must be experiencing, separated from their parents and everything they know. And their parents must be sick with worry. "The Umorfae truly did that, stole your children? And hid them in a cave? Why a cave? What do they want from you ultimately? You said they were using them as leverage." I thought back on my time with them, I couldn't picture the Umorfae doing something so unjust. *Could Opius do that?*

"The warriors were essentially just the henchmen, some of them have sworn loyalty to a ruthless being named Dashelle. I do not know much about him, other than I know he is not one of the typical Fae in Alternis. He is different, but I am not sure what manner of creature he is. Dashelle wants to rule over all Fae, but I do not understand why some Umorfae are working with him. I do not think all are, I am not sure how far the alliance goes. We have been a thorn in their side, so they finally took something we cared about to get us to fall in line. But I believe that we would not just be ruled by Dashelle, I believe he would enslave us. Instead of just doing what he wants, we have been trying to find a way to get them back on our own. The entrance to the cave is underwater, they are using their elemental skill against us. Our fire ability is useless against it."

I sat quietly as I regarded him, the weight on his shoulders was practically tangible. "You're Ignisfae, aren't you. I heard Opius mention that as one of the Fae races."

"Yes."

I regretted being adversarial with him. He was obviously dealing with a lot. *This place just got a whole lot more complicated,* I griped to myself as I rubbed my brow with my thumb and forefinger. "Was Opius one of the Umorfae that captured your children?" I asked carefully, *please say no!* "Also, the Daemalum. Is that a creature of some kind?"

He sighed. "I did not recognize any of the Umorfae when the children were taken. I only knew Opius by reputation, but I know he was not there. I do not know where his allegiance lies. And Daemalum...they are dangerous creatures. Dark hearts and dreadful, they will do anything to torment others. They feed on fear and live to terrorize. Handing them terrified children is like handing them precious gems. Holding them captive promises the Daemalum continuous sustenance."

This was sounding worse all the time. Here I was thinking I had escaped my grievances regarding my own life, and the decisions I didn't want to make, and had found this wondrous place. But Alternis turned out to be more treacherous and convoluted than my human reality. What would my decisions here mean? Choices that would affect more than just me? Life in the human world seemed so easy by comparison.

I regarded the situation for a few moments. Part of me just wanted to run away from this just as I had run away from the decisions of my real life. But what if I could actually make a difference and help these children, help these people reunite with them, and locate Josie? But then, what if he's not telling me the whole story, what if he's only feeding me the parts that will sway me. There had been little indication when I was at the Umorfae castle that this was going on. I wasn't sure who to trust or believe. I flip-flopped in a mental committee until I resigned that I had to help him, regardless of how I felt. If I wanted to either find Josie or just leave Alternis, I would need to try. I was still conflicted as I agreed, "All right, I will help you do this. I'll do all I can to return them safely."

"Who is this friend you want help finding?"

"She's apparently another Vale Born like me. Her name is Josie, we grew up together. I heard from a Syrenni in the castle that she had been here, but Opius didn't indicate that she was ever there. She has been missing for six months, my time." I did some quick math. "That might be over five thousand rotations." My stomach clenched as I realized how long it had been.

"Another Vale Born?" He mused. "I have not heard any rumors of one. But, I agree. I will help try to find her, *after* you complete your end."

I released a breath, with their help my chances of success were probably much better. *I just have to save a whole bunch of kids first,* I cringed.

He gave one sharp nod. "We have our bargain."

I stuck out my hand, and waited for him to take it. He eyed me cautiously, and made no move to accept. "It's called a handshake. In my land, when two parties agree, they shake hands, to bind the agreement in good faith," I explained, still with my hand outstretched. He nodded again, then took my hand. Warm to the touch, strong and slightly calloused, I shook it as I finally introduced myself, "My name is Lily. What's yours?"

His eyes became more intense as he looked further into mine, and pulled down his wrapping to expose his dark, tawny face.

My breath stilled as I took in his features.

"I am called Rannoch."

CHAPTER 16

The words that rolled off his well-formed lips after he revealed his face were almost inaudible to me. His heroic jawline tensed as he quieted. My eyes drifted back to his, which narrowed at me just as I realized I didn't hear what he said. The thoughts of what my "help" might entail swirled in my mind. He abruptly stood to leave. Apparently the interrogation—turned bargaining agreement—had ended.

Rannoch swept aside the tent door, revealing Kerenza waiting outside. He muttered a few quick words to her, then stomped off.

"If you would like to join me for nocte fare, it is being brought over soon," she called in to me.

My stomach answered for me with a rumble. I exited the tent, then walked with her to the cook fire nestled between several tents.

As we sat down on a low circle of seats Kerenza turned to me. "I am relieved that you are going to help us find the children. We are skilled with fire, but there is no way we can control the water to enter the cave." She had a pained look in her eyes as she spoke, and fidgeted with a ring on her middle finger as her brows furrowed.

I held my breath for a moment, I did want to help these people, in spite of their initial treatment of me. Plus I needed their help. But how was I going to control the water in the cave? I could only do a little with the skill so far. It sounded like a big leap to expect that I could affect a large volume of it. "I'm going to do my best. I can only imagine how it's been for the families. Helping get the children back is the right thing to do." I assured her, even though I wasn't sure of my ability to actually complete the task.

She gulped as she attempted to stifle tears, but one slipped over her cheek anyway. She looked down at her ring again as her lip wobbled, twisting the band as she surveyed it. She ran her thumb over the smooth, glass-like gem encased in a burnished gold bezel surrounded by intricate patterns. The jewel was a brilliant burst of red flame, which illuminated and pulsed from within. Another tear escaped as she stammered, "M-m-my Filia. She is one of the ones taken. I look at my ring constantly to see if she is still there. It is connected to her lifeline, the gem glows from the beat of her heart. I am terrified I will look down and see the fire has dimmed. Every so often, I receive images from her through the ring bond. It is both relief and profound sadness when I get them, because I see what she sees." She choked on the last words and closed her eyes as more tears spilled out.

I was stunned, I hadn't realized one of the children was hers. She had seemed so shielded before, to now bare her raw desperation for her stolen daughter caught me off guard. On the one hand, I was honored that she felt she could tell me these things, but on the other it increased the pressure tenfold. It was not just the collective children, it was also Kerenza's child. The personal thread touched that much closer and made it more real.

"I'm so sorry, I promise to do everything I can." I attempted to comfort her, and put one hand tentatively on her shoulder. All the memories threatened to tumble through my mind of the various times that I had done everything I could. When 'everything' was not enough. And the disastrous consequences of my falling short. I held those memories at bay, though the dark thoughts were clawing to get out; to swoop in and render me useless. They would have undoubtedly stunted me from thinking I could actually help.

Kerenza sobbed and nodded her head as she took a few shuddering breaths. She steadied her breathing more and wiped her tears, though her eyes were bleary and brows were in a knot.

"I can only imagine how stressful this has been for you," I tried to ease her further. Seeing her pain sparked an idea. Perhaps emotional pain can be eased just like physical pain. I focused on my energy and channeled it through my hand, and pulsed it gently to her, honing in on her emotional wound. I pictured it turning from dark and heavy to light and buoyant. As I focused the light, my own gnawing thoughts ebbed away. Washed back with the flowing surge. She visibly lifted up, her breathing lightened and she sighed.

I jumped when a strong hand clamped on my wrist. I was so focused I hadn't noticed Rannoch had walked up behind us.

"What are you doing?" He barked, his eyes blared with contempt as he released my arm. Rannoch looked at Kerenza's face, then back to mine. "You should not make her relive that day."

I blinked and lifted my hands in bewilderment. "I was just trying to make her feel better!"

He put his arm around her shoulders and softened his expression as he spoke to her, "We will get Emblyn back. We are doing everything we can. But we need to focus and keep our eyes on the task, for the safety of everyone."

She nodded as she sagged into him. He gave her one last reassuring squeeze before releasing her and walked away. Looking over his shoulder at me with an annoyed glance he declared, "We will eat, sleep, and then head out once we are up."

I didn't respond as he stalked off.

"He has his own way of dealing with the pain," Kerenza offered, "he gets angry, and sometimes directs the anger at the wrong person. You did not do anything wrong, it was my choice to tell you."

I shrugged and shook my head, "Well, maybe he needs to remember that I'm here to help now."

She raised her eyebrows and nodded in agreement.

"Kerenza, I need your help as well. Can you tell me, did you see or hear about another Vale Born that was here? Her name is Josie, she has light brown hair, tall like me. She has been missing from my realm and I'm very worried about her. Someone in the castle told me she had been here."

She shook her head. "No, you are the only one I have seen. I did not hear about another one, and did not even hear about you beforehand. Usually word of a Vale Born travels fast. Historically Fae hybrids have caused...quite a stir here."

I frowned, so far the only clue I'd wrangled was a cryptic teaser from Naiya. Opius was no help, and Kerenza didn't know anything. My stomach tightened as I thought about the last time I saw her. Josie's pretty face and bright smile flashed in my mind.

An older female Ignisfae carried over a tray with three lumps rolled in cheesecloth, which distracted me from the thoughts of my friend. She handed it to Kerenza before bowing and wordlessly left. I watched intently as Kerenza unrolled the packages, my eyes lit up as I saw that the parcels were our meal. A thin, flat-bread covering wrapped tightly around whatever was pouched inside. After she finished unrolling them she placed them above the fire in the hearth, then sat down on the stool across from me.

She made a scooping motion toward the fire, which bloomed in response. I watched the flames dance, part of me was mesmerized by them, the other part terrified. I couldn't help shrinking back any time I was near fire. Treacherous beauty, I supposed.

Kerenza studied my face. "You do not like fire, do you?" She asked in a soft tone.

"No, I really don't. Fire holds many...bad memories for me. Every time I see it, it brings them back to the surface," I responded sadly.

She regarded me for a moment before she countered, "Well, maybe you just have to learn how you have control over it, before you let it control you."

For a split second, her response held immense clarity. If I did have control over it, perhaps it wouldn't hold such power over my emotions and my mind. I controlled it, not vice versa. In that small moment, my logical mind took hold of that thought and I was not under its powerful grip. But then doubt and fear crept back in, as they always did. *It's a force of nature that cannot be bargained with.*

I wanted to change the subject, but the questions I wanted answered were no easier than the thoughts I had floating in my head. "How old is your daughter. Emblyn, is her name?"

She looked into the fire, and called a tendril of flame to her hands. I stared wide-eyed as I watched her cradle it, when she responded, "Yes, Emblyn. She is five cycles old. I could not have anticipated the impact she would have on me. Before she was born, I knew no fear. I could fight anyone, perform any daring task without worry. I was sure of myself as a warrior. Then she came, and suddenly, I was afraid of so much. I did not know myself anymore. Who was this that now lacked self confidence and saw threats to her filia around every corner? I supposed this is part of the natural process of child bearing, to change our will to protect a child. Even still, these were traits that I had seen in others that I had previously thought to be weakness, and now...this was me too. Did that make me weak? It only further added to my new feelings of inadequacy. Eventually I grew past it and learned to adjust, but the day she was taken all those fears and worries that I had quieted returned. And this time, I was angry and dismayed with myself for a whole different reason. Not for having the feelings, but for silencing them. Because now they were legitimate, they were there for a reason and I had sidestepped them. And I had ultimately failed to protect her."

She pulled the ball of flame in her hands a little further, making it grow, before clapping her hands together and snuffed the flame. I squeezed her shoulder and twisted my mouth, I didn't want her to see my lip wobble as I kept back the tears that stung my eyes. Words of comfort evaded me as I released my hand and returned to stare at the fire.

On a whim, I tried calling a flame for myself, after all I had controlled water in this same way. I tentatively beckoned a small bit, using both hands to push it toward itself so that it kept its distance from each hand. Just like pushing water—however I must have been too forceful, as the flame shrank down and disappeared.

"That was good, Lily, a magna first attempt. You just need to learn the balance, if you direct your hands too much toward each other it will shrink the flame into nothing. If you angle your hands just slightly it will maintain it without growing, and if you open your hands the flame will grow," Kerenza instructed as she called another flame over and demonstrated.

I tried again, with more success. It was unnerving to handle fire, it felt unnatural to do it intentionally when everything inside me told me to get away. And yet, a small piece of me healed as I exerted my will over the flame. If only I had this control when it mattered. I thought of Maris's beautiful smile, and my dad's warm laugh. Angrily, I winked the flame out of existence.

"Perhaps you and Rannoch are not so different from each other," Kerenza commented.

I looked at her with raised brows, realizing I had betrayed my thoughts by killing the flame in anger. "I don't have a good relationship with fire. This is going to be difficult for me and may take some time," I confessed as I looked at my palms in dismay. Emotionally drained didn't even start to describe my mood.

She said nothing as she stared at me, waiting.

Well, shit. All right. She'd bared her soul to me, I decided I should do the same in return. I took a shuddering breath as I looked down again. "Where I grew up wildfires happen almost every year. Two years ago, a fire raged through and burned most ranches in our small town called Black Oak Grove. We were evacuating horses when I realized…that my dad and sister had not gotten out yet. I raced my horse over the hill to try…try and save them. But," I sobbed at last, choking back tears, "I couldn't. My horse was terrified. He wouldn't budge and I couldn't run on foot. It just happened so fast, they were gone."

Kerenza returned the comforting gesture and put a hand on

my shoulder, nodding her understanding. What can you say or do when there is a trauma so deep, a gaping wound slashed down the center of the life I knew. Words did not suffice. They never did. I reached up and placed my hand over hers. Somehow, she did make me feel better. Perhaps it was the fact that we both had collected damage that cannot be seen.

I wiped my eyes as I saw Rannoch, approaching in the distance.

CHAPTER 17

Rannoch walked up, as Kerenza began pulling the rolls out of the chiminea. He eyed us suspiciously as he joined, his gazed darted from Kerenza to me.

Kerenza forced a smile as she passed me a wrap and asked idle questions about how I spent my time back home, a meager attempt to circumvent our previous conversation.

I answered in short responses, mostly about horses and shows, as I took a bite. After unloading my horrible history to Kerenza, I didn't want to think about other aspects of my life back home. I focused instead on the scent wafting up to me, comforting my soul. It smelled hearty; shredded beef with hints of rosemary, which satisfied my stomach and my spirit. "This is incredible."

Kerenza smiled and stated, "Illyana is a magna cook, we always appreciate her tortams! So, what is a horse and what is a horseshow? I am not familiar with those terms." Rannoch watched me from lowered brows as he shoved his Fae burrito into his mouth. His quick, intense glances reminded me of a hawk.

I was mid-bite and lifted the wrap up in question, "This is

called a tortam?" I asked around a mouthful. I swallowed and answered, "It's very good. A horse is a...large quadruped herd animal that some humans ride. Horseback riding is a way of life, it demands a lot of time invested and respect for the animal. I live on land that has our own horses and we caretake for several others as well. A horseshow is a contest where skill on horseback is measured against other riders."

Talking about the ranch and home made me think of what time it might be there at this moment. Had they noticed my absence by now? I didn't have a grasp on the time difference, but I imagined they would notice soon enough that I hadn't returned from my trail ride. It dawned on me that I hadn't even told anyone I was going out. Just like Josie. Hopefully Apollo had the good sense to go home. Knowing him, come dinner time he would find his way there one way or another.

Kerenza perked up at my response and babbled, "Oh! We Ignisfae ride a large herd animal as well! They are called equus. We believe in coexisting with them, they have to choose to let us ride them. Some prefer to remain wild, but many choose to come live with us. Rannoch's equus is called Steren, the leader of the herd. Kindred hearts, I suppose. Though his mount is not doing well at the moment."

Rannoch narrowed his eyes at her but said nothing. I smiled, they were horse people, like me.

"What is wrong with Steren? Perhaps I could take a look? I was sort of a healer for our horses back in the human realm, and here in Alternis I have healing power. Maybe I could help?" I offered.

Kerenza looked shocked. "Healing powers? That is...unheard of. How did you discover this?"

"I had healed one of the Umorfae guards after he was shot with the arrow, he was losing a lot of blood and I managed to stop the bleeding and stitch it closed with...magic I guess." I attempted to not glare at Rannoch again over the attack he had committed as I answered.

He sighed and grumbled reluctantly to Kerenza, "Yes, she told me of her healing ability when we were in the tent." He shook his head as he stared at his half eaten tortam. "I do not know what is wrong with him. His girth has been bloated and he is not eating. He is also spending a lot of time on the ground which is not good. I suppose...you could take a look."

I was half-tempted to sneer at him. *Oh wow, thank you so much!* But I filtered myself and responded simply, "I would be happy to."

After I overfilled myself on the burrito, the three of us walked across camp to where I assumed the equus were stabled. My curiosity bubbled to see what they looked like, if they were anything like the horses I knew.

We passed several warriors on the way, all of whom shot me sharp, sideways glances. I realized my Umorfae attire made me stick out like a sore thumb. "Is there an extra set of your clothing that I might borrow? I just realized how much attention I call to myself with what I'm wearing."

"Oh sure, it is *just* your clothes," Rannoch retorted.

I rolled my eyes at him as Kerenza cut in, "Of course, that will be no problem."

We came to an area that had large canvas shelters and troughs of water. I stopped in my tracks, stunned into silence as I beheld the enormous equus that roamed unfenced.

CHAPTER 18

"They're winged!" I exclaimed. *And fucking huge!*

Their large, beautiful wings tucked gracefully around their sides. They weren't feathered, like the depictions of pegasus. Their hair, which was like typical short horsehair, grew partway down the arms of the wings before fading away to smooth, leathery skin. The multicolored wing tattoo winding around Rannoch's right arm flashed in my mind. I crept to the closest one, he snorted a quick breath out his nose, but didn't act perturbed by my presence.

"They're a lot bigger than horses, we measure them according to hand widths at the withers, which is where the base of the neck meets the body. My horse is considered tall, measuring sixteen hands. These are a good five hands taller, if not more," I remarked as I realized I might not even be able to reach the bony protrusion on the top of their backs. *Wow, twenty one hands tall at least, that's a long way down if you fall!* Though if you were flying, their height would be an afterthought.

"Other than the fact that they have wings and are larger, they appear to be similar to horses. I would guess their biology might be similar as well," I commented to Rannoch. His only sign that he had even listened to me was an abrupt nod of his head and quick motion with his hand to direct me to his equus.

I walked up to a stunning, black beast of an animal. Even laying on the ground incapacitated, he was majestic. His labored breathing could be heard before we even approached. I winced at his distended belly, *definitely not a good sign*. He barely responded as Rannoch put his hand on him to comfort him. Another equus—smaller than Steren—paced nearby. Rannoch glanced over, following my eyeline.

"That is Zephyrine, the mate of Steren. She has been fretting near him since he fell ill," he commented as he turned back to his ailing mount.

"How long has he been like this? Is there a caretaker or animal healer that has been keeping watch?" I asked. Steren was clearly in a dire state.

Rannoch nodded. "He has not gotten off the ground for three rotations now. Rovan is a good animedicus, he has been keeping watch over our equus for many cycles, and has been here with Steren almost constantly since he fell ill. I will go find him."

As he departed to find this animedicus, which I took to be their version of a vet, I proceeded to approach the ailing creature. I placed my hands on his belly, hoping to see if my magic could help identify the issue. I surged my power into his gut, right away I could feel the problem. A blockage in his intestine. I could almost see it when I closed my eyes, a dark mass, bound in red. Damaged tissue surrounded by inflammation, his body was attempting to combat the obstruction, but having no effect.

Rannoch appeared with another Ignisfae, who flashed a skeptical glance over me as Rannoch finished explaining who I was. The lean, lithe being with burnt umber skin passed another sweeping gaze—mirroring Rannoch's amber, hawk-like eyes.

I stood a little taller. "Can you tell me about what care he's received? Do you have the capability of surgical procedures if it becomes necessary?"

He regarded me with eyebrows askance for a moment before he responded, "I have been giving him an herb we use to address pain, as well as another for stomach discomforts. I have increased the dosage of both several times, but so far he has not improved. As far as surgical procedures, that is not something we do unless it is a surface issue such as sewing a wound closed." Rovan knelt down to Steren and cupped his muzzle, causing his long braid to swish down, the tail of it brushing the ground. Concern filled his eyes as he looked at the equus, not caring that his black and ruby plait was becoming dirty as it coiled on the ground.

I resisted the urge to gulp at the display of emotion, I needed a clear head and clinical mind for what might come. "I believe he has an intestinal blockage. I want to see if my healing magic can clear the blockage, but if it can't we may have to approach this surgically. This is a grave situation, in my home land by the time an animal is at this stage he has no chance for survival without surgery, which would entail cutting him open and searching through his intestines to find and remove the issue. It may be necessary to prepare for this."

"You want to cut him open?" Rannoch blurted. "How could gutting him help him?"

"By doing it in a careful manner, we could save his life. It is risky but without doing it he will die, *if* healing with magic doesn't work," I responded evenly, as I struggled to maintain my composure. I needed to remove all doubt. And I certainly did not want to start doubting myself.

Even doing a surgery in a fully prepared and sanitized operating room was risky. But, he would die without it if I couldn't clear the blockage with magic. I had only been in one surgical procedure like it when I interned with a horse vet, and it was an intense operation. Still, I had learned at least something to consider attempting it, although horse surgeons train for years to be prepared to handle invasive surgery. I debated internally for a few more moments, but there was no other option. I needed to steel myself for the eventuality that he would need this to survive. It was that simple.

I continued addressing Rovan, when he said nothing regarding my initial diagnosis, "Do you know the dosage of the herb used for pain to render him unconscious? We will need him to be completely out, if it comes to that. Also, we'll need to prepare the area to have it as clean as possible, by boiling a canvas drop cloth and boiling sharp instruments. And one last thing, an antibiotic. Is there something that you use to help the body fight infection? We'll need to help prevent contamination."

Rovan arched an eyebrow and looked to Rannoch. Rannoch's face scrunched, but he said nothing. "We have never attempted a surgery of that nature, I do not know if it could be successful. We could prepare everything as you say, and the herbs can be used to cause unconsciousness," he responded in a measured, even manner, though his expression conveyed more doubt than his voice. "Additionally there is another herb we use for infection. But I must ask, are you sure cutting him open is wise? It is far more invasive than how we usually treat creatures."

"I understand this sounds invasive and risky, but if we do nothing we will surely lose the animal. I will attempt to heal him with magic first, but I think we need to prepare for this, just in case." I answered Rovan, before I turned to Rannoch. "I want to be clear, I am not overly experienced in this area. I know enough to be able to say that he will die without treatment, but as far as the surgery, it is not a guarantee of success. He is at the point where there are few options to save his life. My goal is to heal him and I would not, under normal circumstances, unnecessarily put him in harm's way by attempting a surgery that is out of the scope of what I have been trained to do. However, these are not normal circumstances. There is not another option that will treat him effectively. The choice is yours in how we proceed."

I waited as he weighed my words, his mouth a thin line as he looked at Steren. After a long pause, without breaking his gaze, he uttered, "Yes, do it. I think you are right that he will die if we do nothing."

My mind was already in motion. Steren's immediate need swept aside any doubt. I commanded Rovan, "We'll need the pre-pared supplies. I'm going to start attempting to heal him without surgery first." While he didn't jump to action, he did as I asked and walked off to presumably gather what I had requested.

I knelt next to Steren, and placed my hand on his head to see if I could sense his feelings before I began. I reached in with a thread of golden energy, and eased it up next to his mind. He was in such extreme pain he didn't respond to my mental nudge, I could sense his exhaustion and was at the threshold of what he could handle. My attempts at comforting him went unnoticed by the equus, it didn't make a dent in his pain level. I let the thread recoil and moved over to his belly. I surged in, pressing in at the blockage from two sides. I focused, imagining the mass dissolving apart and slowly moving through his system. The tissues surrounding the obstruction reduced in inflammation and quieted considerably, but the actual blockage didn't change. I tried again, going from two different, opposing directions. Still there was not much improvement. I backed my power out and sat back on my heels.

I glanced at Rannoch, who shot me a questioning glance. I shook my head. "The magic alone isn't working. The blockage isn't responding, only the tissue around it is."

Rovan walked up, toting supplies with the help of another Ignisfae. They carried over a large drop cloth, dripping wet. "We boiled it as instructed. It is completely soaked, but clean," Rovan commented as they heaved the makeshift surgical surface. I motioned for them to lay it down under Steren's swollen girth.

"Good. Let's get him sedated so we can begin. We'll have to do this the hard way." *I must be crazy.*

He nodded and began preparing the herbal anesthesia. Hopefully it was strong enough to keep him unconscious during the procedure. The last thing I needed was a giant hoof whacked in my head, and I certainly didn't want him to feel being opened up.

Kerenza leaned over and asked, "Is there anything I can do to help?"

I smiled at her, at least it seemed I had made a friend. Rovan finished administering the mixture while Rannoch held Steren's head.

"We need to be ready with extra towels and a bucket of hot water. There will be a lot of bleeding. Also, you'll need to restrain the mare. We need her to keep her distance during the procedure,"

I answered. She nodded and left.

Rannoch finally spoke as he crouched, cradling Steren's head as it lolled to the side, "Could magic be used to slow the bleeding?" His eyes darted from the enormous equine's to mine. He clearly loved this creature.

I thought for a moment before I responded, "No, I don't think so. When I healed the injured guard the process of slowing the bleeding also closed the wound. I won't be able to start doing that until I've completed removing the obstruction. Fortunately, because of the magic, I know right where it is. I won't have to search through to find it."

Kerenza came back with the water and towels, Steren now unconscious. I pressed my hand to his head, spooling out a thread to be sure. I could sense his calmness through it, a deep sleep with the absence of pain. I nodded to Rannoch. "Okay, we're ready. I'll work as quickly as I can to minimize the blood loss. Rovan, you and I need to both wash our hands well to be sure they are clean. I'd like you next to me to assist." He nodded and motioned to walk with him.

Rovan carried a cook pot with water over to a fire ring at a nearby tent, and set it on the spit hook. He held up one hand in the direction of one of the ever burning torches that were dotted along the entire perimeter of the Ignisfae camp, and called a runnel of fire. He channeled it to the pit base and surged the flame to engulf the pot. The basin heated within moments, then we scrubbed our hands in the uncomfortably steaming water.

Holding my hands aloft to prevent brushing them against anything and picking up contaminants, we headed back to the ailing equus. He and I knelt side by side in front of Steren's belly,

I took a deep breath and tried to not let the fear show on my face as I picked up the sharp knife they had given me. *Well here goes, please give me the strength to do this.* I struggled to keep my breath from quickening. I felt one last time for the exact location of the blockage.

When I was sure of the most accurate line to cut, I began. Rovan stilled, I could feel his wince as I sliced in a steady, straight manner. Right away Steren's distended innards began bulging out of the opening. I cut back a good fourteen inches on his belly, I needed enough of a gap to pull out intestines to reach the affected area.

Blood surged out, spilling out in a tidal wave of sanguine fluid. I tried not to panic at the massive deluge escaping him.

"He will bleed out!" Rovan hollered.

"You should not have done this!" Rannoch thundered. "If he dies-"

"Calm down and let me think!" The color drained from my face as I rushed to put pressure along the incision.

"Close it back up!" Rannoch ordered. I flashed my eyes to him, his ears pinned back as he glared at me.

I opened my mouth to speak, when I remembered holding the water bubble. *Blood plasma is ninety percent water.* Rannoch was right, water magic can be used on blood. I snapped my head back to the incision, and focused on my hands to push the blood back in. It responded immediately, and slowed to a halt. *But now what do I do, I can't just hold the blood in, I need to pull the intestines out.* I racked my mind, then recalled how the surgery had been done with the horse on his back. *Gravity, gravity will help.*

"Rovan," I ordered, ignoring Rannoch, "we need to turn him

so he's facing up, then I need you to ease the innards out of him until we find the problem. I will guide you through it, so that I can continue to hold back his blood."

He stared at me hard for a moment, before he turned to Rannoch, waiting for his approval.

Rannoch glowered at me, but gave one nod to proceed.

As Rovan struggled to turn the massive horse-creature upward, I could feel the force of the blood surge lessen. Once Steren was facing up, Rovan pulled a few feet of intestine through at a time, healthy but inflamed. By the time he had gotten about ten feet of his small bowel out, the blockage reached the gash, larger than the opening was.

"Now, carefully work it out of the opening," I instructed calmly, "this is what we have to remove."

Rovan gritted his teeth as he gripped and wiggled the mass. My vision speckled as he finally birthed it through the gap, the unhealthy tissue exposed at last. Not only was there a large round blockage of what was most likely an accumulation of feed and dirt, in front of it was another obstruction.

"He has an intussusception and a blockage," I diagnosed after looking over the massive spherical lump. "The intestine telescoped inside itself, the outer intestine began to digest the interior one, causing it to become impassable. This whole section will have to be cut out, and the healthy ends reattached."

I took a deep breath and released my hold on his blood, then picked the knife up. I didn't want to waste any more time talking while he was in need. Using the canvas floor like a cutting board, I sliced at the border of healthy tissue before the beginning of the obstruction, then cut the other side—past the damaged portion.

Blood started to spill over his sides as I worked. I cringed, *must work faster.*

"Rovan, move the discarded tissue out of the way." Silently, he pulled it away as I focused on the now-healthy, open ends. I closed my eyes and centered my thoughts on them, using a thread of bright gold light that flowed down my arm and out through my fingers. I began to stitch them together, working carefully so that there were no gaps. Sewing around and around to maintain the open passage, I worked the magic thread like attaching two tubes together.

I could feel myself weakening, healing Steren was draining my reserve. But I could also sense that the intestine was now healed, and there should be no issue with it, as long as we could put him back together effectively. I broke off the drain on my power and returned to normal vision. Rannoch searched my eyes with careworn lines in his face, still cradling Steren's massive head.

"Everything went great I think, we just have to put him back together now," I reassured him. He nodded and released a breath. I gulped air and focused on the task at hand, then began stuffing his viscera back inside as carefully as I could, but it took some force as things had shifted. I struggled to not empty the contents of my stomach over the sight of his guts. I grimaced, *ugh, that tortam needs to stay put.* I worked carefully with as much speed as I dared, eventually it was all back in place. I unwound a golden thread again, my reserve had returned for the most part. *That must be the key, taking a break before the reserve runs out.*

I closed my eyes and channeled the thread out my fingers again, and started to weave the two sides of the surgical opening back together.

But they were too far apart, spread so wide that I couldn't get the seams of the skin to touch. I pulled harder, and harder. A bead of sweat rolled down my temple. I cracked an eye open to check, sure enough the gap was nowhere near able to close. *Staples. How do I do staples with magic?*

I let out another thread, starting from the middle of the gash. I pulled the thread up to the opposite side and yanked on it. It went taut as I pulled harder on the cord. The opening closed some—but not enough. I could feel the Fae male's worry rising, I had to push thoughts of them aside so I could focus. My panic started to take hold.

I put my foot on the equus's side for leverage, and pulled again on the thread which was still attached. I grunted as I heaved the split skin closed. The sliced borders finally came close enough to each other that I managed to cast a loop through the other side. I lashed three times to create a mock staple, then moved halfway in between the bound center and the apex of the incision. Repeating the same steps, I made another thick binding. Once a third staple was in place, I started to sew the bulging cut from top to bottom. Left with four small openings, rather than one unwieldy pointed oval, I pulled the cord and cinched the end shut of the last one.

I did one more pass, to make sure the suture was solid. The pressure in his gut was still high from his vitals, having it burst open from the strain was the last thing we needed. I snipped the supply of magic once it was done and let the remainder recoil back into me. I had almost drained myself again, but fortunately I retained my consciousness. I dropped back to my knees, panting as my vision faded.

Rovan and I worked together to mop up his belly with hot,

wet towels. Finished, I stood up and wobbled, Rovan put out an arm to steady me, his nimble fingers gripped my shoulder as I swayed. Depleted from the healing—though not as bad as when I had saved Locrien, I regained my composure after a moment. "I'm okay, just a little woozy," I commented, though he hadn't inquired.

Rovan looked back at Steren, stunned. "I had no knowledge that this could happen, or that something could be done about it. We lost an equus several cycles back to a swollen belly like this, perhaps that is what happened to her."

"It's quite possible. Intussusception is somewhat rare, but a blockage is fairly common in quadrupeds that eat their feed directly off the ground, causing the dried grass to mix with dirt. You can help prevent it by putting their feed in a bucket or net, then it is not mixing with dirt."

He steepled his fingers. "Yes, I suppose that makes sense."

I stepped over to Rannoch and held my hand up below Steren's ear. I probed the equus's mind for signs of stress, a subtle exhale was the only response he gave. "I'm not sure how long he'll be unconscious for, but I sense he's pain free. We should let him rest and wake up on his own when the anesthesia wears off. I think he'll recover just fine." I looked over to Kerenza, and signaled that it was all right to release his mate. Zephyrine shook her head and trotted up to his side, sniffed him carefully and nuzzled his mane.

Rannoch tore his eyes from his steed to look at me. My breath hitched at his gaze. Intense. Fiery. But this time it did not hold the disgust I had seen before. "Thank you," he said sincerely.

I was taken aback. For that moment I saw the vulnerable being that cared deeply, and worried for his creature-friend. His eyes, when not filled with anger, complemented his striking features.

In that instant I saw the compassionate individual underneath the rough, rocky exterior he exuded.

The moment passed and he pivoted to Rovan. When his eyes left mine I felt a chill, like moving from sun to shade. "We need to leave on the next rotation. I will be back to check on him before then, but I would ask you to keep a close watch on him while I am away," he stated.

"I will do as you command my-" Rovan responded, stopping abruptly when Rannoch's eyes flashed. Rovan lightly rapped his shoulder and nodded once.

The three of us left the stable area to head back to the main camp. The thought of seeing through Rannoch's facade lingered with me as we trudged back.

Kerenza moved closer as we walked and whispered, "That was impressive, Lily. I have never seen anything like that. Do you think he will heal soon?" I could feel warmth from her, just as I did from Rannoch. It radiated from their soul when they didn't shield it. It made her even more endearing, and lulled me into a sense of possible, genuine friendship.

I smiled. "I think he will. The magic seems to make healing rapid." Relief surged. I wanted to laugh, run, high five myself, light off fireworks, something to celebrate the ridiculous near-failure turned victory, a victory that potentially saved a life.

I was still smiling when we came upon a circle of tents, with an unlit fire ring in the center.

"You will take that tent, Lily, it has clothes in it for you." Rannoch motioned toward the smaller one in the middle. By his tone, his authoritative shield had returned. I glanced at the bigger, more homey looking tent next door. *I wonder if they have me sleeping in their daughter's tent.*

"Come back out and join us for a drink around the fire, after you have changed," Kerenza piped warmly.

Rannoch gave her a hard look, apparently I had not won him over just yet. *Sheesh you'd think after what I did he'd be a little more gracious.*

"What fire?" I asked with a sarcastic smirk.

He shot me an annoyed stare. Without breaking eye contact he threw out his hand to the direction of the closest torch bordering the camp and called a wide plume, then smashed it into the fire pit.

"That fire," he retorted, as he turned his back to me and headed into their tent. Kerenza shrugged apologetically as she started arranging seats around the blaze.

I went into my tent, a small stack of clothing and a low bedroll on the floor was all that waited for me. Not much in the way of accommodations. A loose fitting gauze blouse was folded neatly atop a woven blanket, with a pair of matching billowy pants. As I struggled to peel off the Umorfae leathers, my eyes fell on a washbasin and stack of rags. *Not quite a bath, but I'll take it!* At least I'd get to clean up a little. The scented water emanated an essence I couldn't place, warm and sensual, and made my skin butter soft.

I slipped on the comfortable cream top and pants. The simple shirt hung slightly shy of the fitted waistband, leaving a sliver of skin exposed. The pants were like a cloud around my tired legs, they flowed out and draped down to my ankles into fitted cuffs. I untied my hair and finger brushed it out. The excessive waves, fluffy and full from being braided for several days, fell in a silky, curled mane down my back. I sighed and rubbed my scalp after finally releasing it, Naiya had braided it fairly tight.

I came back out of the tent to find Rannoch and Kerenza, also dressed in their nightclothes, talking quietly by the fire. His eyes flashed over me as I exited, his gaze seemed borderline pleased.

Kerenza's face lit up. "Come sit! We will have a quick sip before bed." She stood up and handed me a nearly round, clear glass. She grabbed a waterskin off the hook of her chair. "This is called vinirubrum, it is my favorite. But be careful, it is strong," she cautioned as she poured a dark red vintage.

They each raised their glasses, then took a sip. It refracted glints of light as I sipped, like it was made with magic. The strong, vibrant taste was full bodied, like a mixture of every berry I had ever tried, with a finish of exotic spices. My insides warmed as I was instantly comforted.

"This is delicious," I expressed. It truly was. I enjoyed red wine back home, while similar, it was different in its complex flavors. I took another sip as she smiled. I started to feel the effects, probably because I was so exhausted from everything that had happened. I was tired even before healing Steren. *All in a day's work: get caught by rebels, march ridiculously far to their camp, make a risky deal, save a magical horse with intestinal surgery. No big deal.* I stared into the fire as I mentally recounted the events, and considered how my captors had turned to friends. Or at least Kerenza had, Rannoch was a tough nut to crack. I had broken through for a moment, but just as fast that split had closed.

Drowsiness set in fast as I finished my glass. "I'm going to sleep. It's been a long day—I mean rotation." They both nodded and bid good night.

I rose on unstable knees and stumbled to my tent. The little bedroll called, and I flopped down with zero grace. Sleep came within moments of pulling the soft blankets in a warm cocoon around me.

CHAPTER 19

"Lily, c'mon, you need to get up off your butt." Felix nudged me with his foot as I lay on the floor of my room.

"I don't want to, Felix. I just want to lie here awhile. I'm just resting," I mumbled.

"If you're just resting, why are you on the floor?"

"...I don't know. I just...don't want to think about anything. I don't want to do anything. I just want to lie here," I whispered.

"Well, mission accomplished. You're officially doing nothing. Is this about dropping out of vet school school? Or...Misty?"

I pressed my lips together. I didn't want to speak. Silence was my friend. I just wanted to lie there, forever, and stay away from the world. Bad things happen out in the world. Hiding in my room wouldn't change that, but at least I wouldn't be so much a part of it.

"Misty wasn't your fault," Felix continued, "we were already going to lose her before you got down to the barn. You know that. The vet wouldn't have gotten here for another hour. No one could help her, or the foal. You did all you could to make her more comfortable at least."

You did all you could. It echoed, over and over. My eyes stung at her name. Misty. She was such a good mare. Losses happen on a ranch. That's how it goes. In my clinical mind I could say that. But I couldn't escape the feeling that I could have done more. I believed I had made a mistake. And if I became a vet, someone else might have to bear the loss because of a mistake of mine. My decisions could cause other people to endure the losses like I have had.

I looked at my hands and gasped. They were huge, unwieldy, and disproportionately inflating. I gaped at them, then looked at Felix. He started stretching, his limbs lengthened strangely and gnashed his now wolf-like teeth.

"It's time to continue your training. Get up and fight!" He grunted in a gravelly rasp.

"What?"

"Fight Lily!"

"I.."

"Lily!" His lips moved, but his voice was not his own. Sweet. Melodic. Female.

I blinked my eyes open as I realized I was not looking at my bedroom ceiling, and Felix was not hovering over me. A bright canvas swath was all that was in my field of vision.

Oh, I forgot. "Yes, I'm getting up now, Kerenza," I called back.

I lay there for a moment, letting the melancholy dream fade away.

I rolled out of bed and scuffled over the canvas floor to the washbasin. Someone had snuck in, given me fresh warm water and a clean washcloth. The neatly folded clothing next to the washbasin turned out to be a strip of fabric that was more like a magician's never-ending scarf as I pulled it out. The long piece of thin knit material was a golden ochre, soft—yet resilient and strong. As I lifted it I glimpsed many more colors woven in than just ochre. Glimmers of red and burnt orange, subtly shifting gradations of faint greens and tawny yellow. Strand by strand, the fine details wended along, reminiscent of sedimentary rock layers, crafted with care by someone's capable hands. I started to wrap it around myself, thinking of how it looked on Kerenza. *Nope, not like that.* I started again. *This is harder than I expected.*

"Kerenza? Could you help me? I'm not sure how to put this on," I cringed as I hollered to her. She chuckled as I heard her footsteps swish in the sand. I wrinkled my nose when she ducked inside.

"Not to worry," she hummed, "a linteum takes practice to get right."

She began with the tapered, narrow tail. Kerenza looped it around my neck to start an anchor point, then widened the swath on the other side and angled it down and around to capture and cover my chest, wound around behind my back, and angled up to cross over the front, forming an 'X'. Winding around several times, and finishing with a short skirt that swooped up around each hip. A bit revealing, but comfortable with a little stretch—and it felt functional. I moved around in it to make sure it was snug.

"I like it!" I pulled back my shoulders and stood taller.

She grinned. "It suits you. The Umorfae think we are uncultured and primitive because we wear wrap—rather than constructed—clothing. But I think wrap clothing is far better, one linteum can be worn in different ways and fit multiple body shapes. Plus it does not get in the way when fighting. Constructed clothing has to be fitted to the individual. Although you should see the beautiful clothing in TerraIgni, when we celebrate. You have never seen such fabrics and garments, I would bet anyway. My favorite holiday—Praetexia—is when we weave the fabrics. Everyone participates, even…high born. We spend an entire rotation weaving together, then we have a great feast and dance until we are all ready to drop. The food and drink, the sativa, it is the best!"

"What is TerraIgni?"

"Our home city, where we live when we are not in our nomadic encampment."

"I hope I get to see that one day. I have to admit, I like this better than the clothes they dressed me in," I said as I admired the weave of my wrap.

She looked me deep in the eye. "You know, I did not expect to like you so much. But you have helped Rannoch by healing Steren, and you seem genuine. Our kind values this trait greatly. When we found you dressed like an Umorfae…well I suppose I expected you to be like them. They are not what I would call genuine, or trustworthy."

I thought back to my time with Opius, I never had an experience that would make me think they weren't trustworthy. But then again, there wasn't anything that happened that made me think they *were* trustworthy either. I recalled how he sometimes withheld information, and was evasive when I asked about Josie. *But that could be explained with the fact that he's the General, or Praetor or whatever, of the Umorfae Army. And I was a human turned Fae hybrid wanderer.*

"Speaking of Rannoch," she continued, which snapped me out of my thoughts, "he is waiting for you outside."

I bowed, then headed out of the single draped doorway. The thick, woven covering brushed past my face, detailed and colorful designs stitched along the edge caught my eye as I passed. *They really are skilled at weaving.* Kerenza followed me out, then went back into their tent.

Rannoch stood facing away from me, his back rippling with muscles which I hadn't noticed were so pronounced before. Lifting the water skins he was preparing made them that much more prominent.

As I approached he turned, doing a double take at seeing me in a linteum. He looked away from my curves and up to my eyes. "Bonum mane," he said...with a smile! I stopped in my tracks. His smile was bright, warm like Kerenza's. And utterly beautiful. I frowned at myself, remembering that I didn't know what happened to Opius, and here I was ogling some other guy—an unavailable one at that.

"Bonum mane," I echoed, unsure of how long this friendliness would last.

"I visited Steren," his deep voice was imbued with a happiness I hadn't heard from him before, "he is recovering well. He was walking around, even ate a little feed." He held out an earthenware cup to me filled with steaming liquid. "Here. Capuli."

"That's wonderful he's recovering so fast," I said as I accepted it. I inhaled the aroma of the morning brew, which smelled rich and robust. I was pleased to find that it had cream in it. *I'm such a baby about my coffee, it has to have cream!*

I took a sip as he continued, "We can go there before we depart, so that you may check on him in case there is something myself or Rovan did not notice." He picked up his cup which was set nearby, and raised it in a short salute.

Akin to coffee, and somehow so much better, strong and dark

with a sweet taste of warm caramel and rich cream.

I realized Rannoch was watching me drink, watching my mouth. "No rotation should start without capuli," he blurted as he became interested in his cup, "it looks like you would agree with me on that."

"Yes, it reminds me of what I drink in the mornings back home, called coffee. I can barely get out of bed without the promise of it waiting for me. Though I think I actually like this more," I remarked as he drained his cup.

"We should prepare to leave," he stated as he clunked his mug down on a folding wooden table, the brusk tone had returned to his voice.

I finished my Fae coffee and set the empty cup next to his. *Ugh, I wish I could have more!* With Rannoch's shift back to coldness, I decided against asking for another. Even with the momentary niceties, there still hung a tenuous air between us.

Kerenza popped out of the tent with a pack on her back and another slung over her shoulder, her striking dark, prismatic hair was tied intermittently from her crown down to the tips in a poofy faux braid. She sauntered over, and took a deep breath as she neared. "Well, we are ready to go. Here, your pack with some essentials. Also, I figured you might want extra protection." She handed me my thigh knife. I thought back to that juncture when they confiscated it, how grim and powerless I felt at being captured.

I turned up the corners of my mouth as I took it, noting the weight of the moment and the trust she had placed in me. Returning the knife was another step for our budding friendship. I closed my hand around it as I looked at her intently in her remarkable cognac eyes, "Let's do this," I asserted with confident resolve. *We will be successful at this, we must. Whatever it takes.*

I slid my gaze to Rannoch, he straightened his back and commanded, "Let us head out. It will take us several rotations to reach the cave. We need to move quickly so that we can catch them by surprise. If the Umorfae realize we are coming they will fortify the entrance with more warriors. The faster we move, the better our chances."

Kerenza and I nodded. He took one last look at each of us before wordlessly turning to march out, leading us to our hopeful victory.

CHAPTER 20

Steren nosed some dry grass that hung inside a rope net, as Rovan brushed the mount's silky coat. *Well I'm glad to see they are already feeding like I suggested!* Steren noticed us and gave Rannoch a pleased whinny. He shook his head as he trotted over, causing his long black mane to ripple.

Rannoch's face lit up as he stroked Steren's muzzle, tenderness gleamed in Rannoch's eyes as he studied his recovered steed's face. I had to turn away. When he smiled, it was...well it was distracting.

"He has improved remarkably fast, Lily, you have given me a new perspective on emergency care," Rovan said, "there is clearly much more for me to learn." Gone was the snide tone prior to healing Steren. He addressed me with respect, the sincerity caused my eyes to well up. Overcome with flooding emotions, all I could muster was a wobbly smile as I held back the tears. Relief after such a stressful situation, gratitude Steren had survived, Rovan's sentiment, satisfaction at seeing a happy reunion; all of it caused a tidal wave hammering to break through the meager emotional dam I had in place. I managed to just barely keep the impending deluge at bay with a few choking sniffles and an appreciative nod.

Kerenza smiled approvingly at me. "I think you have given all of us a new perspective. I believe this is a good omen for the task ahead of us."

My stomach fell, the good feelings I had vanished like a brisk wind had blown them away. I felt like I was on a precipice, hovering over a void of the unknown. My pulse quickened at the thought of what we might endure, and the fact that we would most likely battle a race that had first welcomed me in Alternis added an edge of guilt. Though, it didn't mean I was necessarily doing wrong by Opius, maybe he was against these Umorfae separatists.

Rannoch hardened his face and set his jaw. "Speaking of our task, we should go."

I brightened, snapped out of my downward spiral. "Will we be taking equus to get there?"

"No," he said, "equus are too easily spotted. We would lose the element of surprise. We will go on foot toward the Praegra Forest. There is a creature there—if we can find it—that can help us get to the cave and approach in stealth."

I sagged. *Ride a giant horse in the sky? No, I don't want to do that or anything.*

"Burn brightly," Rovan stated, as he saluted.

Rannoch rapped his chest. "Burn brightly." He trekked away from the equus stables, leaving Kerenza and I to keep pace behind him. I took one last look over my shoulder, to the magnificent creatures as we departed. *Someday, that would be amazing to try.*

Before leaving the bounds of the camp, I followed them to a tent laden with various weapons. They each selected a short sword, Kerenza also took a pair of sais and a spear, while Rannoch chose a bow, quiver of arrows, and a bandolier of knives. I stood motionless, I wasn't trained with weapons. My inexperience felt glaringly obvious. I fidgeted while debating what to do, as my eyes settled on a curved sword placed at the back.

Pushing several small tables aside, I walked over to it, then pulled it from where it hung, centered on the canvas wall with nothing around it. I unsheathed the blade, akin to a machete, like one I had used to cut the brush from overgrown trails. Similar in shape only, rather than being a rusted and roughly hammered piece of metal, this one was stunningly crafted. The gleaming gold sword had beautiful fine embossing and a glinting hilt. The artistry of the precision etched designs left me in awe. Beautiful thick and thin lines arced in perfect patterns. I ran my finger pads over the carved details, absorbing every careful line.

I wrapped my hand around the hilt, testing its weight. After a few unskilled slashes through the air, a tremor reverberated through me, rattling awake something deep inside my chest. An echo from my heart, responding to the metal in my hand. Forged, painstakingly forged. The blade sang as I swirled it around. Like a natural extension of my arm, if I were to dance with it, it would merely be the finishing movement, an expression of grace and power. This was my weapon.

The baldric for it hung loose over my back—it had been fitted to someone much larger. I cinched up the leather until it was snug and practiced sheathing and unsheathing the blade. The last thing I needed was to get hung up trying to get it out at a critical moment. I slid it out one last time and spun it around again, the weapon completed my feeling of empowerment.

I turned to my companions, only then noting their expressions. Their downcast eyes and pained frowns said it all as they beheld me.

"Have I done something wrong? I can pick another weapon," I offered.

They hesitated a moment before Rannoch spoke, "That selwaer belonged to my best friend. I made it for him. No one has touched it since he died. You move somewhat like he did with it, you should wield it."

Kerenza blinked as tears spilled out, she bobbed her head in agreement, though could manage no words.

"You made this, Rannoch?" I asked, stunned. Even my usual snarky retort to him was non-existent.

"Yes, I did. Forging and smithing is one way I enjoy spending my time, dedicating myself to the balance and artistry that a weapon can exhibit. Perhaps one day…" he trailed off as he looked at the blade again.

"I didn't realize when I grabbed it. I should pick another." I flustered as I began lifting the strap off.

"No," Kerenza commanded, and reached forward to lay her hand on my wrist, "You should take it. He died while Emblyn was taken. It seems right that you should use it, while we get her and the other children back."

After a pause, I settled the sheath back in place. "It would be my honor to use it," I said as she dropped her hand from my wrist.

Kerenza closed her eyes and took a shuddering breath. She opened them again to look deep in mine, hope and trust shone from within. Something sparked inside me. My resolve to fight, to do whatever was necessary, hardened and honed equal to the blade I now carried. I would not allow myself to fail. Though untrained in swordfighting and no idea what to expect. I would not fail.

"Lily, have you trained with weapons before?" Rannoch asked.

I gulped, my lack of skill must have been painfully obvious to them. "No, I haven't," I admitted. "I've done hand to hand combat training with my brother, but never with a weapon."

He nodded, passing his glance over my body. "We should spend some time and train."

Kerenza made a sound in slight protest. "We were just about to leave!"

He shifted his gaze to her. "I know you are anxious to finally retrieve Emblyn, but I cannot send Lily out there unprepared. We are all better off if we teach her."

My eyes widened, as I remembered asking Opius to teach me, and how he couldn't be bothered with showing me a few moves with the knife. I knew it wouldn't be easy, but the fact that Rannoch wanted to be sure I could protect myself filled me with appreciation. "When do we start?"

"Now."

CHAPTER 21

He walked to the tent exit and held the flap for Kerenza and I. Marching to an open field with harder-packed ground, he motioned for me to face him. "Kerenza, will you fetch waterskins for us? I will work with Lily for now, then you should switch off, and teach her what you can."

As Kerenza left, he looked me over. "You have a strong stance already, and good muscles. You will do well I think." I tried not to shy from his inspection. "The blade has already keyed itself to you, it will help direct you. But you must learn to maximize the guidance it gives. Here, stand like this and unsheath the selwaer." He stepped one foot back as he lifted the opposite hand to the grip. "By standing like this, I am already set up for a powerful strike, even before taking out my blade. Leverage every moment you can." He demonstrated with a forceful slash.

I copied him repeatedly, he periodically lifted my arm or nudged my foot to a stronger position. Over and over. Sweat beaded on my brow as we worked side by side. Lunges, strikes, parries, he guided me through countless moves while Kerenza watched from a distance, under a nearby awning.

After several hours, he finally motioned to take a break. Kerenza held out full skins for each of us. I gulped down the cooling water as she motioned to me with her chin. "You are learning fast. I will teach you how to use your female form to your advantage."

Rannoch smirked. "Kerenza is the master at that."

He chuckled as she smacked his shoulder. "In *fighting* of course. I do not think Lily needs any guidance on how to swish her hips or how to capture a potential mate's attention."

He narrowed his eyes at her. "Then you should get to it." He swigged from the waterskin again, then plopped down in Kerenza's previous spot in the shade. *No rest for me I suppose.* But I had no intention of complaining, the chance to learn was worth some sweat and sore muscles. I had wanted to learn ever since Opius first handed me the small dagger, I wasn't about to let this opportunity go.

Kerenza motioned for us to move over to the training ground and quickly started some exercises. I remembered how useless I felt, when I had gripped the thigh knife as I wandered through the forest alone. The memory spurred me to push through the difficulty. As I struck in concert with her, my irritation with Opius surged. Why wouldn't he just show me some maneuvers? Always dismissive of me, and he didn't even care enough to make sure I was prepared. Sure enough, I had gotten separated from him and had to find my own way.

I did a combination lunge and strike, then funneled all my anger in a forward motion and released a blast of fire down my arm. It churned in a wide plume from the heel of my hand.

Rannoch shot to his feet, while Kerenza halted her mid-swing strike. I stood panting as I stared after the dissipated flame. I looked at her bewildered. "I got angry, I guess I...lost control."

"That was magna, Lily. *That* is what you need to do. Elemental battles are distracting, there is much more going on than just the clash of weapons. Threats can come from multiple sources. It helps to pick a pattern, strike-strike-element and then change it up. Use your elements as a weapon just as the blade. Also, much of a female's strength comes from the legs. Commit yourself to your strikes by transferring the intensity from the base up. We do not have the upper body strength like Rannoch, our power comes from the root. Push up, and through."

I took a breath as Rannoch sat back down, Kerenza nodded to me—a steady, guiding presence to shepherd me to where I needed to be. She demonstrated once, twisting from the hip as she pushed from below. I could see it, the flow of power from the ground upward. Her strike was a whole body movement, utilizing her rippling thigh muscles to strengthen her follow through with the sword. The blade was the last act, the finishing touch on a graceful, effective move. "The hips are where our ferocity comes from, life and death can be sprung from them. Use them. Those in combination with our minds make us powerful."

She guided me for several hours more, helping me perfect the motions and redirecting my force to maximize its effectiveness, occasionally adding in a discharge of flame to the mix. The first time I had let fire out, it was startling and unsettling. The very thing that had taken those I love now churned beneath my skin. But as I practiced more, I realized the release was necessary, it tempered the anger and stabilized the well which contained the vast amount of energy. The more I tapped it, the more I sensed how deep it was.

At last Rannoch walked over, indicating it was time to stop. I was slick with sweat and shaking for sustenance. "We will eat, and rest," he commanded. "We will do more training on the next rotation, then leave." I silently agreed as I walked back to the camp with them.

I practically fell onto the seat in the common area outside their group of tents. Kerenza bounded off to get us food, as Rannoch sat down near me. I rubbed my sore shoulder muscles and grimaced at how dirty I was. I looked down at my linteum, an entire day of training and it was still secure. I hid a secret smile, I actually *did* like it, a first for me to feel natural in anything not pants-related.

"You did well. And your ability is impressive. Your feminine form belies how powerful you are. Both appealing and strong."

I dropped my jaw and glanced at him, *uh did he just call me hot?* "A married man probably shouldn't talk to me that way."

"What?" He scrunched his eyebrows at me as Kerenza walked up, bearing a tray of food.

"Move over faexhead, quit hogging the whole seat!" She jabbed her knee against his leg.

He grumbled and moved out of the way. "Always so forceful."

"Here, Illyana had these tortams ready!" She handed each of us a wrap, steaming and fresh. I was so hungry, I tore off a bite without letting it cool.

"Is this beef?" I asked after swallowing, nearly burning my tongue.

"What is beef? Is that...meat?" Kerenza asked. I nodded as I ate more.

"It is from the large beasts that roam the Hinterdunes in herds. Huge horns jut down from their jaws," Rannoch said as he mimicked tusks, "and have long hair on their hides. We only hunt a few each cycle."

"I've never hunted, being an animal caretaker I was never comfortable with it. But still, I eat meat so I shouldn't judge."

"I would say it is not something we enjoy, but what we must do to live," Kerenza said. "Plus, we trade with the Caelifae and Petrafae for their goods. Our hunts help them stay nourished as well. Since we are the only race of Fae that fares well crossing the Hinterdunes, it is up to us to provide."

"It's good," I mumbled around my last bite. As my stomach filled I was rapidly losing my ability to stay awake. I rolled my head to stretch my aching neck muscles.

"We have a liniment that will brace your soreness, I will go prepare it." Kerenza said as she got up to leave.

I could have fallen asleep as I glazed over watching the fire. Kerenza fortunately returned before that happened.

I stood, my muscles had already started to lock up from the intense session. Kerenza wrapped an arm around me. "I filled a bath for you, come." I stumbled as she guided me to the smaller tent I had slept in before, which now had a tub of hot water. She motioned to a bottle. "For your hair," she said before excusing herself. I peeled off my linteum and eased into the bath, hissing as my body submerged. A scent of eucalyptus wafted from the surface and soothed my tired body. I ducked under and washed my hair before I got too exhausted to deal with it. I wanted to take the chance while I could, leaving the next day might mean it would be awhile before I could wash it again.

I was tempted to lounge in the water longer, but my eyelids were heavy, and falling asleep in a tub was probably not a good idea. I mustered the energy to get myself out, toweled off, then dressed in my night clothes. I didn't even remember collapsing into my bedroll.

CHAPTER 22

Dressed in my linteum and my stomach rumbling, I headed out to look for Kerenza and Rannoch. The same bright light hit my eyes as I emerged. I had slept a full sleep cycle, I was sure of it, yet the light level remained constant.

My steps were shortened by terrible pain along my shin bones. I hobbled over to the seating area, where Rannoch sat having capuli. "Bonum mane, here, I made you some."

I thunked down next to him. "Thanks." I winced and rubbed my legs. "I knew my arms would be sore, but I didn't expect the shin splints."

"That is normal, I anticipated that and brought this," he said, as he held up a salve. "Here." He motioned for me to shift my legs toward him. He swiped into the balm and leaned down to rub the wide pad of his thumb along the length of each shin, massaging it into the aching tendon. I resisted a moan that wanted to escape.

"Better?" Rannoch asked, as he straightened back up.

I was tempted to ask him to keep going, but I didn't want to encourage a possibly inappropriate situation. However, I was so sore I almost didn't care. I nodded instead. "Where is Kerenza?" I asked as I rubbed the salve in myself a bit more.

"She went to gather supplies for our departure. I will work with you until she returns, then she will train with you again before we leave. It is not enough training, we train for many cycles, but it will be something at least."

"Thank you for taking the time to teach me. I'm ready to start again," I said before sipping my Fae coffee.

He handed me a bread roll and cocked his dazzling smile. "Your tenacity is admirable."

I turned the bread over in my hand, as I thought about Josie. My tenacity wasn't admirable, it was necessary. "Well, who knows what we will face. It's both self-preservation, and my goal of finding my friend. If I fight hard enough, maybe I can save her too. After we save your children."

His smile faded as I took a bite. "I fear Kerenza will never recover if we are not able to accomplish the task. We must succeed."

I nodded as I worked to chew the hard bread. I tried not to think of how far south this deal would go if we didn't succeed...if *I* didn't. After I finished eating I motioned to proceed back to the training ground.

I strapped on the selwaer baldric as we walked across the hot sand, to the harder ground. My feet had grown used to being uncovered, even the baking terrain didn't bother me anymore. A few warriors milling around turned to us, their gazes in my direction no less intense than the last time I had seen them.

I fidgeted with my linteum as they looked me over. "Did I not tie this right?"

The corner of Rannoch's mouth tipped up. "Amusing how you

always think it is your clothes they look at." Just as quickly, he dropped his smirk and looked ahead, to the training area we had arrived at.

"We will try a different approach this time," he said as he turned to face me, when we arrived at the rough arena. "We will face off, you will try to land strikes on me, and I will block them."

My breath quickened. "What if I hit you? I don't want to hurt you."

He grinned. "Think you can land a strike so easily?" He paused, then continued in a more reassuring tone, "Not to worry, I can block your hits. I want you to get used to striking at an opponent. You can unleash fire too, I can redirect it. I will also strike at you, so you can practice blocking."

I rolled my shoulders. "Okay, let's do this."

We clashed blades and traded strikes until I was sweaty. "Harder!" He hollered. "Do not hold back!"

He struck, causing me to retreat a pace, then another. He jabbed forward, which I blocked, but before he completed the move he charged toward me and slammed me to the ground, with his solid arm across my chest. I gasped as the wind expelled from my lungs.

"An opponent like me will use his size to his advantage, use your size to outmaneuver him," Rannoch said as he helped me back up. I dusted myself off and scrunched my brows in frustration.

I gritted my teeth and put more fury behind my hits. I lunged and struck twice, which he blocked with ease. As I completed the last strike, I released a volley of flame. He twisted to the side, pushing his hands to deflect the fire. As he turned, I swung to his exposed side, and stopped my sword just short of hitting him. "Gotcha." I said from under an arched eyebrow.

Kerenza hooted from under the awning, having snuck in sometime during my training. I grinned at her over my shoulder, proud of my win over such an accomplished warrior. As I turned my head back to my sword, still held at his side, his hand closed around my wrist. The world spun, disorienting me as he whipped me around, I lost control over my limbs as I came to a stop. Rannoch's arm locked across my chest as he pinned me in place from behind, then raised his blade to my neck. In one swift motion, he could have eliminated me.

"Never celebrate small victories in battle, while you were busy congratulating yourself, I had the opportunity to turn that triumph into ultimate loss," he said into my ear, as my eyes went round. I nearly dropped my sword, angry at myself for being so foolish. He was right. I shouldn't have been patting myself on the back when we were technically still in mock-battle.

Rannoch lowered his arm, then gripped my shoulder to turn me back around to face him. "You did land a magna strike, that was a good move. You used my distraction from the flame to your advantage, that was smart and shows natural skill," he said as he kept his hand on my shoulder. "Just be careful not to consider the battle won too early. Be sure, absolutely sure, before you name yourself the victor."

I nodded and inhaled sharply, he didn't release his hand until I had visibly shaken off the defeat and mistake. "Again, we will switch off when you have made another stunning win," Rannoch said, as he flashed his brilliant smile and raised his sword.

I smirked as I lifted my selwaer toward his. We traded hits and parries, until Rannoch attempted to redouble an attack in a forceful movement forward. I deflected, and dropped to my knees below his strike, spun, and swung my blade toward his unprotected calves. I halted as I looked up at him, waiting for his response.

My chest heaved as I held my blade, my hand shook from the intensity of the training.

"Magna! That is what I meant by using your size. And while a strike to the legs will not usually be fatal, it can cripple your opponent to set you up for the winning move." He stood down and held out his hand to help me up.

"Kerenza," he called out without looking away from me, "your turn." He nodded to me. "Good work."

I beamed, though already dirty and sweaty before the day was barely started, I felt accomplished. Kerenza sauntered over, with her spear slung over her shoulder as Rannoch left. She planted it in the ground and announced, "We will do something different. You may not always face an opponent wielding a sword, you need to learn to fight against other weapons using what you have. And we will work on using your base more, kicks and spins."

She guided me through slower movements first, demonstrating various responses to attacks. Gradually she sped them up, adding in dynamic kicks to the flow. I worked on committing my body more completely to the exaggerated roundhouses and hook kicks, while working hard to have my core stabilize my movements. She showed me how to interject them naturally between strikes. Kerenza's inspired fluidity displayed just how graceful and powerful a female warrior could be. I mimicked her movements, using the far extreme she was able to extend herself to as a template for what I might be capable of. Felix had taught me self defense moves, and effective punches. But Kerenza was truly a skilled teacher at exhibiting how to use my form to its maximum ability.

She switched the routine to face each other, then began working in direct combat situations. Kerenza whipped her braid around as she swung the staff, forcing me to dodge her strikes. I realized that with the considerable extra reach—and the blunt force trauma her weapon could inflict—direct contact with my selwaer and her spear would prove ineffective. I would need to dodge, deflect if possible, then strike when she would be unable to return the hit. I focused on avoiding her staff, making a showy performance as I spun to dodge and no effort to strike with my sword. After several turns around each other, my opportunity presented itself. She swung the spear wide, I leaped over it as she continued to rotate, and I thrust inward to her back. I nearly hit the tip of the blade against her glistening skin.

She looked over her shoulder and winked at me. "I was hoping you would notice that opening."

I cringed, it was too close, but then released a breath and smiled.

"Come on, you did magna. I think we have done enough, if you are going to still have the energy to travel. Nice job on your linteum by the way."

I flashed her a tired smile as I sheathed the blade. "I did it all by myself."

She blurted a laugh. "Well, *obviously.*"

We chuckled and walked over to Rannoch, who was already standing. "I think you have learned as much as you can in a short time. More practice is required, but for now it is sufficient," he commented. "We will clean up, take a short rest, then depart. Well done, both of you."

Kerenza placed a fist on her heart and bowed. I breathed a sigh, having some familiarity with the sword and being a notch higher in combat skill filled me with relief.

After washing up in the tents, putting on fresh clothes, and splitting provisions between us, we were ready to go.

The three of us set out on our endeavor. The mission to save their children. And to track down Josie.

CHAPTER 23

At the edge of the encampment, Kerenza took out a small glass bauble on a chain. Opening it with a twist, she called a flame from the torch that marked the outermost bounds of their nomadic town. She pulled a wisp of the fire to the globe, a small filament ignited and she sealed it shut. It flickered and refracted in the glass sphere like a tiny, brilliant sun.

I gave her a questioning glance as she slipped the chain over her head. "The Ignisphaera, a special device so that we may take fire with us," she said. "It keeps the flame sustained and the glass does not heat up. It acts as a light and a fire source. We may find ourselves in a situation with no access to fire. This way we will have our own if need be."

"But I can create fire."

She gave me a sidelong glance. "True, but what if you were somehow unable to? Plus, this is special to me. My maeder gave it to me when I turned sixteen cycles. It has always guided me well, a light in dark times."

Giving just a single nod, Rannoch launched into a run.

Kerenza and I caught up after a moment, falling into line behind him. We propelled across the desert landscape with long strides. Rannoch led the way, I kept pace two strides behind him, with Kerenza at the rear. We traveled in almost complete silence, our footfalls raced like cheetahs sprinting through a plain.

The desert gave way to rocky outcroppings, which we wended through at a blazing speed. We hurdled over lower lying mounds of rocks to straighten the path, minimizing the extra distance it would take to navigate everything in the way.

We stopped several times to take short rests in hidden alcoves, when the opportunity presented itself in the intermittent cliff walls that bordered the route. Just enough time to take a quick drink from the water skins and eat dried jerky, before pressing on. Gradually, the Praegra Forest grew on the horizon, and signs of plant life began to spring up through the rough ground.

He broke off the trail and led Kerenza and I into the last alcove before we would enter the forest, to catch our breath and regroup for the next terrain.

After a few moments of heaving his chest and several gulps of water, he managed to say between breaths, "It will not be long before we enter the forest, we will seek out a creature that can help us traverse unseen, if they will agree to it."

I nodded, sick to my stomach from the lengthy run. It had been a solid day, perhaps longer. Understanding the passage of time here still eluded me, without the day to night cycle. With a start I realized it was far less bright than usual, my eyes darted around to see if I was imagining it.

"Is it getting darker? Or are my eyes playing tricks on me?" I gasped to no one in particular.

With her nostrils flaring, attempting to suck in more air, Kerenza answered, "Yes, as it becomes night in the human world, it gradually becomes so here as well. Because of the temporal phase, we have fourteen rotations of light, and fourteen of dark."

Dusk. It was now dusk at home. I hadn't grasped that the time shift would mean it would eventually become night here. The constant light has subdued and softened my concern over what time it was back home. My blood chilled. I had nearly forgotten that my absence would be noticed at some point. My mother may have already realized that I was missing, especially if Apollo hadn't returned home—or if he did return home, riderless. I swallowed at the worry she would feel. The weight of it settled on my shoulders like a leaden cloak. The memory of the moment we found out Josie had gone missing flickered through my mind, and the panic that had rippled through the community when she disappeared without a trace. She vanished in much the same way, left of her own volition, perhaps to go for a hike out in the hills. Which is where her trail went cold and was never seen again. I pictured my mom, sobbing at our kitchen counter, just as Josie's mom had.

"What is wrong?" Kerenza asked with worry-filled eyes.

"My mother must have realized I'm not there by now, in the human realm," I answered solemnly.

They went utterly still, understanding dawned in their eyes. Rannoch's face hardened, as he grasped what that may mean.

"Do you intend to leave us then? To return home?" He asked. "Will you still help us?"

"Wait, do I have a choice now? What happened to the whole death threat thing?"

He hesitated before answering, "It was a mistake on my part, to treat you that way. I thought it was the only way I could convince you. I did not know who you were at the time. I used that tactic to secure your aid. But I see now that I was wrong to do that. I am sorry."

I weighed the situation. Do I return home to safety and protect my mother from worry? Or do I continue onward to peril, and attempt to help these beings, maybe find my best friend in the process? I appraised him as I debated. Kerenza held her breath, waiting for my response. "And what of our bargain?" I asked.

"The bargain remains, help us and we will help you."

Something steeled in me, a resolve deep down in my soul. *I don't know what I am, but I know who I am.* I wanted to be a person that makes a difference, that effected change. These people had asked for my help, and here in Alternis I didn't even know the extent of what I could do. Without me, their chances of rescuing their children was slim. They would likely be slaughtered in the process. No, I would not abandon them. I raised my chin. "Yes, I will help you."

"Do you forgive me?" Rannoch's eyebrows angled out.

"Yes, I do. I can see both sides, I understand how you thought I was somehow wrapped up with what happened to your children."

They both exhaled audibly. Rannoch reached forward and rested his strong hand on my shoulder. Warmth emanated from him, his eyes sparkled in appreciation. I held his gaze, and for those moments the rest of the world faded away. The only world that existed was the one in his eyes. I was captivated, the truth of his nature laid bare for that instant. A caring, strong male capable of so much. Someone who would fight tirelessly for those he loved.

"We should be off then."

His words tore me back into the present. I blinked and nodded. I would do this for them, with them. I would muster all the courage and strength I had. Kerenza beamed at me, then turned to sprint once again.

CHAPTER 24

After a fast trek to the forest edge, Rannoch slowed his pace and nocked an arrow. His hawk-like eyes darted, attempting to weed out potential danger. Kerenza followed suit, and crept along with her spear raised, as she scanned the trees. After several moments of pensive appraisal, he relaxed, and quickened our pace through the woods. We continued on, periodically slowing to sense any threats.

At last Rannoch's ears perked up and he stilled, like a panther on a hunt. He motioned for Kerenza and I to follow. We moved in complete stealth, our footsteps silent on the forest floor.

A great tree loomed before us, giant swaths of puffy moss hung from the bark and limbs like cumulus clouds. The large, waxy leaves that flowered in bursts had glistening dew drops waiting to release from the tips. Waiting—but never falling. Rannoch approached carefully, his steps caused the phosphorescent moss to illuminate in soft outlines. He settled himself facing the great tree with arms spread open, inviting an embrace to an invisible entity. I followed his gaze up to the tree limbs.

"They are formidable creatures, you will find them a valuable ally, if they give their blessing. They are called the Amabilis, and are revered among the Fae," he whispered, without tearing his eyes from whatever lurked in the branches.

I looked up in the tree, and held my breath for what I may see. Will they have fangs or talons? Or just be scary to look upon? I was nervous to finally lay eyes on the mythical beings. I looked all over but saw no such beasts.

"I don't see them, could you point them out to me?"

He looked at me bewildered without dropping his arms. "How can you not see them? One is right there!"

"Ah...um, I only see a squirrel." A tiny, cute squirrel with adorable, large black eyes. He licked his paw and rubbed his cheek. *Aww look at that little face!*

"The great Amabilis is in your presence and you call them a squirrel?" He bellowed in frustration. "...What is a squirrel?"

"A small rodent from the human world. I didn't realize that was him. Can he...talk?"

"Talk! Do not be ridiculous. When the Amabilis wants you to know something you will hear it in your mind," he retorted. He squinted his eyes, as his eyebrows danced on his forehead in extreme concentration.

"What are you doing?" I whispered out the side of my mouth as I watched the creature.

"I am attempting to communicate with them."

The creature shifted his gaze to me and stood on its hind legs. He burst forward, taking two strides along the branch before he leapt off in my direction. I flinched as his spindly arms flung out to the side to reveal iridescent, wing-like membranes attached from the underside of his arms, and continued along the length of his body, tapering at the knees. The Amabilis glided down, but as it descended a soft glow shimmered from its entire body. It became larger, and larger, and larger.

I paled and shrank back as he landed, then stood to its full height in front of me. Its nose pointed down toward my face, and its now massive black eyes peered into mine.

"You are an interesting one, we find you interesting. Yes, yes, very interesting," a din of harmonic voices clamored in my mind.

Hearing the voices rasp in my head and watching the sudden shift in the creature's size stunned me into momentary silence. "You are interesting yourself," I managed. I threw a questioning glance to Rannoch, unsure of how I should proceed. He shrugged his shoulders up. I released a breath, then continued, "We sought you out, and hoped you might help us in our quest." I spoke verbally, not knowing if I could communicate the same way he did.

"Ah, a quest is it? Interesting, yes. We may consider it, perhaps. But first, we would like to know your thoughts," the multi-toned voice echoed between my ears. "May we have your permission to peek?"

"Peek? Uh, yes, you have my permission," I answered, unsure of what I was agreeing to. His eyes intensified and pierced into me. My thoughts shuffled as they were rifled through, I shivered at the feeling of tiny fingers flipping through my mind like it was a large stack of cards. I panicked at the lack of control, as a rapid flow of memories surged. All my experiences flickered past in an instant, leaving me breathless.

He settled back on his haunches as he disconnected from my mind, then turned to Rannoch. During the silent exchange, his fists were clenched at his sides until the Amabilis retracted. Rannoch's face was taut as his eyes darted to me, almost in embarrassment or guilt. I couldn't tell which.

He turned to Kerenza, her eyes went wide as he pored through her mind. As he finished, he brought his long, rodent-like fingers up to her face, and caressed her cheek. Kerenza's face crumpled as she gulped back tears.

He lifted his great head and closed his eyes, then sent a barely visible waveform out, which emanated from his forehead. At last he blinked and looked at us. "We have compassion for your unfortunate situation. But it is complicated. We feel we should not become involved."

Kerenza wobbled and nearly dropped to the ground. She reached forward, clutching his bony fingers. "Please," she whispered. "Please!" Louder this time. "'The children will die without us, we are their only chance. We do not care for the politics or the reasons the Umorfae have done this. We just want our children back."

He regarded her for a moment, then closed his eyes, sending another wave out.

We waited. And waited.

The Amabilis stood taller and faced the three of us, his strange choir of voices rang out in my head, "We will help you on your journey. We do not usually involve ourselves in Fae disputes, however we will take you to a point near the cave. That is the most we can do. It is some distance, and will need to rest at the midpoint, with the Arbor Elves."

I nodded as I stifled tears, Kerenza hands clasped together in a grateful prayer.

He tipped his head up, and sent out a rippling, invisible pulse, different from the previous. Two more creatures appeared out of nowhere. Within moments, the new arrivals grew to match the full height of the Amibilis that had called them.

"Step closer, we will guide you," the voices sang out as they opened their arms.

I took a nervous breath and approached the nearest one. He enveloped me with his diaphanous, webbed arms. In that instant, the world spun and expanded exponentially as we shrunk to a microscopic size. Down, down, down. Like falling through infinite mirrors.

We folded into a different realm, a nebulous, hazy inner galaxy. Beautiful, yet at the same time terrifying; pulsing lights traveled along a network of branching pathways, erratic flashes from indistinct sources, the sensation of wind clashed from multiple directions. It reminded me of the chaos of stepping through the Vale.

"Do not be scared, we will protect you," the voices said, "we are in a sub layer of the realm, the place in which magic flows and disperses. We travel these paths as none other can. It allows us to move from one place to another, unhindered by other beings."

I struggled to keep my thoughts straight with the assault on my senses. "Are you...are you a hive mind? You and the other Amabilis? Is that why I hear so many voices when you speak?" I projected mentally as we hurtled along the cords, zipping from one to another as he navigated our way through the bizarre network.

"Yes, we can all hear each other's thoughts, we are one and the same."

"I'm looking for another, like me. A Vale Born female. I'm worried for her safety. Have you seen or heard of her?" Maybe if they were a hive mind, even just one of them seeing Josie would mean they would all know.

"We have not encountered a Vale Born in many cycles. But, we do not interact with the Fae normally. It does not mean she is not here. Rest, save your questions for later. Your thoughts are scattered, they make us weary," they responded in unison.

My heart sank, still no clues. No indication that she was here—besides the fact that Naiya told me she had been. Nausea turned my stomach as we careened through space. I buried my face into his winged arm, and closed my eyes for the duration of the intense flight, as I tried my hardest not to think about my dear friend.

CHAPTER 25

The world spun again, the sensation of tumbling and inflating made my stomach clench as we returned to our natural size. My surroundings filtered back in, I stood on a platform atop huge trees. Other structures popped into view, no planks, walkways, or ladders connected them. My head thrummed from scaling down and back up, I squeezed my eyes shut as vertigo set in from the height we were now at.

The Amabilis steadied me with a paw to my shoulder as I swayed, my knees threatened to buckle. I stole a glance at my companions, Kerenza and Rannoch looked equally rattled.

"You must sit, and regain your steadiness," the Amabilis voiced in harmony.

I collapsed onto the landing, and placed my hands to either side to keep from swaying. The platform tilted beneath me, my head swam like I had too much alcohol. I tried to focus on the detail below me, to distract myself. Smooth, variegated wood of varying widths composed the surface, planed by skilled hands. Not like the standardized dimensional lumber from my realm, this had a sturdy quality from careful construction. Each piece fit together like a natural puzzle, interlocking to create a stronger bond.

Four flashes appeared surrounding us. Impossibly bright, electrified openings hung in midair, starting first as small tight bursts, and rapidly enlarging to nearly my height. The erratic edge of the sizzling ovals shimmered in every color of the rainbow. The current sparked as the electrons clashed with the air they were forcing open. Leathery, bark-like skin reflected in a greenish hue from the other side of each aperture. Humanoid creatures jumped through the openings with quick, fluid spins, and came to a rest in an armed attack position. Their mossy, wild hair settled a moment after, large volumes that bobbed in delayed movement. The Amabilis nearest me bore his gaze into them, as I froze at the sight of the nimble beings.

The portal-walkers all stood down, a female stepped closer and announced, "I am Aurelian, Venitor of the Arbor Elves. The Amabilis informed us of your need to rest here. You are welcome to stay. We will take you to a more comfortable lodging, though you must relinquish your weapons. They will be returned to you when you depart."

Although smaller than the other Elves—and all were smaller than the Fae—she had a commanding presence and a body of steel. She motioned to her compatriots to separate out, to guide each of us.

I handed her my selwaer and thigh knife, Aurelian holstered them in a scabbard slung across her back, then raised her hands in front. She pulled one hand back like pulling a bowstring taut, while stepping back with one foot to widen her stance. A white-hot oval reopened. She looped her arm around my waist, then guided me like a dance. We stepped into it and spun through, into a round room.

I wobbled, all the inner space and portal-walking was a lot to wrap my mind around. She braced my balance, and appraised me with unyielding, bright green eyes.

Rannoch and Kerenza appeared with their Elven guides.

"I forget that others are not accustomed to the feeling of fenestram, walking through folded doorways," she said as I gradually adjusted.

"Folded doorways?" I asked, blinking my eyes to attempt to clear my head quicker. "Is that like the Amabilis? How they travel the...inner space network sublayer?"

"No, when we open a doorway, we are folding the distance between two points of this plane, then we can pass through. It is a skill only the Arbor Elves have," she answered.

My eyes went round. *Is that like the Einstein-Rosen Bridge theory? Cool!*

I glanced around the partially solid walls, composed of many thin, vertical branches, woven with vines. Greenery from outside peeked through the gaps, allowing the gentlest of breezes in. A cluster of vines looped down from the ceiling, swaying from the soft gale. Three inviting beds fanned out in a semicircle, equally splitting the room. A fourth section was walled off with more substantial woven reeds and wood for privacy, hopefully a bathroom.

Aurelian spoke, "Rest, regain your strength, and feel free to bathe. Join us for food later." She was abrupt, but not unkind. Perhaps she simply did not waste words.

Kerenza replied, "We would enjoy sharing a meal with you."

Aurelian and the other Elves pulled fenestrams open, spun and stepped through—back to some other area of their green paradise.

Rannoch tossed his pack on the farthest bed. "Who is up to bathe first?"

I flopped down on my bed, glad to take a rest. "Go ahead, I'm fine waiting," I muttered with eyes closed, almost too tired to even talk.

Kerenza said, "You go, Rannoch, I will wait also." She set her things down on the middle bed near mine, then padded over to the woven branch wall to peer out.

The door slid closed to the bathing room, followed by the sound of rushing water.

"I am anxious about the next rotation," she said as she gripped two of the wall posts, "I have a good feeling, and yet I am also nervous. It is not like me to be so nervous."

I mustered some energy to get up to comfort her, swung my legs out of bed and pushed myself to stand. She stared at nothing I could pick out in the sea of leaves outside our walls as I approached.

"I know, it must be nerve-racking to be so close to finally freeing Emblyn. I'm nervous also," I admitted.

I gave her shoulder a squeeze as I stood next to her, looking out at the branches as well. I was absently scanning the shifting leaves when my eyes fell on her ring. With sudden dread, I realized the fire had gone out.

My stomach dropped, *the ring is dead*. I panicked, I didn't want to have to tell her if she hadn't noticed it yet. *No, no! This can't be!*

She turned to me, her ears twitching. "Your smell has changed, and I can hear your heart racing. What is it?"

I blanched, afraid to be the bearer of such terrible news. My eyes were wide with terror. "Y-y-your...ring," I whispered.

She gasped and looked at it, still burning bright. I realized that she was looking at the other hand. "Thank the gods, you scared me!"

"I'm sorry, I saw it was dark. I didn't know you had one on each hand," I stammered.

She sighed and responded, "Yes, that ring was tied to my coniunx, Kenneder,"

"Coniunx?"

"Yes, mate. He was killed the day Emblyn was taken. He was Rannoch's best friend as well." She looked down at it as her eyes welled up and over, tears trickled down her cheeks.

"I'm so sorry, that is terribly sad. I—wait...MATE?...I thought Rannoch was your mate!" I blurted.

She coughed out a laugh, still with tears rolling down her face. "Rannoch is my brother! Do not make me claw my own eyes out! You did not know?"

I pursed my lips and shook my head. She laughed again and continued, "Well, do you think I would be okay with how you two look at each other if he *were* my mate?" She cocked an eyebrow as she flicked the tail of her thick bound hair off her shoulder.

"What do you mean? I mean, a few times I felt like...like maybe we had connected for a moment. But I don't think he really likes me. He's always so...I don't know, difficult," I sputtered, trying to backpedal.

She pulled her head back in disbelief, her eyebrows askance. "You must be blind. I have never seen anyone break through his shell like you can."

I flashed her a skeptical glance, *yea right*. She shrugged.

"Do you share a tent though? I guess that's part of why I thought you were his …coniunx. I thought you were in the same tent back at camp," I asked, thinking back on our time there.

"I shared a tent with him after Kenneder died and Emblyn was taken. A tent—but not a bed. I just needed someone to be near me. However, I have been sleeping in my own tent for quite some time now," she said with a sigh.

"…That's why he reacted that way, when I chastised him for complimenting my looks."

"Oh what? What did he say?" Kerenza's eyes glittered as she cooed.

"He said I had an appealing form, after we started training." I giggled. "I told him a married man shouldn't say that. He looked very confused."

"I can understand his confusion, we do not know that word. Does that equate to coniunx?"

I nodded, then realized the water had turned off while we were talking. *Oh god, I hope he didn't hear any of that!* The door coasted open, he walked out a moment later. My glance skimmed over him, wearing variegated green loose pants fitted through the calves, hair dripping from the shorter chunks of hair that framed his face, and his bare, dark upper body glistening. I gulped at the sight of him, color bloomed on my cheeks and down my chest. Conflict tugged as I wanted to stare at him and run away in embarrassment at the same time. My skin boiled, I thought I might burst into flames.

"Is it okay if I bathe before you, Kerenza?" I asked as I rushed past him into the bathroom.

"Of course," she called out smoothly in a lilting laugh. Her smirk from behind absolutely tangible as I reached the door.

I collapsed my back against the wall once the door was closed, then heaved a sigh. *Well that was uncomfortable, way to go, Lily.* I needed to wash the entire conversation off my skin. I disrobed then stepped into the bathing chamber; a gravity fed shower with a lever to release the water. The large basin rained cooling water on me, which steamed off of my hot skin. *Maybe I was close to bursting into flames.* The Arbor Elves had left an assortment of soaps to use, so I scrubbed, trying to forget how embarrassed I was.

Our hosts left clothes to change into, comfortable but pretty dresses for Kerenza and I hung on irregularly twisted wood hangers. *Did they open portals into our bathroom to deliver these?* All the clothing was sized for each of us, it seemed. A light, fitted tank-style top that flowed into a skirt, made from pieces which hung like large, silky petals. Mine was a gradation of various greens, golds, and yellows, the colors blended and shifted into each other, like leaves in a seasonal transition. They were my preferred colors for sure, but dresses were still not quite my thing. Though as dresses go, this was about as close to functional one could get and still have an appealing look.

I emerged, effectively cooled and possibly sanitized from how much washing I had done. I avoided locking eyes with Rannoch, as Kerenza sailed past.

"I am going to take my time. My hair could use a wash!" Kerenza stated emphatically. She flashed a glance at me with her eyebrows raised. I rolled my eyes at her.

I dared to look at Rannoch, he lounged on his bed with his arms up, head resting in his hands. *Ugh, put a shirt on so I'm not tempted to sneak glances please!* I lay down in my own bed, and closed my eyes to get some rest. Unfortunately, my mind was cluttered with wayward thoughts.

I gave up after a while and wandered over to the wall, to where I thought a door would be.

"There is no door. I already checked. I suppose they have no need for doors," he projected from across the room. I snapped my head to him, he had sat up and was watching me inspect the wall. I held his gaze, trying to keep my breathing even.

"Does that make us prisoners then? We're stuck here until they come get us," I responded nonchalantly, tearing my eyes away as I pretended to look at the wall.

"I do not think we are prisoners, I believe it is just the nature of how they design their dwellings. They do not need doors, so why make an entrance that an intruder could use?" He answered confidently.

"Good point, seems logical."

His bed rustled and I realized he was getting up. I stiffened as he strode over to me. *Stay calm.* I turned to him, willing my face into a neutral expression.

"I do not think we have anything to worry about with these Elves. Ignisfae do not have direct relations with them, but we know them to be honorable," he said as he stopped in front of me.

Breathe, breathe, breathe. "That's good to know. I hope you're right."

Silence followed as he studied my face, his ears twitched. I couldn't help myself, my skin prickled as it warmed, the color rushed. He arched an eyebrow and one corner of his mouth pulled up, fire danced in his cognac eyes as he undoubtedly sensed my reaction to him. *Damn his Fae senses.*

I opened my mouth, to try and sidestep my obvious tells, right as a portal opened near us. We whirled toward it as an Arbor Elf twisted through the fenestram.

"Forgive my intrusion, I am Aolis. Aurelian sent me to check if there is anything you need. She also sent this communicator, so that you may call us if you wish to leave your room or request anything. Twist it until it clicks, someone will open a fenestram," he instructed as he handed Rannoch a small box.

Rannoch nodded and thanked him. Aolis bowed, reopened a doorway, then departed.

"Well, I think that should alleviate your concerns," he remarked, handing me the device.

"Yes, it does," I stated, still trying to cool my core as I took a shaky breath.

He quirked another smile and slid his hands in his pockets, then wheeled around to saunter back to his bed. He shot one last glance over his shoulder with one brow raised. "It is a little warm in here, is it not?"

Now he's just toying with me. "I suppose," I answered, as I resisted the temptation to look down to see just how rosy I was. The low cut tank top would've made it hard to hide. I drifted over to my bed and lay back down, attempting to ignore the tension between us.

At last Kerenza came gliding out of the bathroom. "That was refreshing," she crowed, as she flung her long hair out to the sides and sprinkled water on Rannoch in the process. He grimaced and flicked a drop off his cheek.

"Well if you are about done, maybe we can check to see if it is time to eat," he grumbled.

She smoothed her petal skirt of ruby, gold, and amber. "I am looking quite nice I think, so I say yes," she declared. Indeed she did, the dress fit her curves beautifully, and the colors matched the highlights in her hair.

He slid his gaze to me, a small spark of fire still smoldered in his eyes. "Will you alert them, Lily?"

I picked up the box, then gave it a twist, it clicked and emitted a soft light out of the crevice where the two cubes joined. Three fenestrams opened, followed by three Elves. I stepped over to be guided through the doorway, and glimpsed an unbelievably beautiful room through the portal.

CHAPTER 26

I crossed through into a large dining hall, tall trees enclosed the perimeter, arched at the top toward the center and forming a cathedral. Lights twinkled in glimmering strings from between the trees and leaves high above. Several long tables bustled with Elves, some eating and talking with those they sat with, some serving. I smiled as I took in the cheerful bunch, many of them softly laughing as they traded stories. Their appearance was at odds with how Elves had been depicted in human stories, it seemed the only thing people got right was the pointed ears. An Elf guided us to a section of the table where Aurelian sat with several others.

She stood and motioned for us to sit across from her. "I trust you had a good rest." As she sat back down, a female to her side nudged her expectantly. Aurelian nodded to her and announced, "My coniunx, Tenaeran. She is looking forward to meeting you."

Tenaeran beamed with a huge, bright smile. "Welcome! I am glad you have joined us for this surprise visit. Please, call me Ten." Her brilliant, emerald green eyes sparkled with friendliness, and vibrant auburn hair pillowed out in massive puffs, which swayed as she opened her arms.

"It's lovely to meet you," I piped up.

A white sparkling wine poured into tall, tulip-shaped flutes were set out on the table. Ten raised her glass, and everyone followed suit. "May your journey be blessed with success, may you all grow with purpose toward your goal."

"Grow with purpose," echoed the Elves.

I nodded thanks and sipped. The light and effervescent wine rushed across my tongue, leaving a wake of bubbles that fizzled.

Wide bowls of greenish broth were delivered. With no spoons set out, Kerenza, Rannoch, and I lifted our bowls to drink from them. The Arbor Elves, however, placed a hand in the broth. Little root-like extremities branched out from their fingers. I watched in awe as the roots drank up the broth.

Ten followed my gaze. "Our radices—root appendages. We can grow them out at will to drink, and for...other purposes," she chided suggestively and nudged Aurelian with a big grin.

Rannoch's eyes flew wide, as he spit out his broth and coughed in surprise. Kerenza giggled, I blurted a laugh and shook my head. *Oh, I like her.* She reminded me of my Aunt back in Ithaca. My mom's sister Maureen, who always liked a good joke that had at least some shock value.

Aurelian rolled her eyes with a small smile, no doubt used to Ten's humor.

The entirely plant based meal was seasoned with exotic spices, unusual and pleasing aromas wafted out of each pot. Ten was a considerate host, easily making connections with anyone in earshot and interjecting comments or funny anecdotes when she could. Kerenza and I shared small jokes with each other, even worked a laugh out of Rannoch a few times. I had to admit that I had grown to like both of them. Though Rannoch was occasionally a serious grouch, I knew much more was beneath his handsome surface.

After the last plate was finished, Aurelian cleared her throat to garner everyone's attention. All voices quieted as she announced, "The Amabilis told us of your plight when you arrived. I have decided that a small faction of my guard will accompany you when you depart on the next rotation. We will help you clear any enemies at the entrance to the cave, and guard while you are inside."

Silence fell, other Arbor Elves nodded in agreement. Kerenza clasped a hand to her mouth. Grateful tears welled up at the waterline of her eyes.

"Thank you," Rannoch offered with a fist across his chest. Though he was sincere, I felt it was not enough. They needed to know what a difference this would make. They had pledged aid when we had asked for none. They had welcomed us warmly, and extended a further helping hand by putting some of their soldiers in harm's way.

I added, "This is truly generous. We cannot thank you enough for this. This may mean the difference between success and failure. We will be in your debt."

Rannoch flashed me a sideways glance, which I ignored. He relaxed and dipped his chin in accord to Aurelian. *Nothing wrong with a little graciousness to show our gratitude.*

Ten smiled lovingly at Aurelian as she gushed, "This is why she is a great leader. An adept warrior who knows when to lend assistance." Aurelian's stern face softened as she gazed at Tenaeran, and cracked an appreciative smile. I imagined Ten was probably the only one she ever smiled at.

Aurelian's face hardened as she said, "We have heard rumors of the growing threat, the being known as Dashelle is gathering strength. We are assisting you not only because it is the right thing to do, but also because we need to prevent Dashelle from getting a foothold."

"Do you know who this Dashelle is, what manner of creature?" Rannoch cut in. "The Ignisfae have little knowledge of him."

"Unfortunately we Arbor Elves do not know much either, other than being ruthless, and power hungry."

I spoke up, "Is it possible Dashelle is at the cave, with the children?"

"We have had no indication that there is another being, besides the Umorfae and the Daemalum," Kerenza answered. "We cannot be certain he is not there, but we do not believe that he is." She shifted her gaze back to Aurelian. "Will you travel by fenestram? Or request to be taken by the Amabilis?"

"We can only open a fenestram when we know the exact point to travel to," Aurelian answered. "We are not familiar enough with the location of the cave to be able to safely open a doorway there. The Amabilis have already agreed to take a small contingent along. Once we are there, we would be able to open a fenestram home."

I sucked in a breath, then hesitantly asked, "Have you heard of another Vale Born wandering in Alternis? I have been searching for her. She has been missing for quite some time. I was told she had come here, but her trail went cold long ago."

"Here amongst the Arbor Elves? We have not seen another, but we received word Dashelle was with one. That was all we heard, and that was some time ago," Aurelian answered.

I caught my breath, what could that mean? Josie might be with this malevolent being? My mind reeled at the thought. Does that mean she's alive, captured...in league with him even? I finally had another indication she might be here, but still nothing concrete, and no indication of her current state. I nearly collapsed with the weight of worry.

Tenaeran smoothly said, "I think we could all use a good nocte of rest before then." She bowed before she and Aurelian stepped through doorways. It was mesmerizing to watch them pull back and spin between points, like a warrior's dance through space.

Three Elves waited to take us to our room. In a flash, we were back. As we came to a rest after stepping through the fenestrams, Rannoch and I were left standing face to face. The Elves excused themselves and blinked away, leaving us silently staring at each other. The familiar warmth emanated from him, enveloping me in an invisible embrace. His expression was unreadable, but his eyes twinkled with fire.

"Well I am exhausted!" Kerenza exclaimed. I jumped as her voice cut through the silence. I had almost forgotten she was there. She peeked over his shoulder with a mischievous grin and waggled her eyebrows.

I made an effort not to stammer in surprise, "I am as well, good night—bonum nocte—to you both." I turned to my bed without giving him another glance.

I could feel him still watching me, he paused a moment before turning to his own bed. "Bonum nocte," he murmured.

The truth was, he confused me. Some moments we would connect, and before dinner he clearly enjoyed that he had excited me. Other times he would exude little more than an icy exterior with little regard for me. Tonight of all nights, we did not need the distraction. There was too much at stake. What waited for us with the next rotation—the fear of the unknown threatening to hijack my thoughts—I needed a clear head and solid rest. I lay down, then closed my heavy eyes, and hoped for sleep to claim me quickly.

CHAPTER 27

I startled awake to the sound of the bathing room door sliding closed. Rannoch sat on his bed, already dressed with elbows propped on his knees. "Sleep well?" My ears tingled at the deep resonance of his voice.

I stretched and sat up. As hair tumbled down in waves, my mind cleared and I remembered what day it was, what we were about to do. I stopped mid-stretch and didn't say anything, I just looked at him as the sobering reality settled.

"Do you feel ready?" He inquired, his tone strong, stern. A muscle feathered in his jaw as he arched a brow, perfectly framed by the fall of his hair over his forehead.

I stilled as I regarded him. "I think I am. I would like to be better at controlling water, but I believe us having the element of surprise—and the help of the Arbor Elves—may swing the balance in our favor.

"I cannot fail Kerenza, I must rescue Emblyn. And the others. There is nothing more important to me," he stated.

"I understand." And I did. I couldn't imagine having a child

I was related to imprisoned in such a way. It was unthinkable that any creature would want to torment children.

Kerenza exited the bathing room, gone was the emotional, nervous female wrestling with her feelings. A resolute, honed warrior stood before us; ready for battle, prepared to fight for her child, for her people's children. She held my gaze, her unshakable determination siphoned to me.

I wasted no time and walked into the bathing chamber. I wrapped my linteum the way Kerenza had shown me, ensuring maximum mobility. I passed my hands over the tied garment, fitted snug and ready to fight. But was I? I had always been a healer, someone who mended the injured, not who caused the injuries. I pulled back my hair in a segmented braid. As I finished tying off the tips, then released it to swing down my spine, I took one last look at myself. I would fight, with whatever means I had. I set my jaw and squared my shoulders, then turned to open the door—prepared to face whatever came.

When I entered the room, Kerenza waited with the device to alert the Arbor Elves, Rannoch by her side. "Ready?"

I sucked in a breath. "Ready," I affirmed with a sharp nod.

She twisted the box, my heart thudded as portals appeared. Three Elves guided us to the main dining hall.

Aurelian waited with eleven of her guards, and motioned for us to eat. We nearly choked down our food as we inhaled sustenance. The weapons that had been relinquished upon our arrival were laid on a nearby table. After I swallowed the last bite, I stepped over with Rannoch and Kerenza to arm ourselves.

We were still fitting the various straps and baldrics, as Aurelian intoned to all, "The battle may be hard won, but we go to defend the lives of innocents. Do not forget that."

Her words struck deep. I *could not* forget that. I needed to fight, and not hold back until we were done. Against my nature or not, this was bigger than me.

A moment later, the Amabilis appeared, enough to transport all in presence. Each one paired off to an Arbor Elf, then to the Fae. Kerenza was spirited off first. As the next one wrapped his wings around me, Rannoch reached forward and clutched my hand.

"Let us challenge the fates together, you and I," he said in his warm, strong tone that made my core tremble. You and I. Those words together made my heart race. I caught my breath and squeezed his hand in return, before the world spun and shrunk into chaos.

CHAPTER 28

I cringed as another tumultuous passage through the barrage of the sublayer came to an end. The world spun back into focus, the Amabilis disappeared before we could thank them, back into the fold of the network.

A nook of boulders surrounded us, the Praegra Forest was nowhere in sight. A careful peek over the rocks revealed our target in the valley, far below. Massive rocks rose high in the sky, surrounded by a wide, shallow lake. Saturated colors streaked down the smooth rocks, oxidized ore undulated from rich gold, peacock blue, and shimmering purple. We were some distance away, but even from our vantage I could make out at least sixty Umorfae. The water sloshed at their shins as they trudged in a perimeter, surrounding a dark void in the otherwise milky teal water. *How long before blood discolors that otherworldly water,* I thought grimly to myself.

"More than I expected," Rannoch commented.

"Do not let the number concern you, focus on the highest priority shots one at a time," Aurelian commanded. "The use of fenestrams in a battle will be disorienting for them, and will provide us with protection—being able to step through to avoid perilous hits. Each of you will partner with one of us to be able to slip in and out of locations. We will traverse the water plane this way, firing shots as we go. Once we start our assault, do not relent. Push forward as fast as you can."

Rannoch bowed, giving her clear lead without argument.

"It looks like that must be the entrance," I spoke up, "where the lake floor drops down near the biggest mountain. I've seen several come up from there. Their armor looks different from the Umorfae I have met, perhaps they are separatists?" I mused as I focused my enhanced eyes, able to see much farther and with greater detail than with my former human eyesight. Their black armor absorbed the light, the only glint came from a three-armed, red triangular sigil rimmed in gold on the center of the breastplate. I scanned the faces of each opponent, not a familiar one among them.

"I am not sure, I have not seen those colors either. Does it matter?" Rannoch asked.

I shrugged. I hoped Opius had no knowledge or association with this horrible situation.

"They appear to be changing the guard shift, now is the time to strike. We will open fenestrams down there," Aurelian ordered, motioning to a point part way out in the lake. "Archers will release a volley once we step through, then open the next doorways on top of them. Remember to fenestram after the initial strike, otherwise we may be hit by our own arrows."

Rannoch and the other six archers readied their bows, the rest unsheathed their blades. All crouched with their stances wide— ready to sprint—then opened fenestrams. My breath caught and time slowed, as I watched the now familiar circular white lightning open in front of me.

This was it. The battle was starting.

"Now!" Aurelian commanded. We burst through, and spun into place, arrows nocked and released the first volley toward the huddled Umorfae in a flash.

"Blades!" Aurelian shouted. All archers smoothly slung their bows as they drew their weapons. Doorways were opened again as shouts came from the Umorfae. We rocketed through the portals, scattered throughout their ranks as the enemies were still bellowing for back up.

We were upon them in an instant, swords clanged and whirred. Water splashed in arcing waves as we unleashed on them. My selwaer thrummed as I spun through the enemy, I sliced across the bellies of two guards before they realized I was there. Blood sprayed my face, the tang of it coated my nostrils. I didn't allow myself to look—to think—as I had just committed the unthinkable.

"Fenestrams!" Aurelian barked.

All Elves drew back their hands, pulling portals open, I lurched toward the nearest Elf and spun through with him, just as the arrows found their targets. We rotated into place a short distance from the melee. Bodies were already strewn, marring the pristine water.

"Arrows!" Another volley flew. The archers re-slung their bows and opened doorways again.

"Go!" She commanded.

I burst through, back in the fray. Kerenza twisted into the fight with an Elf near me. She speared an enemy guard and unleashed a high, powerful kick to the jaw of another that was fast approaching behind her, slamming her heel into him as she rotated through the kick. Kerenza wrenched her spear free, crouched and spun it wide around her, knocking behind the knees of two more opponents. She then drove the spear home into the chest of another. She launched her spear in a javelin throw at a distant Umorfae, then whipped her short sais out of their shoulder holsters before the spear had even hit its mark. Kerenza hooked a nearby opponent's hand with the prongs, then flung him out of the path of the female Elf she had entered the battle with. Death unleashed from her perfectly executed maneuvers.

I tumbled forward, and ducked a swipe from a nearby Umorfae. As his sword swung wide from the missed target, I thrust the point of my curved blade up into the fleshy underside of his jaw and arced down through his throat. He gurgled as he dropped. The splashing my feet made as I strode away drowned out the sound of his last gasps.

Three, I had already killed three.

"Away!"

I launched myself to my Elf companion, clasped his hand, then burst through the fenestram as I heard the arrows touch down in the water. Some found their marks as we darted away. This time the Umorfae were more prepared for the onslaught of arrows. They pushed great fans of water to act as shields, which blocked out most of the shots.

I appeared farther away this time, on the opposite side from the first escape.

"Arrows! Double volley! Do not give them time to recover!" Aurelian ordered.

Arrows flew, one after another. Doorways opened and I jumped through, back into the battle.

The water bloomed with inky blue blood, chaos and confusion plagued our opponents. Reinforcements had arrived, but so far they had not taken down a single one of my companions.

Aurelian was a force to be reckoned with, she deftly used fenestrams to distract her mark, charging him head on as she raised her sword, before darting through a doorway, and reappeared next to him, to complete the killing blow on his outstretched neck. She was a blur around the battlefield, for each kill one of us would complete, she would finish four. Arcing runnels of water controlled by several Umorfae attempted to encircle her, to catch her and presumably drown her. But it was no use, Aurelian was too fast for them to be able to snare her.

My selwaer sang in my hand, its innate power coursed through me, guided me. I whirled out of the path of one Umorfae and sliced upward across the chest of another. It was an effort to not look at their faces as they fell. Killing was never something I thought I would have to do. Instead I focused on staying in motion, moving on before the gravity of what I had done could settle in, and bolt me to the shallow lake ground. I released a tumult of flame at an oncoming Umorfae, he extinguished it with a rapid slosh of water, but the motion threw him off balance enough that I managed to land a strike across his ribcage.

"Fenestrams!" Aurelian called out.

In a heartbeat I dodged the oncoming onslaught, and appeared a safe distance away, while more Umorfae soldiers fell. Fenestram, fight, fenestram, fight. We completed two more cycles until the arrows were nearly depleted.

The Umorfae numbers were down to twenty when the arrows ran out. Bodies littered the now sanguinous water. It was an effort to not trip on them, as my companions and I battled the remaining horde. I fought in closer range, the Elves opening portals to jump around the skirmish advantageously.

A tall, lean female Umorfae was one of the last reinforcements to arrive, and their only archer. She skirted the battle, attempting to pick us off from a distance. Her arrows arrived a moment after each Elf she targeted slipped through a doorway and out of range.

Aurelian burst into view next to yet another guard, slashing him before she made a rapid exit to another location. The Umorfae archer gauged a point ahead of Aurelian and fired a shot before she opened a portal. Aurelian emerged from the doorway to attack another soldier, swinging her blade to smite him. Just as she summoned a doorway and spun through, the arrow landed its mark, entering the fenestram with her. She burst through on the other side, the arrow had gone clean through her chest. She collapsed out of the portal and into the water. Milky white fluid seeped out of her.

"No! Aurelian!" I gasped. Her body quavered in the water. An Elf nearby immediately opened a fenestram to her, cradled her carefully as he transported her away. He was back moments later, arms empty. I was stunned, the Elf returned to the fray, with no indication of whether she lived or not.

A giant brute of a male squared off with me, he curled his lip and growled. "Murdering bitch!" He spat. Muscles bulging and armed to the teeth, he held a deadly, sharp sword clutched in his white knuckle fist, and an array of knives were strapped in a bandolier across his chest. He shoved his hand forward, creating a wave of needle-like raindrops aimed directly at me. I reflexively held up my hand and pushed, which halted them in their midair position. He grunted, then threw them down—back into the lake.

We strafed around each other as I retorted, "It's not murder to defend innocent children. You all deserve nothing less." He huffed a laugh, then lunged forward, slashing in an arc, narrowly missing my throat as I dodged out of the way.

Warm, thick fluid slid down my neck. My eyes went wide as it dawned on me that his strike had landed. A crimson ribbon gushed down my chest. I fell to my knees in surprise, watching my life blood leak out of me.

He smirked as he circled me, and raised his sword to deliver another blow. I looked up, peering at the face of my executioner. I was a fool to think I could out-maneuver him. An untrained Fae hybrid against a formidable opponent. His haughty expression told me enough, he would enjoy delivering my doom, the fate we both knew was moments away.

"No!" A shout bellowed from behind me. My opponent flicked his eyes away for a moment, and swung. As his sword arced down, I spun on my knees toward him and thrust upward as hard as I could, mustering all the strength I had. I sunk my thigh knife that I had palmed out of its holster into his ribs, just as another knife shot deep into his chest.

He crumpled forward around the blades, his mouth gaped open in a soundless scream, and fell back. He splashed into the water, partially submerged and still. His dark, cerulean blood emanated outward in the water like tendrils of ink.

As I turned, I slumped forward, giving way to the loss of blood or the rush of adrenaline, or both. Rannoch was there in a flash, catching me before I fell.

"You are hurt," he rasped, panting to catch his breath as I

clutched at my slashed neck. "Fenestram!" He called out to whoever would listen. "We need a fenestram now!"

Two Elves appeared, opened doorways then deposited us a good distance away, before they returned to the fight.

Rannoch's eyes were wild with panic as he rushed back to me, gripping my arms to keep me steady. "Can you heal yourself?"

I stared at him dumbfounded, how had I not thought of that right away?

I focused on my hand, and unwound a thread of warmed magic. *Weave*, I willed with what little concentration I had. Slowly the two sides mended back together, the torrent of blood slowed, but I had already lost a fair amount. It was difficult to keep my thoughts clear, fog engulfed my mind and my magic waned like an ebbing tide.

Clarity struck at last, and I recalled pushing Steren's blood because of the water content it held. I pushed my own blood away from the gash, keeping it at bay while I continued to heal myself. Lightheadedness set in with the lack of circulation, the wound finally sealed and I released the invisible dam in my artery. The rush to my head snapped me to alertness.

I dropped my hand from my throat and opened my eyes, the world speckled into view with Rannoch still clutching my arms, as he stared at me. I drew a shaky breath as I settled back into the present.

"I'm all right, I need to regenerate, but I'm okay," I answered his unasked question.

So much killing. All the bodies. I thought about the ones I had already felled, the face of the last Umorfae that nearly killed me. The way his mouth hung open as he died. He was the only one I had looked at as it happened. And it was burned into my memory, forever etched there as a mental tattoo I could never remove. I bent over at the hips and the contents of my stomach emptied into the water.

I stood back up and wiped my mouth with the back of my hand, as my eyes fell back on Rannoch. I clenched my eyes closed and stifled tears as my hands shook. He wrapped his arms around me as I trembled.

"It is going to be all right." His voice was a lifeline that I clung to.

The clang of metal a short distance away rattled me back to the present, and away from my dark thoughts. "The battle! We have to get back!" I shrieked and pulled away from him.

"Give yourself a moment, that was a very close call. Please, just stay here with me until you are stable. They are okay for right now."

I looked up at him, still holding me as war raged. But he wasn't looking at any of them. His solid, unwavering presence was focused only on me. I took several breaths, sinking back into him to regain my steadiness. I closed my eyes, allowing my well to refill from the energy I had spent to heal myself. I ran my fingers over a vacant pocket on his bandolier, the missing knife still embedded in the Umorfae that nearly killed me. Rannoch had defended me. I squeezed my eyes tighter as the images replayed again. Another ring of metal brought me out of my narrowed consciousness.

"I'm ready. Let's go help our friends."

He nodded and released me. The water slowed me down significantly as I ran. There were still foes to contend with, namely that archer that might pick off more of us before this was done. I pushed my legs harder to trudge through the water as fast as I could.

One of the male Arbor Elves opened a succession of fenestrams in a zigzag pattern, jumping through them to reach the Umorfae archer. She launched a double volley to a point halfway between her and where the Elf had been last. The arrows landed just as he spun out of the doorway, striking true to the center of his chest.

"Fenlaen!" cried Aolis. His face creased in pain as his friend fell. The enemy ranks were down to ten, but their archer posed a serious threat. She had figured out how to hit her mark, even with the Elves' ability to jump from one spot to another in the blink of an eye.

He launched into a furious attack against three foes. Aolis had just finished slicing through the gut of one of the few remaining Umorfae when an idea struck.

"Aolis, together!" I thrust my finger in the direction of the archer. He nodded, as he pulled back to open a fenestram, I rocked back on my heel and then sprang forward. I spun through with him and tumbled out right next to the archer, separated from Aolis and darted around her. One to attack, the other to distract.

She dropped her bow and pulled out two short swords, crouching low like a cat on a hunt, ready to spring at any time. She eyed me, no doubt marking me as the less experienced fighter.

She lunged. Her speed was unreal, like her calves contained tightly wound coils. I twisted out of the way, my selwaer circling low around me as I rotated out of her path. The tip of it carved into that muscular calf, slicing a deep gash into her flesh. She yelped as it oozed blood down to her clawed feet.

The archer lurched forward and wheeled around, taking shuffling steps back to try and keep Aolis and I in front of her.

She flicked her eyes to her injury. In that fraction of a moment, Aolis opened a fenestram right next to her. He burst through in a downward arc, his sword pointed, ready to impale her with the momentum of his jump. But she was already waiting, one of her short swords angled up, and drove it deep into his shoulder joint. Tendons and fibers snapped, as the blade all but separated his arm from his body.

He shrieked, his hand going limp as he lost his grip on his sword. He fell to her side, but managed to tumble away a short distance.

I wasted no time to strike her again, I whipped my selwaer in several slashing strokes. For every strike I attempted, she was ready to block. I shifted tactics, opting instead to try and deliver minor injuries to her limbs, pricking her like a pin cushion.

I stood aside as Aolis staggered over to square off with her. She limped from the gashes, and Aolis's right arm hung useless at his side. Both were equally disadvantaged to survive the fight. But the rage that simmered in his eyes and under his skin nearly negated his injury, resolve burned in his gaze.

With one arm disabled, opening a fenestram would be impossible. In a burst of speed, he raced toward her. He thrust his good arm—fingers forward—into her chest. The tips pushed through the surface of her glimmering skin and tunnelled into her, then grew his roots out as he shoved them further into her heart.

The events unfolded in front of me in slow motion. I could see what was about to happen. I threw myself toward them to try and block her move. The archer made one last attempt, one more strike before he could snuff her out.

I was too late.

She slammed her other blade into his chest. Aolis gritted his teeth and squeezed his tendrils, hissing as milky blood sputtered out of his mouth. He squinted his eyes, unleashing his last bit of life force to clamp down, constricting her heart to prevent it from beating. The archer's body went rigid as her eyes widened. They both dropped together.

I ran to them and tried to wrench him away from her, attempting to release his hand from her chest. But the roots had grown into a tangled knot, I couldn't free him. The sword was buried deep in his chest. I pulled it out and tried to staunch the flow, while unspooling the healing thread. The blood didn't respond to my push as he grimaced in agony. The more I attempted to sew, the worse his pain was. I was desperate to help him, but it was no use, the damage was too significant. I rewound the thread and cradled his head. He tried to speak, but the chalk white blood was too thick. He blinked a few times. I held him, looked at him, and was there for him. I caressed his head and watched, it was all I could do. Slowly—so slowly—the light dimmed from his eyes.

A choking sob crept out of me. I sat, holding him, and wept for him. I barely knew Aolis, this magical being that gave his life fighting for people that were not his own.

The battle had ended, the last of the Umorfae had been vanquished. I sat with Aolis, kneeling in the water next to him. The white of his blood mixed with the blue of the archer's.

Water sloshed behind me, and a light hand came to rest on my shoulder. "Come, they will collect their friend," Kerenza murmured.

I looked up at her with watery eyes. "He gave his life for us."

"I know," she said with a tender gaze.

"Did we...did we lose anyone else?" I asked her. "Aolis and I saw Fenlaen fall."

She gulped and nodded. "Auroris, one of the other female Elves."

I lowered my head. They had given so much. "We would not have survived this without their help. And they lost people." It was almost too much for me to bear.

"We are indebted to them, they swung victory into our grasp. We will not forget it," she stated.

I would not forget it. I had never been witness to someone willing to give their life to another's cause. The remaining Arbor Elves came to Aolis, to transport him back home. Kerenza helped me to my feet as they separated him from the archer. I had to turn away as they worked at prying his radices free from her stilled heart.

Rannoch stood a short distance off, waiting for Kerenza and I. "We will do what we can, to show our gratitude, when our task is complete," Rannoch said.

I didn't know what anyone could do to truly show gratitude to the loved ones of someone who had lost their life for a quest they had nothing to do with. I nodded my head, trying to force myself to agree.

One Elf flashed away with Aolis's body, and returned moments later.

The surviving Elves gathered around the three of us. "We will guard the entrance now, as Aurelian promised," one male spoke up.

"Your willingness to help has made a tremendous difference," I responded, my voice shaky, "I'm truly sorry that the cost has been so high. The loss of Aurelian, Aolis, Fenlaen, and Auroris is unbearable."

"They gave their lives in the fight for justice. What the Umor-fae have done here is wrong. Aolis, Fenlaen, and Auroris no longer being at our sides will be hard to overcome. Aurelian, gods willing, may survive. Her wound is grave and she has not regained consciousness, but our best healers are with her now," he answered solemnly.

Aurelian may still be alive! "I will pray also that she lives, with every bit of hope I have in me," I said.

Kerenza issued, "Come, Lily, let us finish this." She had waited as long as she could, knowing her daughter was trapped at the other end of that cave.

I dipped my chin in agreement. *Let's finish this.* We waded over to the lip of the underwater mouth, peering down into the darkened abyss, and prepared to submerge.

CHAPTER 29

"What are we waiting for? We must go!" Kerenza barked impatiently as we balanced on the edge of the dropoff.

"Yes, we should go, but I think I should practice first," I responded evenly. "I have barely made an air bubble for myself before. I need to be sure I can do this for all three of us, and maintain it." The moment had finally been thrust upon me, where it would show if I could measure up...or not.

"Let us just go, I say!" she insisted.

"Lily is right, Kerenza, the last thing we need is to run out of air halfway there," Rannoch stated, placing a strong hand on her shoulder. His set jaw conveyed he would not budge.

I looked at him appreciatively, part of me expected him to hold that solid line and say that I had to do it. No matter what. It lightened the burden—a little.

I didn't waste a beat, I dropped off the ledge as I faced them and let myself sink into the azure void, then pulled a bubble down. Their distorted forms peered down at me, watching, waiting. It was a strange sensation as my lower face broke through the pocket. It took me a moment to trust the breath of air that awaited. Once it was in place it did not take much concentration to keep it there. I swam around, changing directions to test how much force caused the bubble to shift when I turned. After a few course changes I realized it was more about pushing the water on either side of the bubble, rather than the bubble itself. I had control over water, not air. I was merely using water to trap it.

I resurfaced and called to Kerenza, "Come in and let me try it for both of us."

She jumped in, then submerged. *This better work or we're screwed.* I took a deep breath and let the water envelope me. I drew a bubble down for myself, settled it in place, then brought one down for Kerenza.

The pocket of air was more difficult to maintain for her, like it was constantly on the cusp of slipping off. After a few passes around each other it became only slightly more natural.

I motioned to her to surface, we crested the water together and waved Rannoch over. "Okay, let's try all three of us now, try not to swim around too much," I ordered. He nodded and dropped in. I dipped below and pulled my hand in three quick successions to call the precious orbs. I pushed them in place as we drifted down facing each other, holding my hands up to keep the pockets locked to them.

I flicked my eyes for them to swim, they turned to glide through the depth. For a few moments I managed to maintain our breathing reserves, but as I attempted to stroke through the water, both bubbles slipped off of my companions.

Rannoch turned to me with a flash of doubt in his eyes, and worry filled Kerenza's. I shook my head in frustration and swam for the surface.

They joined me, as we paddled in place I suggested, "Perhaps if you each pull me by my wrists, I can maintain all our bubbles. I can kick my legs to propel myself, but I can't use my arms, otherwise I'll lose control."

Rannoch's face was stern and unreadable. He pursed his lips, I had the distinct feeling that his trust in me was waning. "All right, we will try that," he agreed, though his tone said otherwise.

"That will be much slower, it will leave us each with only one arm to swim with while pulling you," Kerenza added.

True. However I was running out of ideas for how all three of us could enter the cave, the only other option would be for one or two of us to go. But I wasn't a skilled fighter like they were. So far I had merely been lucky. There was no way to know exactly what we would face once we were inside. We couldn't risk splitting up, not with an ominous Daemalum inside, and most likely more foes than that.

"What about asking the Elves? Maybe they can open fenestrams in there?" I looked up as I thought, as if the sky could give me another idea.

Rannoch shook his head solemnly. "I already asked. They said they could end up in a point inside a rock, which would mean instant death. It is too dangerous. The other problem, will a bubble last long enough for us to make it through the whole cave? We know the Umorfae can make the trip, they are reliant on air as much as we are. But they are not slowed by having to bring someone."

"Perhaps they were slowed the first time though, when they took the children into the cave. How did they get them in? They must have done the same thing, and formed a bubble for each child," I mused.

They both nodded with pursed lips. We had to try and make this work. Even with the risks, this was our path.

I was about to submerge when Rannoch spoke up, "Keep your wits when we face the Daemalum. I have never faced one myself, but I know they can enter your mind and make you believe things that are not real. They feed off of your terror, so they will try to evoke that from you."

Great, that sounds like fun. Having my mind invaded and the terrible, dark sludge of memories past dredged up sounded like something I did not want to experience. *One problem at a time, Lily. Focus on the current issue.*

I steeled myself and forced my fingers to unclench, which I hadn't noticed had formed into tight balls again, then gulped down as much air as I could. Kerenza and Rannoch copied me and filled their lungs, then we dropped below to attempt our fools errand again. I pulled three pockets down, then slipped them into place as they gripped my wrists. We proceeded down toward the entrance, marked only by a gaping black maw that awaited to swallow us.

CHAPTER 30

The dread from the darkness that enveloped me was magnified by the powerlessness I felt at being dragged. It took significant effort to not thrash away like a terrified animal trying to avoid its inevitable slaughter. I focused all my will on the pockets of air, and tried not to think about what would happen if they slipped off.

Fortunately, Kerenza's Ignisphaera flickered to life and cast a warm glow onto the rocky tunnel walls. I honed in on that light, clinging to it like a lifeline in the dark.

I continued behind them through the rough, pitted formation. Occasional large holes pocked the porous surface. Kerenza and Rannoch used the openings to pull us faster, climbing and swimming at the same time. The space narrowed as we swam further, and jostled against each other for room as it tightened.

I concentrated on the life-giving bubbles, and pondered the formation of the tunnel to distract myself. Claustrophobia set in when I had to wiggle past a choke point. As I passed one of the larger fissures, I caught a glimmer, deep inside the recess of the opening.

I wound further through the tight quarters. A shift in upward movement caused us to bump along the top of the passage, signaling the cave was rising in elevation. *Hopefully it's not too much further, I can't imagine there's much air left.*

Another glimmer shone in my peripheral vision, then another. My blood turned to ice. *Eyes, those are eyes shining back at us.* Kerenza and Rannoch swam on without noticing. Rannoch angled his face around to survey my sudden change. My eyes were round with fear. He cocked an eyebrow in response—wordlessly asking what slowed me—when one of the owners of those eyes shot out of its burrow.

It snaked through us and looped around; a sleek, eel-like creature with fangs as long as my arm, which jutted up from its lower jaw. Another eel burst out. I panicked, our reserves lost their hold as I flailed my arms. Rannoch was instantly armed and ready to drive a knife into the guts of the serpentine creatures. The fact that our time was now down to seconds did not seem to cloud his mind. Kerenza pushed onward, kicking her legs hard to escape. I followed her and swam as fast as I could propel myself. My lungs screamed to inhale, my face scrunched in desperation. The terror rose inside me as the oxygen waned and the threat of unconsciousness increased.

Kerenza and I broke through into a cavern, gasping for air. The cramped area just enough space for us to catch a breath.

"Rannoch!" I shrieked, as I bumped my head on the low ceiling. I had barely caught my breath before I turned back around to help him. Kerenza ripped her Ignisphaera off then put it on me, to illuminate my path. I pulled two quick bubbles down, settled one on my mouth and pushed the other out in front as I dove down to find him.

I raced down with the extra pocket of air before me. I knew I had to reach him immediately. The water was murky with blackish blood, the visibility significantly cut down by the sanguine dispersion hanging in the already dark volume. Even with the glow from the Ignisphaera, it was difficult to see.

Finally he came into view, floating lifelessly. The carcass of one creature hung unnaturally in the water, slowly drifting down the passage.

I reached him and shoved the bubble to his face, hoping that he would take an instant breath.

He did not. His stern, handsome face didn't have the slightest tremor when he had oxygen available again. I shook his shoulders while holding the pocket there for him. His head rocked back, then sagged forward.

I gave up on the bubble, and instead pulled him to the open cavern. His dead weight was a struggle to drag through the passage. We inched up the tunnel, drawing closer to the cavern where Kerenza waited.

Something blasted by my cheek and knocked me into the rocky surface, a shiver ran up my spine from the slickness of the massive, slimy body coming into contact with mine. Dazed for a moment from the impact, I shook my head to refocus my senses, when I realized I had let go of Rannoch's hand. *I don't have time for this!*

I reached down and grabbed his hand again, in one quick motion I pulled him up to me, then wedged myself underneath his back and pushed him from below using both feet on the tunnel walls.

The eel shot toward me again, but this time I was waiting. With Rannoch balanced on my back, I pivoted to the side and latched on with both hands and brought all frustration and anger to the forefront of my mind. I sent searing heat through my limbs as I focused the raw energy on the water snake. The tunnel illuminated and steam bubbles rushed upward, as I released scalding fire. The creature tried to wrench itself away, but I had already burned into its skin. It writhed, attempting to snag me with its massive fangs. Gnashing a hair's width from my face, I angled my chin away as I gritted my teeth, clamping down harder on its now crackling neck.

It slumped away at last, as I gave one huge push to move Rannoch the last distance to the surface. *I told you I did not have time for that!* I thought angrily at the dead creature.

The steam filled the cavern, but there was still enough oxygen for me to replenish.

"Rannoch!" Kerenza screamed.

"Help me hold him up," I ordered. She looped her arms underneath his limp body and held him from behind.

I pinched his nose and put my mouth around his, and gave two breaths to force his lungs open. I couldn't get the pressure needed to do chest compressions while we were stuck in the water, so I unwound a golden thread through my hand and pulsed it into his heart, forcing it to beat like a defibrillator. I counted pulses out loud, "...Twenty-nine, thirty." I withdrew my hand and gave two more breaths. Thirty more pulses.

I was starting to give two breaths again when he coughed to life. His eyes shot open, he gagged and sputtered water. Both Kerenza and I cradled him as he panted, spitting out the last of the vile liquid.

"How did you..." Rannoch stared at me, still gasping.

I shrugged. "Something from the human world, combined with healing magic."

Kerenza gripped his chest with her arms. "I thought I lost you!" she cried.

"I thought you did too," he admitted through gulping breaths, "thank you, Lily."

I held back tears as his warmth cocooned me, the rush of adrenaline subsided. All I could do was bob my head in answer. I wanted to hug him with all my might.

"The other snake!" He exclaimed. "I was only able to kill one of them."

"I killed the other one when I went to get you."

His mouth dropped open, and nodded his approval. "Yet another surprising feat from you. Why is it so hot in here?" Rannoch asked, as he looked at the steam in the confined space.

"Well...that's how I killed it. I burned its neck to a crisp with my hands. The process heated up the water," I confessed.

He raised his eyebrows, and Kerenza gave me a sidelong glance.

The air thinned, we had depleted the cavern's oxygen. "I think it's time for us to go, we're running out of air in here," I said. I took off the Ignisphaera, then handed it back to Kerenza.

Kerenza agreed as she accepted it, her face painted in worried lines as she slipped it on the jewelry.

A thought struck like lightning. "Kerenza, you've mentioned that you get images intermittently from Emblyn through the ring, which is how you knew what was in the cave with her. Are you able to send images back?" I asked.

"Yes, well...there is no way to know for sure if she saw an image

I sent her, but if I concentrate, I can send a single image through the ring bond."

Rannoch snapped his sharp eyes to me. "I see where you are going with this," he declared, the fire flaring in his pupils.

I nodded as I continued, "If she knows we are here to rescue her and the other children, perhaps she will send us an image of what to expect, where the foes might be, to help us gain an advantage. Maybe if you send her a picture of us in this part of the cave, she will know."

"Perhaps," Kerenza said, "it could be worth trying. But she is just a young filia, she may not think to send back a picture of her surroundings. And what if somehow it alerts her captors to our approach instead?"

I hadn't thought of that, I admitted to myself as I puffed through my lips. "Well, it's your choice, whatever you think is best. I do think they already know of the possibility of us reaching the cave. They sent out as many Umorfae as they could."

"Emblyn has keen senses and a knack for survival, I think it is worth the risk," Rannoch said as he laid a hand on her shoulder.

She regarded him for a moment, then nodded in agreement. She clutched the stone of the ring and squeezed her eyes shut. As Kerenza re-opened them, she confirmed, "It is done."

"Let's proceed, with you both pulling me. Hopefully this time we don't have any unexpected encounters," I commanded. The stern resolve in my voice surprised me, though neither took issue with it.

I pulled three pockets down once we submerged, and settled all into position as we began our watery trek onward.

CHAPTER 31

The remainder of the tunnel was thankfully clear, no perilous snakes or other fun surprises. A wide surface loomed above us, light refracted off the top and filtered down into the dark volume we were about to emerge from.

We crested the water, allowing only the top half of our faces to slip through. The chamber surrounding us was devoid of signs of life. Rannoch lifted a finger to his lips, and used his other hand to indicate for us to move.

Firelight danced on the rounded walls, emanating from a hidden source across the chasm. Howls, mixed with whimpers and clicks, echoed from deep within. We glided through the water to the lip of a large flowstone, which ramped out of the water toward another tunnel.

One by one, we climbed the rocky lip onto the floor. Rannoch's ears pricked up, trying to discern any movement nearby. We prowled through the passage, burnt umber stone glittered on the walls and stalactites jutted down like the teeth of some great beast.

My heart was in my throat as we entered the tunnel, wider

than the water-filled entrance passage. Deep grooves scraped along the surface, like a reaper dragged his scythe countless times along it, waiting for his next victims.

We were coming to a bend in the passage and just about to peer around it, as the clicks increased. Kerenza gasped and grabbed Rannoch's arm. Her eyes wide as she leaned over to whisper, "She sent an image! The Daemalum is near her, and I saw the entrance to the chamber that they are held in. It is guarded by-"

Oh fuck! Large, claw-like arms swiped toward us, their hulking width was more than half my height.

Arthropods. Unsightly shelled creatures that were a nightmarish amalgamation of scorpion and crab with compound eyes and fangs. The blood drained from my face as I took in their plated bodies the size of Rannoch's equus. Their blue-black carapaces shimmered in the low light as they rushed us.

We darted back, Rannoch used the wall of the passage to invert himself and flip out of the way.

"Spread out! We will not be able to battle them in close quarters!" He barked.

The ghastly crustaceans scuttled after us, their claws clicked and mouths drooled as they anticipated their next meal.

I dashed down the tunnel and whipped out my selwaer, whirling around to face one of the creatures that had been right at my heels. I spun and struck, but my blade clanged across its armored back. It swung its massive claw, narrowly missing me as I managed to leap out of the way.

Kerenza's short sword did the same, everywhere she tried to strike was met with an unyielding exoskeleton. It snapped a spiked claw, attempting to snare her by the ankle. The claw arms were slow, however their clamp force looked to be deadly, enough to crush a man's skull like an egg.

Rannoch was the first to land a blow, he ran and skid on his knees underneath one, as he jabbed one of his longer knives into its tender underbelly. Oily orange goo gushed out of it. A stream of it sprayed across Rannoch's arm, leaving an acid-like burn in its wake. The creature slumped off as it shrieked at the fatal wound.

He bellowed as the heinous blood marred him, and hissed through his teeth at the pain. He narrowed his eyes, his muscles so taut it looked like the sinews might snap. "Go for the belly or between the plates! Avoid the blood!" Rannoch raised his sword up and back, then charged forward with stunning speed.

Another crustacean was already winding up a swipe with its unwieldy appendage, when Rannoch flew at him. He drove his blade deep between the narrow sliver where the shoulder plate met the neck. The creature instantly dropped, Rannoch was already whipping around to target another one.

More and more clacked their way down the cavern, the clicks of their bony parts scratching on the walls grated against my ears.

I had avoided the strikes from the arthropod that was squared off with me, I circled around it as I looked for an opening to wedge my selwaer under its plates. As it slashed its claw again, I went to dart away, before I realized I had become hemmed in by the rocky wall. There was only one option to prevent the bone crushing claw from finding its mark. I leaped up toward its other shoulder, and scrabbled over—onto the beast's back. It spun wildly, trying to fling me off so it could crush me or stab me with its barbed tail.

I clung to the ridge of the back plate behind its neck, gripping it until my knuckles were white. It stopped spinning and began shoving into nearby walls. I slipped a little and caught the glimmer of iridescent wings under the back shell. *Female! This might be a female.* An idea struck. I reached forward in between her rocking and slamming, and laid a hand on her head.

Listen! Calm. Calm. I blasted out as I unwound the thread down my arm. *Hear me! Calm. Stop.* She shuddered to a halt, and stopped clacking her claw.

No more fighting, calm. End this. I pulsed down the cord. She listened intently, waiting. *All stop. Ask others to stop.*

I sensed nothing from her, other than perhaps curiosity. I received no thoughts in return, but she stilled as I spoke through her. The shell on her back began to split open down the center, her wings emerged and fluttered. I inched further up her back away from her wings, keeping my hand to her head.

She lifted off the ground, as all other arthropods stopped their attack.

Rannoch was about to sink his knife into another creature. "Rannoch, stop!" I yelled at him from down the corridor. He hadn't noticed what was happening. His mouth dropped as he beheld me, riding the hideous, fell beast.

Her ascent was slow and clumsy, I hunkered down further so that my center of balance was as close to hers as possible. We rose above the bodies of the other crustaceans.

Forward, cavern. She teetered over the domed heads of her kind, buzzing down the tunnel past the stunned faces of Kerenza and Rannoch. I shrugged at them as I passed by, equally as surprised by the turn of events.

The teeming arthropods followed her and filed into the open space beyond the tunnel. Huge stalactites and stalagmites jutted angrily into view in the expansive chamber. Wide ruts ran horizontally, like troughs for some ancient waterway. Across the eerie cathedral, light flickered and whimpers echoed. Small shapes cast shadows through the steamy haze that permeated the area.

My mount twittered toward the huddle, her walking legs dangled and scraped over the crest of the channel walls. The other crustaceans scuttled over the rises, scratching and rasping against them. A chill ran through my blood as my eyes fell on another being.

CHAPTER 32

A jet black creature, standing fifteen feet tall, ambled from behind a large column. It parted its thin lips and smiled a rictus grin, which made my bones shudder. Closer it strode, the sinews of its lanky limbs held in by papery skin.

"Come to claim your prize, filia?" It hissed through its unnervingly white, fang-like teeth.

I gulped down my fear at the sight of the living nightmare. "We have conquered all in our path to this point. Give us the children and we will leave in peace," I announced, the stammer that threatened to squeak out held back by sheer willpower.

A low laugh rumbled from all sides of the cavern. "Leave? In peace? You greatly overestimate yourselves if you think you can leave at all."

The sound of its voice rasped against my ears, against my very soul. I began to sweat, and a creeping sense that I was bound by chains swept over me. I barely blinked before he was mere inches from me. A taloned nail scraped along my cheek, drawing a bead of blood in a curving path down the length of it, ending under my throat.

"Besides, I do not think you have near enough forces to fight all of us," he cackled in wicked delight, as he poked in harder to the fleshy underside of my jaw.

Another Daemalum appeared, then another, and another. They walked out from hidden alcoves all around us. Rannoch and Kerenza leaped across the ruts, springing off the ridge to cross the gaps. The melee started in a flash, Rannoch launched himself toward them, his blade whirred through the air.

But the Daemalum were too nimble, they shifted in a haze of smoke and reappeared a short distance away, unscathed. Rannoch tried over and over to slash at them, each time his sword fell short and the creatures dispersed. Kerenza spun and kicked her way through the fray, stabbing forward with her spear. But again, she never found a mark.

Rannoch's face clenched in frustration, he burst forward, a cyclone of power and metal. A Daemalum slipped out of the way, then materialized again with its claws outstretched, into the path of his abdomen. The force of momentum propelled Rannoch onto the deadly talons, they ripped into him until they were poking out the back.

"No!" I screamed. The chains around me tightened.

Kerenza gasped as she saw her brother fall. She charged the nearest Daemalum, who slid in a wisp of smoke and grabbed her spear as he went, fluidly taking it from her hands, then flung her off in another direction. She careened to the side, where the Daemalum reappeared with the spear held aloft.

She collapsed onto her own weapon and stared down at it in astonishment, before falling to her knees.

The world retracted from me, my legs wobbled as I tried to rationalize what had just happened. My friends were gone. Rannoch was dead, I couldn't stomach it. Beautiful Kerenza had been snuffed out. Emblyn, still trapped by these monsters, now alone in this world.

My heart raced. The faces of my father and sister smiling at me jumped into my mind, then contorted in pain as they met their end and flames enveloped them. The powerlessness that I felt that day choked me, debilitating and overwhelming as I was forced to watch, again. I stood uselessly, as the Daemalum pressed his talon further into my neck.

"Submit, or I will kill you," he promised in a dark whisper. All I could do was blink, my body went numb, I was lost and alone. Everything was cloudy and indistinct, like a disorienting fog.

A faint clang sounded behind me; metal ricocheting off stone. The Daemalum in front of me distorted, like looking at him through a thin film being blown by the wind.

Another metallic ringing cut through, along with a muffled voice. *Something doesn't feel right. Spear...Kerenza had left the spear with the Elves. She only had her sword and sais.* I started to doubt what was around me, what I felt. How had everything happened so quickly? The visage of the Daemalum quavered. *This isn't real, none of this is real.*

He disappeared, along with all the other Daemalum, and Rannoch and Kerenza's bodies. The monster reappeared as a single entity where I had first seen him, when he had walked out from behind the column. I was still sitting on the giant arthropod. I looked to my side, and there stood Kerenza and Rannoch. Unhurt—and furious.

My blood rushed when I realized I had fallen prey to the Daemalum's mind tricks. *Oh, this asshole is going to pay.*

"Well, well. Stronger than you seem. That will make it all the sweeter when I ensnare you for good," he sneered.

"Actually, I think it will be all the sweeter for us when we repay you for all that you've done," I countered. All fear melted away. Only my goal remained, our mission. We had reached our target and would not falter.

I launched myself off the lip of the beetle-like back and sailed toward him, hands outstretched. I unwound my power, channeling all of my anger at him. *Using images of my father and sister against me? I don't think so!*

I slammed into him with my hands imprinting on his chest, they seared deep as he tried to evade my burning grasp. His mouth opened wide in a shrill cry, his papery skin scorched. He wrapped long, spindly fingers around my wrists and ripped them away from his chest, his hands smoking at the touch of my skin.

"You will pay for that, cunne!" He hollered. The Daemalum pulled me closer. A rank, putrid smell emanated from within his horrible body. I cringed, trying to angle my face away from his threatening fangs and ghastly scent of death.

As I struggled to free myself, a giant fireball erupted and engulfed him. It felt like the heat from a thousand suns. The rush of it going past me blew my hair aside and singed my arm. I panicked, as I tried to wriggle my wrists out of his grasp. With one strong outward motion, I snapped my arms free and tumbled back. Rannoch caught me, scooping me away from the flames, then tucked me into his chest.

The Daemalum's scream nearly burst my eardrums as he withered. My eyes traveled from the monster encased in the blaze, to the river of fire—which Kerenza blasted in a mighty stream from her Ignisphaera. She held it aloft, while the other hand pushed the flame into a powerful, unyielding current. Her eyes danced with the fire, entranced as she pummeled him. Her hair reflected the flames in brilliant ruby glints, she curled her lip and gave one last hard jolt.

The shrieking ceased. He was beyond death, held up only by the rush of fire around him, as his limbs dwindled to vanishing sticks. Nothing but embers and ash remained of the fear monger.

Slowly, she lowered her hands, the Ignisphaera swung from the chain wound through her fingers. Tears slid down her face as she dropped to her knees. Smoldering charcoal was all that was left of the evil being, a fitting end.

She hung her head and sobbed. I was still catching my breath as I pulled back to look at Rannoch. He smiled down at me with the warmth that I had only rarely felt from him. I could have cried, it had been like clawing our way up a mountain made of mud, and against all odds we had finally reached the top. I wrapped my arms around him and buried my face in his chest.

Little voices sounded from behind the columns, full of hope and optimism, yet quietly cautious. They grew closer, when the first face appeared. A young girl partially emerged, with pointed ears and long black hair, matted with debris. She crept further out, a skinny wisp of a girl wearing a tattered sack dress.

Kerenza caught her breath as she looked at her, their eyes went wide as they held each other's gaze. I gasped, the sound startlingly loud as it cut through the silence. More children appeared. They were all so thin, so horribly thin. Their furtive eyes darted around looking for their captors.

The denizens of the cave, the arthropods, stood where they had been left, waiting patiently. They made no move whatsoever as the Ignisfae children peeked at them.

Kerenza clasped her hand to her mouth as she waited, and watched. The little girl burst forward with a huge, beaming smile. She sprinted for Kerenza, and threw her arms around her as she collapsed into her.

"Maeder! Maeder you did come! I knew you would!" Emblyn cried and smiled. "I always told the others that you would come!"

Tears rolled down Kerenza's cheek as she rocked her, holding her tight. "I am so sorry my filia. You should never have been taken. I am so sorry, Emblyn." She wept into her child's hair.

They sat, holding each other and crying happy tears. Rannoch and I looked at the other children. A bright smile spread across Rannoch's face as he motioned to them to come forward. They ran toward us as fast as their legs could carry. They clamored around, encircling us excitedly. They glanced curiously at me, hugging and chittering questions.

"How will we get home?" a male, who looked to be no more than four, asked him.

Rannoch stood taller and held up his hands. "Do not worry! We have a plan to get you all safely home."

I raised my eyebrows at Rannoch in response, then smiled and nodded my head to the little ones.

"This is Lily, a Vale Born. She has powers over water and can swim the great length of the tunnel. She will swim back out and retrieve someone who can help us," he declared.

Oh, is that what she will do? He turned toward me, cocked an eyebrow and twitched his mouth to the side before turning back to them. "I am so pleased to see all of you, we have all been so worried about you and have worked tirelessly to bring you home. Give me a moment with Lily so that we may plan to leave," he said.

They cheered and danced in giddy excitement, they were finally so close to escaping this horrible place. He pulled me aside. "I thought perhaps you could swim out and retrieve one of the Arbor Elves, and then swim back with him. He would be able to open a fenestram to a place they have already been. Once one is inside they can shuttle the children out through the doorways," he suggested.

I eyed him carefully, I didn't want to admit that swimming through the tunnel alone sounded terrifying. I nodded my head as I responded, "If you think that's the only way."

"The only other option I can think of is you swimming the children out one at a time. That would be exhausting for you and more dangerous for the children," he countered.

I pondered for a moment before agreeing, "You're right. It's a good idea. I'll swim and ask an Elf to join us."

I still needed to convince myself. This was safer for the children, there should be no question. However being completely alone in a dark tunnel was a daunting thought. I was mulling it over as Rannoch spoke quietly to Kerenza.

He jogged back to me, a tendril of his dark hair had escaped the crown of his high braid, which came to a rest as he stopped in front of me, framing his perfect arched eyebrows. I had to resist the urge to reach up and sweep it back. "I will go with you to the edge of the water, and wait for you there," he stated.

I took a deep breath and mustered my courage. *I am Lily Brennanfalk. I can do this shit!* "One moment, I want to do something before I go," I told him.

I walked over to the female arthropod, then reached up to place my hand on her head. *I will be back, guard them. Do not hurt them,* I said down the thread of magic. She buzzed and clicked lightly in response. *Hopefully that was an agreement.* In that moment, her eyes didn't look so scary, the reflections I saw in them almost looked...cute. Her shell was pretty—appealing even. I stroked one hand down her back, the same way I would stroke Apollo. The smooth surface had faint ridges that caused the light to bend and the colors shift.

I turned from her and nodded to Rannoch, ready to make my way out of the cave. I hopped the troughs and went around the corner to the antechamber, to head down the corridor, leaving Kerenza in the main cavern to manage the children until he came back. I took the ten minute walk with him through the tunnel to the edge of the water, rallying my courage. The thought of entering the confined lengthy space filled me with terror. We turned toward each other when we reached the lip of the drop off, my eyes must have been the size of saucers with concern.

"I could go with you," he offered, as he studied my face.

Yes, dummy. I don't want to go alone. "No, I'll be okay. If the arthropods change their minds and attack, you should be here. I don't think they will, but...you should stay," I answered. It was how I should have responded, but not how I wanted to.

We stared at each other, the silence created tension that made me want to either leap in the water or leap into his arms.

I opened my mouth to say something, when he said, "Here, I borrowed this from Kerenza. So it will not be so dark in there."

He took a step closer to me and slipped the Ignisphaera over my head, then gently adjusted it and slid my braid out to rest on top. As he let go of my hair, he brushed his hand along my shoulder, down my arm, then picked up my hand.

I looked at his forearm, burned from the fight with the arthropods. "You were so brave," I whispered as I took a step closer, remembering his skill and heroism, and tireless fighting for his people. I lifted my other hand to the injury, and unwound the healing thread as my vision tunneled into his skin. It was healed in a flash, and I blinked back into the present. I placed my hand on his now-smooth arm, feeling his corded muscles underneath.

He looked down at me, his eyes were soft with tenderness and warmth, then glanced at my mouth. The warmth turned to fire that flickered in his pupils. Desire welled in me, I parted my lips and leaned toward him. He shifted closer, but waited. His eyes searched my face. He blinked several times, then pulled back his head, his gaze going dark.

"Be safe, Lily. Burn brightly. I will see you soon." His deep voice carried a crestfallen undertone.

I released a breath I didn't realize I was holding, disappointed by the moment flickering out. "I will," I answered, trying not to let my disheartened feelings show.

I dropped his hand and turned to the water, then jumped in without looking back.

CHAPTER 33

I dove down, then flipped around to call an air bubble. As I adjusted it, Rannoch watched, his image distorted and refracted by the water's surface. I stared back at him, wishing he had kissed me. It was worse to almost kiss me, and then abandon it, rather than not at all. It seemed a cruel joke, one that I didn't get in the least.

Was it to distract me, to get me to think about him instead of the terrifying passage? I shook my head to shake off the thought, and turned to head down the tunnel. The darkness descended into the small opening, waiting to swallow me. I couldn't help but feel the malice of the cave, the sense that it would like nothing more than to forever contain me in its innards. The walls closed in around me, the Ignisphaera was a meek candle against the cold, Stygian passage. Goosebumps rose on my limbs as I entered the narrow tunnel, my heart threatened to beat its way out of my chest.

I hope there are no more eels. No, don't think about them. Think about...Rannoch. No, don't think about him. You'll be too distracted. Think about...light. Just think about light. Be a light in this hateful place. You are not scared, you are brave. You will not falter. You are

Lily Fucking Brennanfalk, and you can do this thing. Be the light that this world needs.

Onward I swam. I came to the chamber where we caught our breath on the way in. I paused only briefly to gulp a few breaths, before I proceeded and called a fresh bubble. I swam as fast as I could, hoping that focusing on speed would help distract me from the depressing darkness.

I passed the lifeless corpses of the water snakes, twisted and strange as they drifted from the slight current. Already developing the whitish mycelium fuzz on the surface of their skin, my hand brushed one as I swam by, sending a shudder through my spine. I hurried, half afraid they would come to life and strike at me.

Hand over hand I pulled myself along the wall of the tunnel, periodically scanning the recesses for light reflected back by little beady eyes. Fortunately, none were there to be seen. It didn't stop me from being hyper-vigilant though. I kept expecting that one cavern would be occupied, its resident just waiting to lash out and wrap its wretched body around my neck or snap its jaws at me.

As I pressed on, the sadness of the oppressive cave ate into me, my thoughts of "being the light" were nibbled away. I slowed as the positive, optimistic thoughts finally ebbed away completely. The images the Daemalum had tricked me into seeing flickered in my mind, Rannoch, Kerenza, my father, and sister...dying. Those horrible, final moments. I stopped swimming, the tragic loss that I felt in that moment choked out my will to paddle onward, and arrested my ability to move. The claustrophobia I had felt from believing I was alone with that creature, all the way inside the rocky prison took hold. Terrible loss—both real and imagined—in both worlds. There was no escaping it. Anything I cared about could so easily be washed away from existence. It was all so futile.

I started to feel lightheaded, and for a moment forgot where I was. Everything was so dark and foreboding. *I was going somewhere. I think I had to do something, what was it?* I looked around for an indicator, but the rough tunnel walls yielded nothing.

The necklace I wore twinkled. I looked down, and remembered what it was. *The Ignisphaera! Rannoch! I need to get to the Elves!* I realized with sudden clarity that my reserve had run out of oxygen and hypoxia was setting in.

I let go of the useless bubble, no longer holding it in place freed me up to use both arms fully. I kicked off from the wall hard and pulled myself down the tunnel.

Faster and faster I went, down, down, down. My vision speckled, I didn't know how many seconds I had left, but I knew it wasn't many.

The walls widened and dropped away, I was at the bottom of the lake that the cave opened up into. *Push!* I had to get myself to the surface. It was still full night, and hard to see where the surface was. An endless, inky volume loomed ahead of me.

I fluttered my feet, and pulled in mighty breaststrokes to propel myself up. I gritted my teeth as I gave my quickly vanishing consciousness the last jolt that I had in me.

I blacked out just as I burst through to the open air.

Images filtered in; the great splash I had created when I crested the water, being dragged by my underarms, people crowded around me as someone propped me up from behind in shallow water. A slap to my back expelled the water trapped in my nose and mouth. I greedily inhaled as I choked, my surroundings clarified as my vision returned.

"You are all right, just give yourself a moment," a female Elf reassured as she rubbed my back.

"Can you tell us what happened in there? Where are Rannoch and Kerenza? And the children?" She asked, once I had regained my composure.

"They're all okay. They're waiting inside. Rannoch had the idea that one of you could swim back with me. Once you have been to a place you can safely open a fenestram there, correct?"

"Yes, that is true. Once inside I can fold a doorway and retrieve more Elves, to assist moving everyone out. Can you hold enough air for one of us?"

I turned to her. "Do you breathe more air than an average Fae? I maintained air for both Kerenza and Rannoch. It was difficult, but we managed."

She pushed a woody finger to her chin. "No, I do not think we do. We have never done something like this—spending an extended period of time underwater—so we will just have to see."

"One thing though, I will need help to swim. In order to maintain the air reserves I need one hand free to hold them in place."

She nodded. "Have you recovered?"

"Yes, let's go. I'm sure the children are anxious to be finally freed and returned to their families."

She helped me up, then we slogged through the water to the drop off of the lake shelf. My toes hung over the craggy edge, as I steeled myself to return once again to that wretched place. The devil's large intestine.

"What's your name?"

"Dendris."

"All right, Dendris, let's do this."

Rannoch, Kerenza, the children. Just this last time, then they are safe. Dendris and I looked at each other, took a deep breath, then jumped in.

CHAPTER 34

I shook out my hands, which had reflexively balled up at the thought of going back into that tunnel for a third time. The prior trip was more than I could handle. The greatest threat turned out to be my own mind. *At least you're not alone this time. Just keep it together, they're depending on you.* That was perhaps the only thing keeping me from outright running away. They needed me. At this point, without me, none of them would be able to escape.

I closed my eyes as I drifted down, bolstering my resolve to soldier on. I opened them to find Dendris watching me intently. I realized she was waiting for me to give her air. *Whoops! Coming right up.* I pulled down two bubbles and set them in place, then held out my hand to her so she could pull me. She grasped it, then dragged me slowly. Her long, mossy hair floated out in a swirling mass inches from my face. Multiple types of fine plants wove through the volume, like its own ecosystem. Miniature flowers of pale yellow and white, their tiny round petals bloomed with the increasing water pressure as we descended.

We made several passes before we surfaced facing each other.

"What do you think? Did it feel safe to you?" I asked her as the water dripped from her mottled bark skin. It struck me how strangely beautiful she was. Her self-assured nature and the confidence she exuded practically glowed through her, and her intense jade eyes conveyed thoughtful intelligence.

"Yes, it felt safe, it was an...interesting experience. It is not common for us to swim, it is hard to keep my radices from growing out to drink up the water. They do that naturally when submerged. But if I maintain my focus I believe I can do it. Is it a long journey?"

"It's somewhat long, but cleared of dangers, so it should be fairly easy going. And there is a rest point a little past midway. It's hard to tell how long it took for us to get through it, perhaps thirty minutes at most," I answered.

"How long is a minute?"

"Oh, um, sixty seconds," I responded with my palms up and eyebrows askance, hoping she would know what that meant.

By the look on her face, she didn't. "One, two, three...that is the length of a second." I indicated using my fingers to count.

She gave a single nod. "Let us be off."

I flashed a smile and motioned with my chin.

Dendris returned a small smile that did not reach her eyes, and dipped down under to wait for the air reserve. She reminded me of Aurelian in a way; a little blunt—maybe too serious. Focused.

I situated the bubbles, then we descended to the opening of the cave. Back to that dark, awful place. At the very least, I could be optimistic that this would be my last time having to slog through it.

My heart stuttered as we entered, the panic was already rising and quickened my heart rate. The familiar feelings started to take hold as we began the suffocating traverse, the numbness and disembodiment that I would feel whenever the memory of the wildfire came to mind, how it choked out any rational, logical thoughts. *Focus on the finish, get to the end. They need you. You will be okay.* I shook myself back into the present, not only did I need to get to those currently stranded on the inside of this hell hole, I also was now responsible for the other soul with me.

She tugged me along steadily, for not being accustomed to swimming she was quite powerful. A little awkward at it, but each stroke pulled us swiftly through the passage. I kicked my feet constantly, giving all my physical effort to propel myself, so that she was not having to haul me like a sack of grain. Focusing on my feet helped to keep my mind occupied as we traversed the rugged formation.

Dendris slowed and looked at me with an alarmed expression. We had reached the dead eels. I motioned to keep going with my free hand. I probably should have been more specific about what "cleared from danger" meant. We skirted their fuzzy corpses, using only one hand made it impossible to sidle past them without touching. One ended up sliding down the whole length of my back. I shuddered in disgust, it left phantom tingles there for minutes afterwards. I gagged and wanted to wretch at the slimy contact, it took all of my will to keep it from happening. Puking through my air bubble would most likely not be ideal.

The ascent was slow, but I knew we were nearing the rest point. Finally, we broke through to the small cavern. It was low on air, but held enough to at least breathe for a moment.

"What were those back there?" Dendris asked as she inhaled.

"I don't know, in my realm we'd call them eels. They attacked us on the way in the first time. Rannoch killed one, and I killed the other," I answered as my chest heaved.

"My pace is slowing, my body is starting to absorb too much water. I tried to prevent it, but it is not working anymore. Is it much further?" Her forehead creased with concern. Dendris's skin had plumped, the normally thin, bark-like layer appeared puffy and spongy. Her lush hair had grown longer and fuller, the weight of it pulled her head back.

Now I was worried too, if she became too slow she may not be able to help. If she was unable to pull me I would not be able to maintain air for her. We were past the point of turning back, and we couldn't stay in the rest pocket much longer.

"Can you open a fenestram from inside a water volume?" I inquired. If we had to get her out, perhaps that could work. That would leave me ferrying everyone inside one by one, but it could be done.

"I do not think it has been done before, but I will try." She looked doubtful as she slipped below, pulling her right arm back like an archer readying an arrow to fly. But there was no portal that opened for her. Not a glimmer of a window to the outside.

She resurfaced, visibly frustrated. "No, it does not work. I cannot feel the tension that I usually do when I pull it open. There is no resistance, as if nothing is there. Sometimes, when we begin to open a doorway, we have trouble connecting the end point. This time, it is like the start point does not exist."

I considered, then announced, "All right, we'll swim. When we get closer I can release both our air reserves, so that we can switch and I can pull you. I will tug twice on your hand, so that you can get as much air from your bubble before I release it. We will need to hold our breath until we reach the main chamber."

She widened her eyes, her emotions betrayed her previously reserved exterior. "Will we make it? I do not know how long I can hold my breath for. As I said, this is not something we normally challenge our bodies to do."

I kept my face neutral and controlled, willing an air of confidence as I answered, "We are not that far from the cavern. We will go as far as we can with the air reserve, if you get to the point where it is too hard to continue, we will resort to releasing them so that I may swim us to the end. We can do this." I laid a hand on her shoulder and mustered all authority in me. We had no other choice. Second guessing ourselves could waste precious time. Her skin had increased in volume since stopping. "Let's go, the sooner we get there, the sooner we can get you out of here," I commanded, trying to keep her focus on me, so that she wouldn't notice the bark layer had risen a good half inch off the normally nearly smooth surface. It gave her skin an alligator-like appearance.

We sucked in a breath, then ducked down. With the now familiar scoop motion toward myself, I brought down our two life preservers. Dendris moved much slower, her legs more awkward and lumbering. Her labored kicks barely made headway for us.

Not far enough. I had hoped we'd get a little more distance. I couldn't remember how much further it was to the end. I squeezed her hand twice. We took a breath in unison, then I released the reserves. I pushed myself off the wall, gripping her swollen hand, and used my other hand to pull us. At least we were heading upward, rising was certainly easier than swimming down.

Her heaviness increased, as she swelled Dendris became additional drag. *Push on!* I used handholds in the pocked surface whenever I could, and kicked off the larger dips for more propulsion. The air I held inside screamed to be released, my lungs were desperate to take another breath.

I could see the surface, we were near breaking through. I squinted my eyes in my last efforts to reach the top. My whole body strained as I pushed with all my might. Dendris's weight made the last few feet nearly unbearable, my muscles burned.

I burst through the surface and gasped for air, as I pulled Dendris up. She had been inert and rigid for the last sprint, I half-expected her to be unconscious. I prepared myself for the worst as the top of her head bobbed slowly up.

I pulled hard to get her face above water, and found her eyes wide open and staring at me wildly. Her body had become immobilized from the water she had absorbed.

"I've got you, it'll be okay," I comforted her, as I struggled to drag her to the rocky lip that gradually rose from the water's edge. Rannoch appeared at the mouth of the barren cave. He rushed down the ramp, then jumped into the water and swam over.

"She's full of water, she can't move," I managed to tell him between breaths. I got her to the ramp with Rannoch's help, then pulled her up. Dendris's previously shapely legs had become nothing short of huge trunks. Her skin tightened in bands to accommodate the extra fluid.

Her shallow breaths couldn't fill her lungs, no more than feeble inhales as we settled her on the stone.

Dendris's radices branched out from each limb, her phalanges had grown into long, fibrous roots.

"She told me that they didn't swim like this. She did not know this would happen. Maybe...I can pull the water out of her?" I conferred with Rannoch as we knelt beside her. "Dendris can you blink your eyes twice if you want me to try that?" It was the only thing I could think of to help speed her recovery. There was always the possibility that she would be just fine, once she dried out. But who knew how long that could take.

She didn't hesitate to blink twice.

"I'll try drawing the water downward, toward the radices. Rannoch, can you help me turn her on her side? That way we can lay her arms on top of each other and I can try pulling the water all in one direction." I motioned for him to adjust her, so that her hips were stacked.

He propped Dendris up, and stabilized her from behind as I began. I pulsed down my arms and out my hands to sense the water volume. I could feel it within her, I sensed a gelatinous, indistinct form. Situated near her hands and feet, I pulled it toward myself, cast an invisible net and yanked it taut.

Rannoch grunted as he crashed into Dendris. "You pulled me also!" His voice was muffled from his face being smothered by her hair.

"Oh! Sorry Rannoch," I apologized as I released the volume. "I guess you can't be there. I must have pulled your blood from inside your body."

"That was strange!" He exclaimed as he stood up, then walked a safe distance away. "I did not know you could do that."

"I didn't really know either," I responded. Although I had held blood at bay more than once. It would make sense that the opposite could be true, even if it were contained within a body.

I pulled again, drawing the fluid down. I had to sit back and prop a foot up on her hip to keep from pulling her over. She groaned as the water ebbed away from her head, down her chest, then toward her limbs. Her arms swelled even further as the water retreated to her extremities, but the radices slowly began dripping the excess out.

I yanked in a rocking motion, rowing back to keep the flow of fluid steadily seeping out. A small rivulet ran down the rock, back into the aquifer. Dendris's face returned to a more normal size, the spongy appearance of the bark texture reduced considerably. She breathed a sigh of relief as her chest slimmed down, finally the skin loosened enough for her to breathe comfortably.

"Now I know why we do not swim," she stated.

"I apologize, Dendris. This is what we call in my realm "learning the hard way." I appreciate that you took the risk to come with me. Hopefully you'll feel better with a little more time."

I started to get dizzy, my vision flooded with dots. *I'm nearing a burnout. I've used magic a lot today.* Though I did notice I was able to use more and more, as time went on. The first time I used magic it did not take much to reach the point of unconsciousness. *It must be like a muscle, it gets stronger with use. I'm getting better!*

I eased off as I rewound my power, letting it spool back inside to curl up. "I need to take a break," I stated. "I think-" and then, darkness.

CHAPTER 35

A deep voice hummed, and trickled into my slowly emerging consciousness. I cracked an eye, like a turtle checking to see if it was safe to come out of its shell. A hand stroked rhythmically over my hair, as I was cradled by a warm arm. I opened my eye more, and squinted at the throbbing pain in my head. Rannoch held me, he paused his quiet song and smiled as he looked down at me.

I blinked my eyes open fully. I tried to sit up, but he gripped me with the arm I was slung across, preventing me from rising.

"Do not sit up," he cautioned. "You fell and hit your head on the stone. You should rest, and get your orientation."

"I think you mean 'get your bearings,'" I corrected, as I winced from the pain and put the heel of my fisted hand to my head.

"You say it your way, I will say it mine. At least you are feeling well enough to give me a difficult tempus," he admonished with a coy smirk.

I rolled my eyes. "I think it's you who likes to give me a difficult "tempus" as you say. What was that before I left to go get Dendris? You confuse me, Rannoch. Why are you so back and forth with me? You like me, you don't like me, which is it?" I snapped. It was probably not the time to bring it up, but finding myself in the position of being gently cared for after the way he had cut himself off from me yet again left me frayed, and annoyed.

"I do not dislike you. You have been a true friend to the Ignisfae. The aid you gave us is immensely appreciated. Emblyn is back in our care, as well as the other children. I have you to thank for that."

I stared at him, my mouth opened as I dropped my hand from my forehead. *Are you kidding me?* "*Friend* to the Ignisfae? What the actual fuck, Rannoch. I asked how *you* feel, you're being evasive! I don't like head games," I blurted.

He gaped. "I do not understand that phrase-"

"Don't play dumb. I'm sure you can guess its meaning based on my tone," I interrupted in a clipped voice.

I instantly regretted what I said. I wanted to know his answer, but clearly he wasn't ready to tell me, for whatever reason. And my head was pounding.

A fenestram opened near us, Dendris stepped through a moment later. *Saved by the bell, I suppose.*

"The others are all safely out, are you able to stand so we can move you out as well, Lily?" she asked warily.

"Yes, I'm ready to go." I abruptly got up and ignored Rannoch, still sitting on the ground. I should have been relieved by the news, all the others had been rescued from the cave, and we are the last to leave. I should've been delighted, and it should have lifted an enormous weight off my shoulders. But instead, I was too pissed at Rannoch and clouded by our argument. And I was tired—so tired. My patience was stretched thin from the relentless swimming, pulling, pushing, trying, trying, trying.

I wobbled, and pressed the heel of my hand to my head again as Dendris opened a bridge. I dropped my arm with a sigh and noted some blood on my hand, from where my head had met stone. She gently guided me through the portal. As I rotated in, my gaze swept Rannoch. His brows furrowed, the sadness in his eyes wrenched my heart as he watched me step through.

The other end of the bridge opened to where we had first arrived, the overlook where we spied the Umorfae and developed our plan. Stepping through the portal was a chance to leave the issues in the cave. Maybe it was that dreadful place, and all the effort I had spent that finally broke me. Maybe now that I was out, I could breathe a sigh of relief and move on. My part was done, I fulfilled my promise. But though I was finally on dry land, the darkness had not left me.

Kerenza bounded up and swallowed me in an exuberant hug. "Lily! You are all right! I was worried! I am so thankful for everything you have done. I cannot stop crying, or laughing, sometimes both at the same time. Having my filia back means everything. I want to scream and leap and drink all the vinirubrum in celebration. I—what is wrong?"

"Nothing, I'm so happy that you're happy," I said, faking cheerfulness. "And that all the children are safe. It's truly a miracle." I wanted to leave the ill feelings in the cave, but clearly they had yet to release their hold of me.

She looked me over with a knowing expression. "Rannoch is... complicated. He has things that he will not even tell me. He cares for you, I know he does," she expressed confidently as she squeezed my hand. "Come, I want you to meet Emblyn."

Rannoch twisted through a fenestram, we glanced at each other for one heavy moment. I gave him a small, pursed smile. I wanted to say I was sorry. But I didn't. My eyes welled, the emotions of everything that had happened threatened to tumble out. I felt like I was held together by fine string wound around me, and it was about the bust from the pressure of my raw, anxious state. I needed some rest, and distance. Maybe it was time to go home. I frowned at the thought of leaving. *Leave these wonderful beings? This amazing realm? To go back to ordinary? And still no sign of Josie.* I gulped at the thought of going home without her.

Kerenza snapped me out of my wandering thoughts, when she pulled my hand to drag me over to her daughter. *I probably shouldn't decide anything when I'm upset, anyway.* I nodded and smiled at Kerenza, and took a deep breath. We didn't let go of each other's hands as we stepped over to where Emblyn was waiting, Kerenza practically danced her way there. I savored the warmth, and focused on the friendship that had grown with her. Her wild ways, her enormous loving heart, her occasional brazenness, I had come to admire and adore her.

Emblyn's huge doe eyes flitted over me as she rushed to hug her mother's leg.

"Filia, this is Lily."

I knelt down to her eye level, and propped a forearm on my bent leg as I spoke in a soft tone, "I've been looking forward to meeting you."

She eyed me as she gripped her maeder's knee and ducked further behind. Kerenza rubbed her back and motioned with a subtle nod.

"Thank you," she said meekly, "for coming to save us with my maeder and Avuncul Rannoch."

"I am glad to have been able to help you all," I answered.

Emblyn toed the ground as she fidgeted. "I think, I think that Daemalum, he was bad, he should have known. My maeder is strong, and you are strong, now they will know that they cannot do those things. Bad things." She rambled on with her story about how this will teach the Daemalum to be nice; a version of her own continuation of the events, perhaps to rationalize in her mind the things that she and the other kids had to endure.

I sighed as I stood up to Kerenza. My heart broke for those children, that she had to design some narrative to make sense out of the injustice, to explain in their minds why they were used as pawns.

Kerenza gave me an imploring look as she said, "Will you come back with us? We are getting ready to take the children home to our camp. We will begin dismantling to make our journey to return to TerraIgni. My faeder will be expecting us there."

"No, I can't. I'd like to go back to the Arbor Elves, to check on Aurelian and see if there is anything I can do to help her. After that...I'm not sure," I responded. "But, someday, if I'm ever able to return, I hope I can come visit TerraIgni with you."

She grabbed me and held me for a long moment. I buried my head in her hair and squeezed her tight. I truly would miss her. There was the possibility that if I went home, I might never be able to return to Alternis. I had no way of knowing. I drank in her scent, her warmth, and clung to it. I hoped that it would imprint itself forever upon me.

She released me and gave me a huge smile. "Until we meet again. Burn brightly. I mean, you are pretty much always burning *something.*"

"Burn brightly," I answered and laughed with a smile equal to hers. We clasped hands one last time, before she turned to guide the children over to the Amabilis that had appeared.

Rannoch spoke briefly to Kerenza, before walking over to me. "Kerenza said you wish to return to the Arbor Elves, for now."

"I want to try and help Aurelian, if I can. I feel we owe her that much. After that, I'm not sure."

He nodded. "We should inform them, the Elves are ready to fenestram back to the Arbor Boles."

One by one, each child was whisked away, the Amabilis shrank into the fold of space that only they could travel. Kerenza saluted us, with her hand over her heart as she blinked away.

I was tempted to say something to Rannoch as we walked to the Elves, there was so much hanging between us. I mulled it over as we approached Dendris.

"I would like to come back with you," I stated, "and help Aurelian."

"I will come as well, to aid in whatever is needed," Rannoch added.

"You are both welcome to join us. If you can help our Venitor, it would be most appreciated. The last we heard of her condition was very grim." She pulled open a bridge, then guided me through.

CHAPTER 36

We stepped through directly into the great hall, which was even more beautiful than I remembered. The thousands of lights that lit the high wooded ceiling twinkled softly like stars.

Rannoch appeared a moment later with another Elf. We studied each other briefly. I yielded nothing in my expression, not the disappointment in myself for what I said or the frustration I felt for how he affected my emotions.

I shook the thought from my mind as I turned to Dendris. "Can you take me to Aurelian?"

"Yes, she is in the infirmary."

She opened another portal then guided me through, leaving Rannoch to assist the Elves in the hall.

We exited the aperture onto a landing high up in a tree, outside a curtained opening.

"Tenaeran," Dendris said from outside the room, "Lily is here. May we enter?"

"Yes, come in."

Ten was bleary eyed and sat wringing her mottled hands at Aurelian's bedside. "She has not regained consciousness since it happened," Ten said. "Her life force is slowly waning. There is nothing we can do. We tried soaking her radices in water, if an Arbor Elf is injured we can encourage the radices to soak up water to heal themselves. Apparently the wound is too grave."

"I'm so sorry Ten. She fought bravely, and risked much for us. I thought that I could try to help her. I have healed others before. I don't know if I can, I don't want to offer false hope. But, maybe there's something I can do."

"If there is anything you can do, I would be forever in your debt. Please, proceed."

I sucked in a breath and peeled back Aurelian's sheet, as I hovered over her. They had removed the arrow, milky fluid oozed out of the opening from under a cloth bandage pressed to her chest. I carefully took the folded linen pad off to inspect the wound. A branch-like system spread out within the walls of her chest, many of them snapped and frayed from the path of the destructive arrow. Her chest barely budged from her shallow breaths. I pulsed my power to push the white blood and staunch the loss, but it didn't react to my water ability. Whatever the fluid was, it wasn't water based.

I looked at Ten bewildered, "Does your blood not contain water?"

"I...I am not sure."

"I can't effect a change on it, which tells me there's no water in it. I should be able to push it to stop it from hemorrhaging."

I shrugged, and unwound a thread of golden healing light down my arms. I pulsed it into the wound gently, hoping to stimulate the branches to reconnect somehow. She didn't wake, but moaned loudly in response and arched her back, her face held a pained expression.

I stopped and let the magic recoil. Tenaeran's face fell as she looked at me. "It will not work, will it." A statement, rather than a question, one that made my heart stutter.

"I don't know why, but my healing powers don't work on your kind," I confirmed sadly. "I tried to help Aolis when he was dying, but I couldn't. I thought it was because he was beyond saving, rather than my power having no effect. But it looks like that is the case."

I sucked on a tooth and thought for a moment, then remembered my time I spent as an understudy to one of the local horse vets. *Kathleen told me a good vet thinks of every avenue to treat a patient. I can't heal, and I can't push the blood. But what about the water?* "I'm going to try one last thing. I want to try pulling the water into her. Has something like that ever been attempted?"

"I do not think so. As only Umorfae or Fae hybrids have the power to control water, I would doubt it has ever been tried. They are not known for...helping others," Dendris answered diplomatically.

I get it, everyone thinks they're all assholes.

I padded across the room and fetched bowls of water they had set aside. I placed Aurelian's hands in the smooth wooden vessels, then went to the head of the bed.

I called the volumes, pulling them upward toward her arms. It promptly collided into me, soaking my shirt rather than entering her fibrous roots. I shook my head and chided myself for not thinking it through first. Dendris scurried over with a large tear drop shaped jug and refilled the bowls.

I pulled the water into her, angling myself so that my pull

went through, rather than over her. At first the water went around her hands, and slid up her arms, encasing them in upward streaks. Slowly, the radices began to open up. I could feel through the tension of the water a trickle running within her arms, the force of my pull wedging the capillaries open just enough to allow some in.

"Add more water!" I shouted.

The receptacles were getting too low, most of the water was lost as it was drawn up along the skin, rather than into the root-like growths. It was now steadily spritzing me as the water continued along its trajectory. Dendris poured fresh water from the smooth container, as I pulled the last drops from the bowl.

"Is there such a thing as too much water for healing? I don't know if I can tell when to stop," I panted as the excess water dripped from my hair and face. I steadily pulled the liquid, and could feel the radices allow in a miniscule amount more. The water inside her body was slowly creeping up toward the open wound.

"Yes," Dendris responded, "when the water begins to drip from the wound, the hands should be taken from the water. We would then have to wait for it to do the work."

Almost there.

As Dendris poured in the last of the jug the first signs of fluid started to bubble out of the wound. I gave one last gentle pull, the radices now fully open and allowing the water to pass through.

I released a breath and the remaining water, as Dendris slid Aurelian's hands out of the bowls. Ten waited anxiously, and caressed her coniunx's face as she said, "Open your eyes."

Aurelian's stoic face remained still. We all stared with bated breath and waited. "Damnatus, Aurelian!" Ten cried, "Open your eyes!"

The tension was unbearable. Aurelian hadn't so much as fluttered an eye and had gone completely still, even the shallow breaths had ceased. Tenaeran let out a sob and hung her head. I reached over and placed a hand on her shoulder. I knew that though I had said I didn't want to give false hope, that's exactly what I had done. Ten shuddered under my touch, and drew in ragged breaths as she wailed for her beloved coniunx.

Dendris kneeled and bowed her head in reverence for their leader, their Venitor. All I could do was watch, as these beautiful, generous people grappled with the fact that they were losing Aurelian.

Aurelian's radices twitched. The movement was almost imperceptible. Another movement, this one stronger. She took a breath. I gripped Ten's shoulder, her head shot up and she stopped crying. Dendris realized something had changed as well, and rose to her feet.

Aurelian let out a small moan, and cracked her eyes open. "Tenaeran," she muttered, barely moving her lips.

"I am here my love."

"What..."

"Shhh," Ten hushed her as she held her mate's weak hands, "just rest, and heal. We managed to get water through your radices. It will take some time now, just rest."

Ten glanced at me and gave an appreciative smile. I nodded and let out a sigh. She was not out of the woods yet. Even still, I could have collapsed from the relief that surged through me.

"I will leave you to recover, come and get me if there are any changes. Dendris, we should return to the hall. I will stay as long as you need me to, if I can be of further help." I leaned over to inspect the wound again, the trickle of water continued, and the branch like structure appeared to be improving. The broken frayed ends were growing toward each other—slowly, but they were growing.

We flashed out of the infirmary, and were back in the great hall. Rannoch was busily helping set the long table for a meal. He looked at me with an inquiring glance, I nodded and smiled.

I wasn't ready to speak to him yet, so I ventured down to the far side of the dining hall, to a splash of color that caught my eye. As I approached, I realized the color was far more than I had first glimpsed, the image unfolded as I neared. A huge scene painted with both extreme attention and reckless abandon, the various hues melded together to tell a story of life and growth, love and loss. The colors blended and bled into each other in shifting gradations of saturated values. I stared at it, my mouth agape as I tried to take in the entire scene, which spanned the whole wall. The stunning beauty of it was unmatched to any painting I had ever seen, and made my heart ache with the sheer emotional power the depictions held. I put my hand to my head in disbelief, when I realized what a riotous mess my hair was. I had not cleaned up since we returned from the cave.

As much as I wanted to gaze at the painting longer, I felt awkwardly aware of how dirty I was. I spotted Illaran from across the room, then padded over to her to guide me to somewhere that I could clean up.

She promptly opened a fenestram and deposited me in the room I was to share with Rannoch, a smaller treetop yurt with two beds. I went straight into the washroom and peeled off my clothes. I washed my hair as I thought about all that had happened. The little sticks and mossy bits stuck in the mass of tangles from all the swimming and constant questing were difficult to remove. I finger brushed all the debris out as my mind wandered, good thoughts mixing with the bad: feelings for Kerenza and Rannoch, saving the children, killing Umorfae, losing Arbor Elves. There was more to process than I had the capacity to deal with.

I finished cleaning up and dressed, then called for a guide back to the hall.

Rannoch was where I had last seen him, helping with the preparations. I went to his side and began working. He had apparently cleaned up earlier. His dark skin glowed with a luster that made me want to touch it. We stood next to each other, sorting dishes and folding napkins. It was comforting, to be near him and focus on the menial task, and to put all other concerns aside.

Bowls of food and broth began to fill up the table. We sat on the long bench together. There were no words exchanged between us, but it was not an uncomfortable silence. It was a mutual unspoken accord, perhaps there was a lot to say—but not now. Others spoke to us sometimes, or talked around us. We occasionally shared small smiles, but were both clearly exhausted. It was the first time I felt content in a long time.

The Elves' sparkling wine was served, and their version of a toast was given for the health and continued improvement of their Venitor. I finished my drink and leaned against Rannoch, his muscled, warm arm a comforting support as I released a breath.

CHAPTER 37

I woke up to the comfort of the Arbor Elf dwelling, tucked in a cozy bed. I stretched, then wriggled further into the plush blankets. I peeked up at the branches, vines, and leaves of the natural ceiling, woven in intricate patterns to create the domed shape. Their enclosed rooms gave me the impression they must have been able to control plant growth, to be able to create such structures.

"Are you feeling rested?" Rannoch's rich voice called out from nearby.

I poked my head out from the blankets far enough to eye him, without losing any of my comfy coverings. He lounged on his bed, once again without a shirt on. *I swear he's doing it on purpose.*

"Yes, but I'm at maximum comf, I'm not moving!"

"What is that?" A laugh rolled out of him as he shook his head. "You have such a funny way of speaking."

I adored his laugh. He rarely let it out, but when he did, it was warm and honey-like, with an undertone of a guttural, animal sound. My hybrid ears twitched in delighted response to it, tickled by the reverberation.

I giggled. "A product of my upbringing, I suppose. And I like to be silly. It makes life more fun somehow."

I breathed a sigh. The weight that had been pressing down finally felt lifted. Rannoch and I had not resolved anything, but at least it did not feel uncomfortable to be around him.

"I love your silly ways."

My heart fluttered and my eyes went wide as I stilled, hidden in the mound of blankets. "Love?"

"Yes," he responded, "I find it endearing. It reminds me to not be so serious all the time. I know I can be...difficult."

I hesitated, unsure how to respond. "That means a lot to me."

"Can I bring you food? So you can enjoy your maximus comf longer."

Oooo breakfast in bed, yes please! "Maximum," I corrected with a grin, as I propped myself up on my elbows to peer over at him. "That sounds wonderful."

The smile that he gave me lit me up from the inside out. "I will be right back." He threw a shirt on and picked up the summoning cube, then gave it a twist. The bright blue light flashed, followed by a fenestram opening near him.

An Elf I didn't recognize spun into view, I sunk back down to hide myself. "Greetings, Rannoch, where may I guide you?"

"To the dining hall."

I remained encased in warm blankets, with only my eyes showing. "Thank you!" I called out, muffled from all the fluff.

I collapsed back and squirmed in even more. To rest— finally rest—was heavenly. I closed my eyes as I enjoyed the peaceful warmth and quiet.

Light clinking sounds nudged me out of the sleep that I had drifted back into. I stretched and sat up, letting the covers fall down around my waist.

"I brought an assortment, hopefully something is to your liking." Rannoch grinned as he laid out a tray on the small table between our beds. "Would you like to eat here, or are you still in maximum comf?"

I laughed. "I'll come join you."

I got up and realized I had been changed into a short sleep dress. I looked at my exposed legs, then slid my gaze to Rannoch.

"I swear, it was not me. A female Elf escorted you back and changed you after you fell asleep at the table."

"Mmmhmm, sure." I chided him.

He dropped his jaw, then quirked a smile as he took a sip of green juice.

"What do we have here? It looks great." The tray was covered in an array of unusual fruits arranged artistically, some pastries, a second glass of juice and, "Coffee! I mean...capuli."

I snatched the earthen carafe from the tray and poured myself a cup. "Would you like some?" I asked without looking at him, as I filled mine to the brim.

"If you can spare any, it looks to me like you want it all," he teased as he handed me an empty mug.

I rolled my eyes, and smiled. It was true, I did want it all for myself. I poured a cup equal to my own and held it out for him. He grazed my hand with his fingers as he accepted it.

"Thank you," he said as we waited, motionless. I didn't withdraw my hand, and he didn't completely take the mug. My eyes flicked to his curved lips. We locked our gaze for a moment, I was tempted to drop the steaming cup and kiss him deeply. Run my hands through his unbound hair and...I took a steadying breath, realizing that the heat inside me was flaring.

"Did you hear if Aurelian is improving?" I asked, as I released the capuli to him and averted my eyes. I had no doubt he knew of my desire, his keen Fae senses probably picked up on it instantly.

"Yes," he responded smoothly, "the Elves in the dining hall mentioned her condition is getting better. We can go check on her. Are you wanting to depart?"

No. "I suppose I should. I've been here a long time."

He nodded. "What are you looking forward to about being back in your realm? Do you have...companions waiting for you? Or someone you care for?" He studied my face intently as we ate.

I was about to take a bite of a pastry, when I paused and dropped my hand. "Well, I miss my mom—maeder, my brother Felix, and of course my horse Apollo. I haven't had anyone I was close to, since my dad and sister passed away. Only Felix and Josie. I pretty much stopped talking to all other friends, and didn't really get involved with anyone. Not seriously anyway." I knew what he was truly asking, but he also seemed genuinely interested. He searched my face as I mulled over my words.

"What happened to them?"

I took a shaky breath, but kept myself steady. "There was a wildfire, which happens almost yearly where I grew up. I tried to ride my horse into it to save them. But the embers were burning my skin, his skin. I couldn't make him go forward. The truth is I would have died too if I had gotten him to go." I looked down at my hands and gulped.

His warm hand on my face made me lift my eyes back up to his. He spoke gently as he cupped my cheek. "Dealing with loss has been the hardest task of my life. I am sorry, that you had to endure that."

My eyes welled and I nodded, praying my tears did not spill.

"And now, you control fire, it is...strange, that turn of events."

"Yea, we call that a cruel irony in the human world." I breathed a sigh, then became more aware of his hand on me. I savored his touch, and leaned into it.

"And what about your dreams? Your wishes for yourself, your future?" he asked.

My breath hitched as he lowered his hand, searching my eyes with his. "I don't know anymore. I used to want to be a horse vet—like what Rovan is here. But after my dad and sister, and a few losses on the ranch...I became scared I guess. And I was so consumed by guilt, that it should have been me and not Maris. I turned away from the dream. I spent a few years wandering around school, avoiding any real commitment to what I was going to do with myself. The truth is, I wasted time. I didn't do anything of note. I just hid." I gulped, I had never admitted that out loud before. "Maris would never have done that, she would have excelled. Then Josie went missing, and I wasted more time. I should have followed the pull here much sooner. I'm just so disappointed with myself, not finding more clues about her whereabouts, it fills me with dread. I have a lot to make up for." I paused as my mistakes weighed on me, then pulled myself back from the impending downward spiral. "What about you? Your dreams? What will you do now that Emblyn is back with your sister?"

He exhaled through puffed lips. "I have been thinking about that. My faeder will want me to return to TerraIgni. I would like to not think about such serious things for awhile, and spend some time in the forges there. Make some new blades. Though if it were up to him I would not forge at all, he would rather I leave that to the appointed ferrars and that I tend only to my assigned duties. I have been having dreams of things I would like to create. It has been too long since I last crafted anything. Perhaps it is one reason I can be so disagreeable. I work out many of my frustrations hammering the metal. And it makes me feel more useful, I make not just weapons, but tools that help my people. I thought of a blade I would like to make for you, but I do not suppose you will be here to use it." His eyes dimmed.

"And what about companions, or someone special?"

He perked up and twitched a smile. "No, there is no one in TerraIgni who holds my heart." His looked at my mouth, which made my heartbeat stutter.

"How nice that you want to pound on a piece of metal for me." I giggled and pushed his shoulder.

He belted out a loud, guttural laugh that twanged in my ears. He shook his head and smiled broadly. I took a congratulatory bite of my pastry, proud of myself for making him laugh so hard.

I smiled to myself as I started to eat the remaining food on my plate. After I finished a bright pink stone fruit, I said, "I'm going to wash up."

A huge grin spread across his face. "I already washed before you woke, so I'll be out here getting ready to go." He held his breath, I could sense a laugh threatening to burst out.

"Okay—wait, did you just use a contraction?"

"A what?"

"Contraction! You said "I'll" not "I will". That's the first time I've heard you do that! Oh no, I'm rubbing off on you! You're going to start talking like a human country girl!" I snickered.

He laughed and glanced aside, then back to me from under an arched eyebrow. The look he gave me made my heart leap. "Well, I suppose your mannerisms are altering mine. I think I like it. In fact, I love it. You've brought a lot in my realm that I hope stays. You have changed me."

I fluttered my eyes, speechless. There was that word again. Love. I hadn't used it—not genuinely—in a long time. I gave him a bashful smile, before I turned to the sliding door of the bathing chamber.

I went in, then stripped down as I sighed. Was I truly going to leave today? I took a leisurely shower and thought about the things Rannoch had said to me, how I changed him, and how I have brought something of myself to Alternis. Just by being here, I had changed things.

Fresh clothes were hung on a gnarled branch rack. I dressed in the pretty yet functional attire; pants of a soft, thin material that draped loosely off of a fitted wide waistband and then tapered at the calves, and a matching camisole with a low neckline. The dreamy colors were reminiscent of sunlight filtering through trees; variegated greens and yellows with blurred, light lines throughout. *Arbor Elf camouflage.*

I padded over to the mirror on the wall, to run a comb made of smooth twigs through my hair, when I did a double take. My lips were a brilliant shade of bright pink. *Ha, the fruit, nice. Free makeup!* I tied back my hair in a loose fishtail braid.

I gave myself one last look, was this the last time I'd see myself like this? I had almost grown used to my appearance, and enjoyed it. But I missed my mom, and Felix. They must have been so worried. I knew they already had to know I was missing, but for how long had they known? Going back without Josie was unthinkable, but as long as I could come back through the tear afterward I could look for her again, once I had reassured my family. I couldn't just leave her here, wherever she was.

I left the bathing chamber and found Rannoch sitting in the armless chair, waiting. "All set," I said, "complete with lipstick even." I puckered my lips at him and tilted my head up, modeling my new makeup.

He grinned. "They are...colorful."

I smiled, wishing he was admiring my lips with his own. I wanted to sit astride him, and feel his mass underneath me, kiss him, hold him. My skin prickled with heat as his eyebrow twitched, the images rolling through my mind made my cheeks flush. My breasts swelled at the thought of him. His glance lower told me he noticed my peaked curves. I walked closer, tracing my fingers along his shoulders as I walked behind. He caught my hand, stopping me. I turned to face him—hoping to collapse onto him, hoping he would pull me atop his lap.

"Regarding our bargain," he said, clearing his throat.

My stomach dropped. "Yes?" I resisted clenching my hand as he held it.

"Faeries. That is how you can leave Alternis. They are the only beings that can pass back and forth through the Vale. One can guide you through the passage back to your home. They can get the aperture to open, and then you follow it in."

"Oh, right. I almost forgot you were going to tell me how to get home." I was relieved he didn't say what I thought he would, the part of our bargain I felt so much guilt over. I pulled my hand back as disgust in myself washed over me.

He merely nodded, his eyes darkened to coals as his ears angled down slightly.

I hesitated, I didn't want him to mention the rest of the deal that still remained. Fortunately he cut through the silence.

"I will call for a fenestram." He twisted the summoning cube, and a portal promptly opened.

The Elf from earlier stepped through.

"Lily and I are ready to depart," Rannoch announced, "she would like to check on Aurelian first."

"Of course," the Elf answered as he twisted a wooden disc on a woven wristband. The same blue light glowed from the center, and alerted a nearby Elf to come to assist. Another doorway opened, then Dendris stepped through. They guided us through fenestrams to the entrance of the infirmary.

"Venitor? Tenaeran?" Rannoch's Elven guide called into the darkened hospital room, "Lily and Rannoch are here."

"Please come in," Ten's upbeat tone filled me with relief.

We entered to find Aurelian propped up in bed, with Ten sitting by her side.

"I think you will be pleased with her improvement. The wound is nearly closed!" Tenaeran bubbled over.

I beamed at them both. "I am so glad to hear the good news! Are you able to draw up water on your own now, Aurelian?"

Though still bedridden, she looked remarkably better. As stoic as ever, she answered, "Yes. I can draw it in as needed now. Without your assistance, I would not have survived."

"You were so generous to help us, I wanted to do everything I could to return that immeasurable favor."

She dipped her head in response. "You are welcome to stay and rest, until you are ready to depart."

"As you are on the mend, I think we will be departing right away. I have things to resolve here before I return to my realm." I glanced at Rannoch.

Ten smiled and said as she stood up. "We understand. We will send you with supplies for your journey. And come back to visit, if you can." She stepped over to me and raised one hand, with fingers splayed out. "Grow with purpose."

I hesitated. She gave a soft smile and nodded to my hand, so I lifted it to match hers. "Grow with purpose," I answered.

Her radices fanned out as she pressed her hand to mine. The tendrils wrapped gently around my fingers, and an image flashed in my mind, beautiful, idyllic and unearthly. A place outside of time and space, where all things flourish. Life, created in an unending cosmic cycle, where death is merely rebirth. To burst forward in a new way, one life leaping forward to the next. I knew this image, my breath stilled as I realized it was the mural from the great hall.

The vision faded as she retracted her radices, then lowered her hand. I stared, speechless, my skin tingled from the emotional impact of the incredible vision. The solace that the brief image gave me was both heartening and saddening. That life must end, but can continue on as something else. I thought of my father, my sister. I never truly faced if I believed they existed still in some way, I couldn't bear to think about it. The only belief I allowed myself was the natural law that no energy could be created or destroyed. It was the only thing I could cling to. Their energy went somewhere, it had to. But where, that was the question that was so hard to confront.

She leveled her gaze at me, a serious expression painted her usually cheerful face. "As the roots grow, so do the branches. The circle of life affects us all, though the length of time that may take depends on many factors. You were the arrow shot forth from your faeder's bow. Never forget that. As we say, grow with purpose. Live intently and move forward, and perhaps one day, you will shoot forward an arrow of your own."

I blinked at her, dumbfounded by her counsel. I opened my mouth to respond, but no words came. I had no response, as all she had shown me sunk in. There weren't any words that could suffice.

She gave me a knowing nod, before turning to glide over to Rannoch. Ten held her hand aloft to him. "Grow with purpose."

"Grow with purpose," he said. She grew her tendrils out and encased his fingertips, they stood for a few moments before she retracted. He shifted his gaze to me, his eyes heavy and face weary.

"Dendris, Kaerlis," Tenarean said, "Escort Lily and Rannoch back to the main hall, and pack supplies for them."

"Mere words do not convey our gratitude," Rannoch said as he rapped his fist across his chest and bowed.

I smiled at them. "I hope I will see you both again."

Tenaeran smiled brightly and nodded, Aurelian dipped her head in recognition.

Rannoch and I stepped out of the room to the waiting Elves, they opened doorways to the hall, then guided us through.

Kaerlis and Dendris readied supplies for us, loading them

with dried fruits, nuts, bread loaves, and bed rolls. They collected our weapons from storage, which we relinquished when we had returned from the cave.

I slung the sheathed selwaer across my back, then hoisted a pack onto my shoulders. I slipped the knife into the thigh strap, which I had put on over the Arbor Elf pants. Rannoch finished adjusting his pack at the same time. I nodded, ready for this last adventure.

"We will take you to the edge of the Arbor Boles," Kaerlis said. "Where are you going so that we may guide you to the closest point at our border?"

Rannoch looked at me. "To Opius?"

I hesitated. Pangs of guilt washed over me. I had only thought of Opius when I remembered my looming departure, and the fact that it was the final piece of the deal I had struck with Rannoch. I didn't think of Opius with any sort of longing, it had merely become the crutch I used to stay with Rannoch. I had been dreading this moment, but as I had no alternate location, I nodded my head.

His eyes shuttered out their fire, and his jaw flexed. His lips became a thin line as he pressed them together. "We will be going to Lacausia," he answered coldly.

The Elves shrugged, then reluctantly opened fenestrams to the edge of their realm. I spun through with Dendris, the last dance through space with an Arbor Elf that I would take—maybe ever.

CHAPTER 38

Darkest night greeted us at the edge of the forest, the familiar, minuscule energy flickers flitted through the air. Dendris and Kaerlis bid their farewell, then promptly portaled back to their majestic home.

We started our trek in silence. Rannoch angrily charged ahead, his forward motion nearly an attack, rather than a walk.

I mulled my thoughts over, the vision I had seen and all that happened since coming to Alternis replayed in my mind, wonderful things, horrible things—all of them startling and extraordinary. Even with the awful things that happened in this realm, I did not want to leave it. I didn't want to leave Rannoch. *Maybe I'm just an erratic girl with a fickle heart that ends up attracted to every Fae male she meets.* But the more I thought about it, the more I knew that wasn't true. The feelings I had for him were different. The vision Ten shared had shaken me to my core, its message echoed within me: life is short, grow with purpose. I knew that, but for the first time I saw and understood it. Life cannot be hidden from or avoided. And I should never wait to say what I want to say, when it's important.

"Rannoch, stop," I ordered as I halted in my tracks. "Stop, I want to talk."

"We need to keep moving if I am going to get you to Lacausia to find Opius," he ground out, while he pushed onward.

I dropped my pack and ran forward, grabbing his hand as I dug my heels in the forest floor to pull him back. "I have something to say."

He swung around and glowered at me. "What is it?"

Anger flashed in his eyes. After a moment I realized it wasn't anger, it was hurt. His ears pinned back and his eyebrows angled outward.

"I don't want to find Opius," I blurted. "I haven't wanted to find Opius for a long time. Our agreement was that you would help me find him, after I helped you. I was afraid to say..." I lowered my hand as I searched his face, which softened slightly.

I took a step closer to him. "I was afraid to tell you the truth, that it's you that I want to be with. Our bargain kept you with me, I didn't want you to go. Tell me how you feel. I need to know."

"After everything, you think I would just leave you? And all that happened, that we talked about when we were with the Elves, did that not tell you anything?"

"I just thought...I don't know. I didn't know what to say when you asked where to go. I could have said to look for Josie, or find Faeries. It's been a long time, since I've allowed myself to have feelings—real feelings."

"Hearing that you wanted to go back to that male, I just could not stand it, could not believe it. You have given me so many signs—physical and otherwise—that you are interested. When we spoke in the Elves dwelling, I thought for sure you had feelings for me too. And then you said yes to going to him. I wanted to find him and tear his head off. But I would not even be able to do that, because you had made me promise that I would not attack him when I delivered you to him!"

"I'm sorry, it was a mistake. I didn't mean to hurt you."

He hesitated and looked down at my hand, which still gripped his. He opened his mouth several times to speak, before finally mustering words. "There is too much to say."

He cringed, and didn't look at me. I lifted my other hand to his face, and ran it along his strong jawline. He finally brought his gaze up to mine, the smoldering embers began to dance deep within his eyes.

He turned his hand over to hold mine, and ran his thumb over my fingers, looking at our two hands joined for a few moments.

"When you healed Steren," he took a deep breath, "I started to see you as someone special, different. I do not mean look different, *you* are different. You are kind, and generous, and wear yourself out for anyone that needs your help. The friendship that you gave my sister, I do not know if you know how much that did for her. But, every time I would get a spark and think these thoughts about you, I would remember, you wanted to get back to Opius. And I would die a little inside each time. I would make myself shut off, because I thought, I was not who you wanted to be with. And I was not supposed to fall..."

A lump developed in my throat, my heart ached for all the times that his feelings made him anguish. All the missed opportunities for either he or myself to say something. "I was wrong," I confessed, "I was mad at you in the cave for not telling me how you felt. But I now see I did the same thing. I should have just told you. You make me want to live, Rannoch. Instead of hide."

I took another step closer to him, and angled my face up to his, as his eyes lit up. I leaned into his warm, planed chest, and parted my lips expectantly.

He slid his hands around my lower back. "Fae males are notoriously territorial. Opius will challenge me in a battle to the death. I will fight it gladly, but you need to know that. I would fight endlessly for you, Lily," he breathed, our lips nearly touching.

"He has no claim on me, but I would fight that battle with you, if it came to that."

"There is more...that I need to tell you."

"Shut up and kiss me, Rannoch."

He stilled as he looked into my eyes, his preternatural ways appeared to take over—an apex predator readying to pounce his prey.

I am not your prey. I put my hands behind his head and pulled his face toward me, and locked onto his full lips. My back instinctively arched and hips went achingly pliant.

He kissed me more and more deeply, our canines scraped against each other as the kiss heated and I opened my mouth fully to his. A low, guttural sound rose in his throat, which made my core burst into flames. My ears twitched and tingled to the rumble, the sensation skittered down my spine.

He licked my neck and nipped my ear, his sharp teeth marking me just a bit. I squeezed my eyes, wanting more, so much more.

The heat rose to my chest, and up my neck. Fire danced off the surface of my skin. Rannoch placed his hand on me, pushing the flames back down inside. But his touch made my desire even stronger. I wrapped my legs around him as fire roiled down my arms to my hands, which were still clasping the back of his head.

He wrenched back from the heat momentarily, then slid his other hand lower and hoisted me up. Rannoch's eyes were alight with flame.

"I don't want to burn you," I panted, as he moved his mouth lower, toward my half-exposed breasts.

"I am already burning for you, I cannot deny it, cannot hide it any longer," he said as he pushed my back up against a nearby tree. I couldn't think straight with his solid mass pressed into me. I ground against him, feeling the sheer size of him as I did. I wanted to mesh our bodies completely, to join them, as our hearts were becoming, and finish the bond.

Rannoch grazed his teeth along my clavicle, then over the ridge of my lower neck. He breathed heavily against my skin, I ached for him to bite me where he hovered. A deep, animalistic need for him to sink his teeth right there surged through my whole body, for him to grip his canines into my flesh as he thrust himself into me. And to not let go until he had emptied every ounce. I wanted it all.

Let us challenge the fates together, you and I. His words echoed in my mind, the times our bond had gone taut, the moments I had felt our connection. I wanted him. I wanted to know each glorious inch of him. I wanted every inch of him inside me. I wanted to feel and know all of him, melding with all of me, combined as one. I needed him. This beautiful male. This caring, compassionate, moody, sometimes cranky warrior male. The warrior who fought for those he loved. *I would fight endlessly for you.* I wanted everything that he was.

He slid his hand down further, under my waistband, down

to where I silently begged he would. To the ever-growing ache between my legs. He growled his approval at the proof of my desire he found there, I gasped as he glided his fingers in further, my mind unleashing all the times I just wanted to be closer to him. He pressed down on the center, taking my breath away in process.

Rannoch pulled his hand out, then nudged himself against me, the hardest part of him teasing, taunting. "Tell me what you want. I want to hear you say it." He dragged his nose along my jaw as I moaned. *Merciless.* I was nothing short of liquid fire as he rolled against me.

"You," I breathed. "I want you, all of you, right now. I want you inside me, pounding me against this tree." I couldn't wait another second.

Rannoch obliged me, immediately.

Our clothes were off in the blink of an eye, he was already sliding in as I raked at his back. He cradled my head with one hand, and held me hoisted up from below as he thrust himself into me. My body threatened to climax with every heated stroke. His power felt endless as we hammered into the tree over and over again. I lost all sense of time as we forged ourselves together in burning bliss.

He tugged my hair, angling my chin up higher as he scraped his canines on my neck. His growl against my skin sent me over the edge. He threw back his head as his eyebrows pinched. All his muscles went taut as release shuddered through both of us. I cried out as he wrung the last of the pleasure from me.

We stayed together, panting against each other's skin for countless minutes. He traced circles over my shoulders, then across my collarbone, as he admired me. He toyed with the spot he had hovered his teeth against, staring at it before running his lips over it again. I was sure he wasn't breathing as I released a long exhale, my eyelids drooped with satisfied exhaustion.

"That was...intense." I laughed a little.

Rannoch lifted his lips from my neck, then brushed a kiss to my cheek. "That was more than intense, that was...I don't even have a word for it. Magic, maybe."

"Magic," I agreed.

We released our grip on each other at last and dressed, though part of me just wanted him all over again. I needed more, so much more. He cocked an eyebrow at me the moment I thought it, and I knew he sensed my desire pooling again.

Rannoch circled his arm around my waist, pulling me close as he leaned in for a kiss. I moved forward to meet his lips with mine, when he halted.

His ears twitched and he stilled, listening intently for barely a moment, when a loud snap shot through my sensitive ears like a bolt of lightning.

We whipped our heads in the direction of the sound, just as an arrow pierced Rannoch's underarm, the tip of it a hair's-width from my heart. He howled and stumbled as blood sputtered from the wound. I reached up to break the arrowhead off, when a blunt object whacked down on the back of my skull. I collapsed to the ground like a felled deer, as darkness washed over me.

CHAPTER 39

Memories of being dragged along a forested floor dredged in, I slipped in and out of consciousness for hours, perhaps days. Images of trees flitted by, which eventually turned into the beginnings of a barren, rocky landscape. Finally, a steep, mountainous area. Every time I would stir and begin to open my eyes, a pad of fabric soaked in a horrible smelling solution was placed over my mouth and nose. My vision would narrow to pinpricks, then go out completely as I went under again.

Round after round of waking and drugging continued, until I was being hoisted up by my bound wrists. A low, clunking sound reverberated with every notch, as I was raised higher. My whole body hung heavily, my head was a leaden weight that I couldn't lift, my legs dangled and swayed. I opened my eyes a fraction, trying to seek out any details without giving away that I had awoken—afraid that I would incur another suffocating, toxin-laden ministration.

My head pounded from the awful anesthesia. An inky black void loomed below, murky and indistinct. I couldn't see anything without moving my head up. A male voice groaned in pain near me.

Rannoch.

Even the slightest noise and I knew it was him. A small comfort that at least we were together. I angled my head to catch a glimpse, to see if I could ascertain his condition, and figure out where we were. What had happened? I remembered the arrow, and being struck. I could see his lower limbs, his body was slack, and caked amber blood ran down his legs. I struggled to raise my head higher, to peer at his face. His eyebrows tightened, Rannoch's eyelids were heavy, but open slightly.

I shifted my glance the other direction, and hoped that my movement would go unnoticed by our captors. The lip of a rough rock platform came into view. Only a slice of the massive room we were in was visible, the darkness punctuated by cold shafts of light.

"I was hoping you would wake soon," a smooth, male voice rang out across the expanse. "I was trying to find you for so long, however it looks like another male has captured your interest. Shame."

I knew that voice.

"Opius?" I asked as I squinted from the pain, which throbbed from the back of my head.

"How did you find me? Can you get me down? I feel terrible."

"Questions, questions, it is always questions with you. Here is one for you, why would I get you down when I just finished hauling you up there?"

My pain subsided as his words hit me like a bag of rocks. "Why are you doing this?" I looked up to see him standing near the edge of the drop off, wearing the same colors I had seen on the Umorfae at the cave, the tri-point sigil emblazoned at the center of the black armored chest piece.

He slid his hands in his hip pockets as he strolled, and gave me a sidelong glance. "I am having a bit of fun, before I hand you over. It was going to be quick and painless, until I scented *him* all over you."

"Fun? Hand me over?" My aching head and screaming limbs made it difficult to think clearly.

"Yes, a deal I made, to ensure that I become ruler of Umorfae territory. Hand over three Vale Born, and Dashelle will eliminate my cousin, to make me the leader of my people."

I cringed from the dull, persistent ache, and tried to muddle through all he was professing. "What does that even mean? What does Dashelle want with me?"

"Dashelle means to take your powers, as Josie's were taken. You see, Vale Born can absorb each other's powers, upon death that is. All they have to do is be in proximity. You human filias are so easy to seduce. A few smiles and some vocafortis, and you are willing to follow me anywhere."

My blood turned to ice as it drained from my face. *Upon death.*

He killed Josie. He intended to kill me. Opius had given her to that bastard, whoever he was, and murdered her. My heart sank, to finally know what happened to Josie. Bile rose up my throat, and I wretched down into the void at the knowledge of her death. I failed her. I knew she felt the pull to the Vale, why didn't I go in sooner? Why did I waste such precious time? I prayed that it was over fast for her, a small consolation for such an unfair end to my dearest friend's life. I hung helplessly, and wept as my heart shattered for her mother, still unaware of her daughter's fate. I deserved this bleak end. I didn't follow her when I should have, I wasn't there to protect her.

Rannoch moaned again. The sound rattled me back to the present, back to him. I couldn't give up. I had one more chance, one more person I could make a difference for.

I wriggled in my rope shackles. "Don't do this Opius! Let us go!"

"Well, sometimes a greater purpose has costs. This is what must be paid. Celestine will be...collateral damage unfortunately. I am tired of a lackluster empress that yanks my strings and orders me around. Of course for me to rule, she must die. But I cannot do it myself. That would invalidate me for the throne. Dashelle has agreed to manage that bit of business, as well as removing her offspring to prevent them from being eligible in the future. And for her to die, you must die."

Terror strangled me as I hung over the massive pit, trapped by my former flame. My mind reeled. It dawned on me that the first time I had met him, my first instinct was to run, that he was a predator, and dangerous. That cunning bastard had seduced me, smoothed me over with his unnatural good looks and free flowing wine. I had been such a fool. A shallow, foolish girl. I made a mistake not looking deeper than the surface to discern what lurked beneath.

"Culus!" Rannoch seethed. "I will not let you harm her. And I will kill you for this, that is a promise."

Opius chuckled as he glided closer to Rannoch. "And you, Rannoch. Or should I say, Prince Rannoch. Prince indeed. Prince of Primitive, perhaps. Prince Rannoch Ashwani Albericus. What a mouthful, is it not, Lily?"

My jaw dropped, I had never considered his full name, or whether he had a title. A flash of irritation surged, at the reveal of this lie by omission. *It doesn't matter, he had his reasons for not telling me. Opius is trying to drive a wedge between us. But we will have it out about this, that's for damn sure.*

"Oh, perhaps you did not know, Lily. But the truth does not end there, does it Prince? No, it is far more interesting. You knew of Lily's presence in Lacausia Palace, and had planned to steal her from me before your attack on us. In fact, it was you who commiserated to cut the power from the Imperiductus to draw her out with me."

I was stunned. I twisted my head to eye Rannoch, to try and gauge the truth in Opius's words.

His face contorted in guilt. He grimaced at me, the truth laid bare. "How did you know that?" Rannoch bleated to Opius, as he panted in pain from his arrow wound, which still seeped blood.

"Excellent question, dear Prince!" Opius cajoled as he clapped his hands condescendingly. "Bring out that traitorous fish!" He bellowed out to the darkness behind him.

Two Umorfae soldiers dressed in the same black and red armor marched out, carrying a rough wood stretcher between them. A small lump laid on top, flaky and crusted. It moved feebly, its mess of black hair congealed to the board it rested on. The guards dropped the stretcher with a clatter at Opius's taloned feet.

"Well, well, Naiya," he cooed in a silver-tongued voice, "it looks like all of your sneaking around divulging information has gotten you into quite a bit of trouble. And poor Locrien, you roped him into your schemes. It was unfortunate to have to execute one of my own because of your designs."

My stomach dropped. She had dried out so badly that I couldn't recognize her. How long had they prevented her from going in the water? And Locrien. When I had healed him I got the distinct impression that he had an empathetic heart. His toothy grin flashed in my mind as I gulped.

Opius stepped on the spine of one of her fins, then crunched down and flexed his claws into it. She shrieked as he raked deep, shredding it to papery bits. "Seducing Locrien was brilliant," he seethed, "that stupid bastard. He actually thought you loved him. Little did he know you were using him, to gather information that you could pass on to this filthy rebel Prince."

She sobbed with a creaking voice, "I did love him. But m-my people have been oppressed by the Umorfae for so long. It was the only way. I would do it again."

"Finally, a bit of honesty from you. And all it took was me killing your love, and breaking your wretched body."

He took another clawing step onto her, crushing her hips. The crunching sound was sickening, as was the unbearable wail that emanated from her. A cry so hopeless, it carried not only intense physical pain, but also extreme emotional anguish.

"Water for life, remember, Naiya? As long as we control water, we control life. You live by our grace, or die for insubordination. You were warned once, you do not own your bones, you merely rent them from us. Now, I will repossess them."

I cringed at her condition, as he continued to break her apart. My heart bled for her, and the terrible position she had been in. To have to choose between her people and an Umorfae she loved. To love one of the enemy, and then to sacrifice him to attempt the only chance she had to make a difference. *Water for life! Maybe, I can break free and help her, and pull water from somewhere to save her. Maybe I can heal her.*

As I struggled against my bonds, wriggling and pulling them to see if I could escape, Opius took another step onto her body. He unfurled his claws wide, then punched down hard onto her chest as he tore a hole into her.

Naiya let out one last puff from her gills, then all movement stopped. Her eyes glazed over and her nictitating membranes slid to half closed, the milky white film eerily covered her vacant stare. Opius sneered down at Naiya, his face painted in contempt. He stepped off of her, then wiped away the fragments of her broken skin from his feet with a disgusted grimace.

I cried out for her, for her lost life and the futility of it all. With one great kick Opius shoved the board off the rocky lip, into the abyss. Her lifeless body separated from the stretcher and floated free for one moment, before she was swallowed by the darkness, and fell to wherever the void went. A discarded husk of former life. Tears streaked my face as I looked down into the Stygian hole, straining my hybrid ears to hear if she ever landed. At long last, far below, I heard her body impact.

"Well, now that the messy business with that cunne is over, I can proceed with you, Lily." He dusted his hands as he strolled closer to me.

"That is faex, you culus!" Rannoch spat, his voice strained from pain. "Water for life? You Umorfae are domineering elitists. Do you see the Caelifae trying to take over Alternis? They have power over air, do you not rely on air as much as water? They could draw the breath right from you and leave you flailing on the ground. Yet they are peaceful. And for that, you butcher them. Probably because you fear them."

"Weak-minded Ignisfae with a dimwitted view of life. You are not fit nor worthy of reproduction. I am surprised this *hybrid* likes you. Though, she is easy to entice."

Rannoch growled through his teeth as he thrashed his body.

"For fuck's sake, get on with it Opius," a female voice called out from above. I craned my neck to see where it had come from. A figure emerged into a shaft of light, then settled to a stop on an elevated platform, high above the plateau that Opius stood upon.

I stilled as I beheld the newcomer.

CHAPTER 40

Pale skin reflected the light in a cold, otherworldly way. I had never seen her before, though I recognized something about her. Familiarity with her features struck me: shorter, pointed ears, no talons like the Fae, elongated limbs, and a slightly angular face.

She was a Fae hybrid, a Vale Born—like me.

"I enjoyed you," Opius said quietly to me, I shifted my gaze from the female overlooking us to him, "while it lasted. But alas, Dashelle wants her prize." He jerked his chin up in her direction.

My heart dropped. She was Dashelle. She—not he—as I had thought.

"I will only need one more Vale Born," Opius continued, "to complete my end of the deal. I wonder how long it will be before your brother, Felix, ventures here. I sent Faeries to whisper to him once I had captured you. I imagine he will be along eventually. It may take him some time to make his way to the tear, but with you gone, I shall have all my time to focus on him." His grin was an evil slash across his face.

Rage bloomed inside me. *Too far, asshole. Now you've gone too far.*

"You will not harm my brother," I said with calm, deadly seriousness, "you will not harm Rannoch, or me. Or anyone else again."

"Oh come now, Lily. What can you do? And you must know, I do this for my people. For them to have the ruler that will forward the interests of the Umorfae. I do this not for myself, but for them."

"Whatever you say, shithead." Anger burned in my eyes, as I stared down at him from my restrained position. Outrage boiled in me, as the list of injustices he had committed continued to mount. How he had seduced Josie and given her to Dashelle, facilitating her murder, how he had brutally killed Naiya, and what he had done to Rannoch and I thus far. How he had seduced me, and sullied my heart with his hidden agendas. And, apparently, he was a part of the imprisonment of the Ignisfae children, as well as Kerenza's mate's murder. *I'm going to make this son of a bitch pay.* I let the fury spark the fire, it exploded in my chest and churned up my arms, to the bonds that held me.

His eyes flashed to the sizzling ropes that held me, the skin of his shimmering face blanched as he realized I could burn through them.

I gave him a haughty smirk and a wink—a promise of what was to come—before I turned my face upward toward the disintegrating rope. There were just enough of the fibers destroyed for me to break one hand free. Before the end of the line gave way, I reached higher and grasped it, worked my other hand out, then climbed.

I ascended enough that I could grip the lower part of the strand with my feet, and swung myself toward the platform Opius stood upon. Slowly at first, I swung closer. The rope withered beneath my hands, the tumult of flame still spread onto the twisted cable.

He retreated a step as I took one last mighty swing, then let go of the rope as it broke away completely. Time stood still amid the rush of falling. I arced down toward him, my hair flapped behind as I sailed to the edge.

I realized that my trajectory would bring my path just short of the rim, and leave me falling into the abyss. I thrust my arms forward, and gave a hard yank toward Opius—and the blood his body contained.

He lurched from the forceful pull, the extra nudge pulled me the difference I needed to clear the lip. I crashed into him, the impact sent us tumbling away from the dropoff in a careening mess of blonde and opal hair.

I sprang up into an attack position opposite him, rocked back on one foot and ready to fight.

"You were right Opius," Dashelle called out cooly as she began descending down the side of the rock face she had been standing upon. "Her abilities are surprising. Though far more intense than you suspected. With the ability to not only wield fire, but also create it, I will be unstoppable."

My jaw hung agape as I watched her drop down from high above, she effortlessly slid out portions of the stone into rough stairs. Dashelle smiled a wicked grin, as she flicked her hand, rhythmically creating a step while destroying the one she had just dropped off of, never once tearing her eyes from mine. She took slow, deliberate steps down, stalking me like a cat. The closer she got, the greater my feeling of dread. I sensed in her true malice, a disregard for life that I had yet to encounter in a being. Even the

Pythonnisamul, deadly as she was, did not seem as intrinsically evil. That witch at least inhaled lives out of the need for consumption.

I panicked. My fight or flight instincts clashed causing indecision, and left me frozen in place. *Focus, Lily. Decide.*

Opius ignored my aggressive stance and took two confident, long strides toward me, like I wasn't more deadly than a common mouse.

In a flash he closed the distance and had his hands around my neck. He lifted my feet off the ground, and held me captive as Dashelle swaggered her way toward me. I kicked and struggled as he gripped me tighter, he chuckled in response at my inability to break free.

"No!" Rannoch shouted, still hanging helplessly over the void. I strained my eyes to look at him, his pained face knotted with worry.

I remembered a self defense move Felix had taught me, one that could break a choke hold.

I slid my hands—palms together—up between his wrists, then clenched my hands into fists and snapped them outward, away from each other. He lost his grip on my neck and I dropped to the ground.

I reached up and grabbed his armored collar, then pulled it hard down, as I brought my knee up to his abdomen in a rapid succession of blows. I jumped back a step, thrust my hands forward, then yanked on the volume of blood inside him. He stumbled toward me, as I wound back my right fist. I shifted to the side to avoid the oncoming mass and released all of my might into one forceful, epic punch. I committed my whole body to the expulsion of energy, using my base like Kerenza had taught me, and delivered a stunning blow to his perfect jaw.

A loud crack echoed in my ears and shook through my body. He continued on his path past me, the force of the pull and punch I had given him sent him hurtling through the air.

The rush of wind swished my hair as he sailed past. Opius came crashing down like a lifeless marionette. He slid across the plateau a short distance, then settled to a disheveled, motionless heap.

Ha, bastard. You deserved that.

Rannoch blasted out, "Yes! Magna strike, Lily!"

The win was momentary. I turned to find that Dashelle had nearly reached me. I ran toward the direction the Umorfae guards had come from, my heart raced and hand ached, as I reached a rough wall across the huge plateau. I scrabbled at the surface, looking for an opening. I spun around as she approached, with my back up against the impassable barrier.

"I control this fortress," she taunted, "in fact, I created this whole place. If you can't control earth, you can't open the doors. Looks like it's the end of the line for you, *Lily*." She cackled. Her smooth brown hair shifted over her shoulders as she squared off with me.

I gulped and took a steadying breath. I had no choice but to fight, flight was not an option. *C'mon, Lily, kick this bitch's ass.*

I steeled my courage and launched myself at her, then unleashed rapid punches, constantly changing the direction I approached from. But she was faster. She deftly blocked and avoided each blow, dancing around me with the swiftness of an agile boxer. Clearly, she was trained to fight.

The hits that nearly landed just miffed off of her, never connecting a complete impact. I swung and jabbed, each time Dashelle blocked and dodged, never attempting to land a blow of her own. I started to get frustrated, when she stunned me with a hard knock to the face.

I barely saw it coming, stars twinkled and my vision blurred. I shook my head, trying to clear my double vision.

I thrust my arms outward and pushed Dashelle's blood to send her backward, then squatted down low and pulled the volume within her, to knock her off balance. Her legs came out from under, she toppled onto her back with a whack.

I took one running lunge to push again, trying to roll her toward the edge of the drop off. She flopped over twice. *A few more and I'll shove her into that abyss!*

The extra inertia from the lunge added more force, so I tried again, this time running forward as I pushed. As she tumbled over on her side, she made a strong tossing motion with her hand.

A thick sheet of earth erupted upward out of the ground directly in front of me, blocking my view of her. My forward motion propelled me smack into it, causing me to bounce backward from the impact. As I staggered, another sheet burst up and knocked me from behind, wedging me with little space.

I shimmied to move out from between them, when two more jutted up on the open sides, encasing me in an earthen box.

"That was actually fun," her sickly sweet voice called out from the other side of the wall, "and I got to see those powers of yours—soon to be mine—in action. Nice to know I will be able to push people around with their blood."

My stomach dropped, as the realization of what she'd been doing set in.

A rumble sounded through the rock, and a low tremor worked its way up my legs from the ground.

"Hello down there."

I snapped my head in the direction of her voice. She perched on a rocky overhang, near the top opening of the stone cage she had grown for me. Dashelle smiled her evil grin again.

"Why are you doing this?"

"Why would I even bother wasting my breath? You'll be dead soon. That's all you need to know." She waved a hand and rolled her eyes.

"You killed my best friend. You claim you're about to kill me. I want an explanation."

"Ugh fine, only since I'm a fan of villain monologues. I heard the story about Vitus Augustus, the Vale Born that ruled here over a millenia ago, he had supreme power because he took it from other Vale Born. And I thought, ya know what? Why think small? I've had enough of small. Nothing good was ever going to happen in my hick town. Then I came here, and I saw the possibilities. A whole realm I could actually rule. He did it, so why couldn't I? I figured I'd need to collect as much power as I could, hence my need for you."

"You are absolutely nuts."

Dashelle shrugged. "Now, time to relieve you of those powers," she said as she held up her hands facing each other, and began to push.

The walls shrunk in around me. I panicked, claustrophobia and terror took over my mind, and blotted out any rational sense I had left. I pushed helplessly back against the encroaching surface.

"Please! Don't do this!"

"Well, sweetie," she drawled as she stopped pushing for a moment, "I got all I could from the two other Vale Born in my small town. Tragic." Her face darkened. "Those bastards deserved it, after what they did. And they both had the gift of earth. As did Josie. There's only so much I can do with all this earth ability." She interlaced her fingers and stretched her palms out, then shook her hands. "Your skills will really round mine out. I promise to make creative use of them. I understand you got your second set of skills from your sister, you're more like a two-fer!"

My jaw dropped as I narrowed my eyes up at her, I wanted to scream at the hateful, evil bitch. *My sister's death a bonus? Oh hell no!*

A succession of loud booms followed by shouting echoed through the chamber. She whipped her head toward the clamor, as I watched her from my prison.

"Shit!" Dashelle hollered as she disappeared from view. "Guards! Get your asses out here! Opius! Get up, dammit!"

I strained to hear what was happening. Metal clanged, followed by shouts. The now-familiar sound and feeling of earth being manipulated shuddered through, from all around.

I have to get out of here. The walls were close, but not so constricting that I couldn't move. I pushed my back up against the wall and slid one knee up, as I braced myself with my hands on the rock in front of me. I pulled up my other knee, and began walking myself up the chimney. The rough walls scraped my legs as I rose higher. The scant protection the fabric of the Arbor Elf pants offered wore through before midpoint of my ascent, my knees cracked and bled.

I reached the top, and poked my head out to peek at the battle

I had thus far only been able to hear. My eyes flew open as I took in the scene.

CHAPTER 41

Ignisfae. Tons of them. And another race of Fae I didn't recognize. They whirled around the enclosed battlefield, pushing and pulling rock formations. Their rich, tawny skin and blazing auburn hair streaked colors around the gigantic space, as they slammed earthen objects into their Umorfae opponents. *They must be the Petrafae!*

The battle raged in a turbulent blur. Weapons clashed as elements collided; fire arced, earth moved and shattered, and water coursed through the air.

I saw the flash of an unmistakable thick black braid whipping around the ensuing chaos. Her powerful kicks had her spinning through the battle, against the Umorfae that had come streaming out of whatever hole they slithered from.

Kerenza had come, and brought friends.

Dashelle was on the far end of the fight, opening crevasses to swallow up my allies. I could see her cruel delight as she felled Fae after Fae, opening the earth and then closing it back up, crushing them beneath the surface.

As I crawled to the top, I dropped my jaw at another familiar sight. Ears like mine, and a male face that mirrored my own. I went rigid as I beheld my brother, that foolish boy had ventured into the Vale.

I snapped my eyes back to Dashelle, who now faced off with several Petrafae, still on the far end as before. *Good, it looks like she hasn't noticed him yet. I hope one of them takes care of her.*

I scrambled out of my rocky coffin and leaped off the lip. I made the fifteen foot jump without thinking, then did a tuck and roll to divert some of the force of the impact. I sprang up and sprinted toward him.

"Felix! You shouldn't be here! We need to get you out!"

"I came to find you, I was worried when Apollo came home without you. I ended up here, met Kerenza...we tracked you...it's a long story." His skin positively gleamed as a Fae hybrid, and his chest barely huffed from running. *Naturally, he's perfect in both realms.*

"You shouldn't have come. This place is dangerous."

"All the more reason that you need me. Who's the trained fighter again?" He smirked at me in his cocky way.

"This isn't a joke, Felix. Just being able to fight is not enough. This chick is crazy. She wants to kill us both and take our powers. She killed Josie. I have to get you out of here."

His jaw dropped and he started to respond, when three Umorfae peeled off in our direction, charging with the force of a freight train.

"Shit, looks like escape is not an option," I said as I went to push him behind me. He blocked my hand with one arm and reached up over his shoulder with the other.

"Here, Kerenza said this is yours." Felix whipped out my

selwaer from a sheath on his back and tossed it to me. The blade sang in response as I closed my grip around the pommel, twirling it gracefully once, a greeting to an old friend.

I took a deep breath and looked at him. "If you have powers, now is a good time to figure out how to use them."

He grinned and answered, "Well, they aren't battle-tested, but I have a feeling I'll do okay." He held up his hands and stirred the air, which whirled up twin cyclones.

I didn't have time for amazement, the Umorfae were upon us, swords raised and ready to strike. I swung my blade instinctively upward, and deflected their downward swings. Felix pushed the cyclones into them, the Umorfae on the farthest left lost control of his sword as the swing continued from my deflection. It sliced clean into his neighbor's side, sending a wave of blood gushing out of the deadly gash.

The warrior gasped and clutched his waist as he fell back, scrambling to keep his blood contained. I yanked a runnel of the blood out before he could get a handle on pushing it in himself.

The two remaining barely even glanced at their fallen comrade, as they continued their assault against us. They spread out, keeping enough distance from each other so that Felix couldn't use the same trick twice.

My eyes darted between the two, now too far apart to effectively watch them both completely. They struck in concert, while I was still debating a plan of action. Their parries came at a stunning speed. I blocked and flinched, as I fell back a pace. Falling back widened the view to encompass the other warrior and Felix. I shifted my angle as I retreated another step. With several quick shoves to the volume of blood inside him, I pushed the Umorfae further away to give myself some breathing room. He tripped over a crack in the rock and fell, giving me a momentary reprieve.

Felix did not appear daunted by the fact that his opponent was far larger than he, or that he had no weapon to wield against such a foe. I tried to focus on my own adversary, but I couldn't stop myself from staring at Felix's skill. He threw one forceful twist with his hands, which blew the Umorfae in a clumsy spiral. As the warrior quickly regained his footing, Felix was already onto his next move.

He blasted an air current toward the ground as he leaped up, arcing toward his attacker. The strength of it boosted Felix higher, putting him in a perfect line to come down on top of the warrior. He had switched their roles, and put himself in the offensive position. Felix sailed into him and delivered a brutal punch to the bridge of the Umorfae's nose. He wasted no time as the warrior stumbled back, Felix rained strikes down on him, until his foe's body slackened with unconsciousness.

"Lily!" Rannoch cried from the background, "Watch out!"

I had gotten distracted by my brother's fight, and I lost track of my assailant. I snapped my eyes back to where I had seen him last, only to find him in mid-strike to my side. I pulled on the felled Umorfae's blood to help propel myself out of the path of the onslaught. But it was too late.

His blade sliced into my thigh, the Arbor Elf fabric bloomed red as I hemorrhaged out of the long slice.

"No!" Felix yelled as he threw himself toward me. He funneled a draft of air down and launched himself in a gymnastic tumble up and over, then came down behind me—onto the bastard that cut me. The fury Felix unleashed was unreal.

I backed away to Rannoch, and unspooled healing energy to

stitch the deep laceration. Felix was holding his own as I hobbled away, giving me a reprieve to fix myself. *Then I really need to help Rannoch, he has been hanging there for too long!* I sewed the two sides back together. The suture was haphazard and incomplete, I had to save enough energy for Rannoch.

I eyed Rannoch from my vantage, he grimaced as he hung over the pit. *Well, at least he looks marginally okay.*

My selwaer clattered to the ground as I lifted my hands. I pulled Rannoch's blood within his suspended body, to start him swinging. Within a few passes he reached the maximum distance the rope would allow, I couldn't swing him any further.

"It looks like you could use my help." Kerenza bounded up holding a ball of flame aloft, her black braid flounced as she approached. "Let us do this before one of those culuses notices."

I gave her an appreciative nod as she pushed the flame in a current, toward the rope he hung from. I gave one more hard yank on his blood, as the rope snapped. I gritted my teeth, pulling him hard. Down he sailed in an arc. But not enough of one. He would fall just shy of the edge, just as I had.

Harder and harder I pulled, Kerenza readied to grab him as he approached. *He won't make it!*

A flurry of air whipped up underneath Rannoch, and gave him just enough lift to come flying down at the edge of the crevasse. Felix arrived just in time to lend a hand.

Rannoch crashed into me, we tumbled across the rocky surface. We settled to a stop and I hurried to move off, to inspect his injured body. The arrow was still impaled in his arm, it had punctured from the underside of his armpit and grazed his chest. I broke the arrowhead off, then pulled the shaft through.

His face scrunched.

"It'll be okay, Rannoch. I'll get you healed as fast as possible." I caressed his forehead for a quick moment, before I called the healing magic, sending waves of it into his torn flesh. *Stitch! Stitch fast!*

I sewed faster than I ever had, though it still was not fast enough. It dawned on me, *I have two arms. Perhaps that means I have two threads.* I visualized the strand splitting in half, twin needles weaving a brilliant gold thread. Side to side, they worked in unison, each one the mirror to the other. As I reached the edge of the wound I pulled the strands taut, then released it. Both filaments snapped back into me.

I panted, my vision speckled. I had nearly reached burnout. "Rannoch," I whispered feebly.

"I have you, Lily, do not worry." He scooped me up and cradled me. I let myself relax into him, and closed my eyes. *I just need a minute.*

"Greetings, again," Opius called out. "That was quite a strike you managed to land. I shall have to return one to you."

I cracked an eye to peer over at him. *This jerk just won't quit.* I sighed. "Put me down, Rannoch, time to take out the trash."

He set me carefully on the ground. As I went to get up, Rannoch burst forward toward him, his canines bared and strong feet clawed the ground to propel him.

They collided in a stunning display of Fae savagery. They traded intense blows to each other, each hit landed squarely. Every time a punch landed on Opius, I cheered. When one connected with Rannoch, I almost thought I could feel it myself.

Kerenza propped me up from behind as I continued to recover. "It's like they aren't even trying to block the hits," I muttered as we watched.

"You are correct. This is the battle for you. This is how it is done."

"Well that's stupid."I said, as Opius cracked him hard in the cheek. "I've seen enough. Time to finish this, before he wrecks your brother's pretty face." I pulled my legs underneath me, then rose, straightened my shoulders, and readied to strike at the silvery charlatan.

I rocked back on one foot, and shot myself toward him. When I was within two paces, I leaped forward and launched myself into a flying kick. Opius's intense focus, as he tried to pummel Rannoch, distracted him from my rapid approach. My heel connected into his side, just above his hip bone, sending him in an off balance spin.

Opius let out a surprised grunt, but got his bearings again as he lurched around to face me, seething.

"I will deal with you later, cunne! First I will take down this filth you have associated with, as is my right."

"I don't have to play by your rules, Opius. I'm not Fae. So fuck you," I retorted as I circled him.

He gnashed his teeth and growled.

One corner of my mouth lifted up. *Now I am the shark.*

I thought about everything he had done. His lies. His sinister ways. Josie. Naiya. Luring Felix here. I let it anger me to the point of boiling. My heart felt like sputtering lava, a churning pit of destruction waiting to consume him for his maliciousness.

I blasted out, sending two wide swaths of flame churning toward him. He dashed out of the way. I released another spout of fire, aimed at the same side. One branded his right arm as he attempted to evade it.

"You will pay for that!" He hollered as he clutched his fried forearm.

I didn't bother with a response. I sent another dual flare at the same side. He dodged again, then finally caught onto my plan.

He had run out of real estate. Opius was now at the edge of the drop off, and had nowhere to go.

His eyes widened as he realized I had trapped him. I struck my arms out in a vee, and unleashed the turbulent flames once again. I began to close my arms together, to make the flames meet in the middle, where he stood.

"No, Lily. You do not want to do this." Opius's strained voice wavered between confidence and pleading. "Would you truly burn me, kill me in the same way your family died? No, I do not think so. You cannot do it, you do not have the strength."

I gasped a cry at the thought of them. My flames sputtered, and went out. He was right. I couldn't do it. Having this power meant that I could use it for good, when possible.

He smiled his sick, crooked smirk. "I knew you could not do it. Leave the killing to the trained warriors, the battlefield is no place for a filia like you."

I snapped my eyes back up at him, something sparked in me. Killing would never be natural for me. But in this case, he was wrong.

His skin paled and opened his mouth to speak, when I pushed. I pushed his blood and forced him backward at the edge of the cliff, teetering above the chasm.

"Lily," Rannoch's voice was strong and soothing from behind, "you do not have to do this. I can do this for you, I told him I would, and I will."

I halted a moment, just one, before I responded, "No, I got this." For Josie, and Naiya.

And I pushed.

Time stood still as his eyes went wild and he flailed his arms. Our eyes locked, one last time, before he disappeared. I held my breath as I waited, everything shrank away from me as I disconnected from the reality around me. Far off in the distance below, I heard the thud.

I sank to my knees and sobbed. I hated him for what he did. I had wanted to make him pay for all he had done, and was going to do. But I wasn't really a killer. *Though I guess I am, officially. I have killed more than once.*

Rannoch rushed to me, picked me up and embraced me protectively. Clangs echoed nearby, the battle waged on without us.

I angled my head away from him, to gauge the remaining players. There had been heavy losses on both sides, but the Petrafae and Ignisfae were prevailing.

"We need to go help them," I said to Rannoch as I looked back up at him. "We need to turn the tide and end this." All I wanted was for it to be over, to take my brother, Rannoch, and Kerenza, and run. But I couldn't leave the others and have more die.

"Felix," I called out, "stay away from Dashelle. No matter what. She is cunning, and extremely dangerous."

He shrugged in response with a non-committal head wag.

At that moment, across the battlefield of her making, Dashelle spotted us. The thing she wanted, the three other powers she lacked, wrapped up between Felix and myself. All she had to do was kill us, and they were hers. I pulled away from Rannoch, then hurried over to my brother.

"Please, Felix. Go and let me deal with this," I begged as I gripped his arm insistently. "I can take care of this, just go."

"No. You need me, I know you do. And, I promised you that I would always be there. I am here, and I'm not leaving you." He stood taller and angled his chin upward, how he always stood when he was telling me that it didn't matter what I said, he was going to do it his way. He would not budge.

I searched his face imploringly, but it was no use. I knew it. I let out a breath as I dropped my hand from his arm and let my head sag forward. I closed my eyes and took a beat to console myself, to tell myself that he will be okay, that we will all be okay. It was not convincing, but I had no choice.

Felix shook my shoulder, forcing me back to attention.

Dashelle had pulled up a wide path high above the melee, and was running swiftly along it toward us. My blood went cold, the dread drained the warmth from my face. My hands shook with fear as she sprinted headlong. She shoved her palms down as she neared us, the path descended like a rolling wave that she surfed.

She glided to us, then dug down to raise both hands in the air, like she was lifting an invisible, large object. The earth rumbled as an octagon of thick rock walls shot up, cleaving between Rannoch and I. She had cut Felix and I off from the others. The top of the barrier went all the way to the ceiling.

"Now I have you all to myself," her silken voice oozed. "Let's see, who's first. I pick...you, Lily." She flung one hand upward and another blockade shot up, closing Felix off on the other side.

She danced around, moving backward, eyeing me from under

slanted brows. Quick as lightning, she darted forward and popped me right in the mouth. I felt my lip split and tasted the tang of blood. She cocked a grin as she sprang away, her fists held up loosely, ready to strike again.

Again, she was upon me before I realized she had pitched in my direction. Dashelle unleashed a rapid release of punches to my abdomen, so quick I didn't know how many it was. Six? Eight? My gut sucked in and I hunched forward, as the wind was knocked out of me.

Her smirk grew. *Cat and mouse, and I'm the mouse.*

Dashelle's jabs kept me from thinking, I was too focused on what attack would come next. *Switch it to the offensive, she has you on defense right now.*

After a few more lithe steps around each other, she once again flew at me. This time I reacted quicker, I dropped and spun with a leg outstretched. As she lost her footing and I completed my turn, thrust my hands and pushed her blood hard. She smashed into the nearby wall. I sent a plume of flames after, but she tossed up a rocky barrier between her and I, blocking the flares from hitting their target.

As I was preparing to unleash another stream, the barrier rushed at me, forced forward by Dashelle on the other side. It smacked into me, and pushed me along as it raced toward the thick wall enclosing us. The speed of it flattened me onto the moving surface. I managed to roll off, just before it crashed into the obstruction it was hurtling toward.

It burst into thousands of rocks from the impact, the loud crash shuddered through my delicate ears. I tumbled across the ground, and scuffed my extremities in the process. Part of the skin from my elbow remained on the rocky floor, torn off by the rough surface like a greedy animal snatching a bite off its prey.

I hobbled away from Dashelle, who smoothly advanced toward me without concern. Her form fitting leather creaked as she swaggered her hips, I wanted to smack the insufferable simper off of her face. As she lifted her arms to raise another flake, a rumble resounded through the chamber.

She whipped around, a hole had opened in the side of the structure. Two Petrafae stood a few paces away from the opening. Rannoch and Kerenza charged in, both wielding immense fireballs, followed by Felix riding a gust of air.

They lobbed spurts of flame at her, which she deflected with earthen shields. Felix spun his hands diagonally, sending the fiery runnels in an arc around her blockade.

She cursed from behind the wall, the smell of burning skin filled the air. The ground shook and separated, she shot upward on a round plane, while the rest of us sunk down. She had given herself a buffer to regroup.

The Petrafae did not allow it. They pulled the mighty plateau down. She came into view as it lowered back into place. Dashelle was hunched over, clutching her ruined leg. The leather pants had been melted into her skin in three large licks that wrapped upward, from the cyclone funneling the fire in a spiral.

She seethed and panted from under a slash of hair across her alabaster face.

I opened a fighting stance and lifted my hands, as I released my own flames from them. "It's over Dashelle. You've lost."

Her eyes darted between all of us, like a caged animal backed into a corner.

Without tearing my eyes from her, I questioned the group, "What should we do with-"

Dashelle let out a shrill war cry and hurtled herself toward me, one last attempt at taking me down. I scrambled to unleash spurts of fire, then let the flames die out so I could push her blood. But she was already moving past me.

When she reached the edge of the gorge, she jumped without any hesitation. Time slowed to a halt as I watched her sail down, her long hair fluttered behind her like a flag. My body shook as all senses dulled. Nearby voices were muffled. At last, I heard the crash of rock impacting far below.

Just like that, she was gone, jumped into her own nearly endless pit. After all that, she just ended it herself.

I stood dumbfounded, and aghast. Appalled at everything. All she had done, and for what? It was all so senseless. The other Vale Born she had killed from her hometown. And Josie. The Fae that battled and fell. All killed for Dashelle's greed and lust for power.

"Absolute power corrupts absolutely," Felix said. I jumped as I looked to my side, I hadn't noticed he had come to stand next to me.

I frowned as his words sunk in. Our dad had said that phrase. Absolute power. "So...what does that mean for you and I?"

He looked at me, shook his head and twitched back the corner of his mouth. *I guess time will tell.*

CHAPTER 42

"You took my kill, Lily." Rannoch said, as he wrapped me in a tight embrace. "Though I am proud of you." His voice strummed my ears.

"Sorry to make you break your promise, but I needed to do it myself. That son of a bitch deserved it." I breathed against his skin. I just wanted to let all of the madness of what had happened wash away; the insanity of controlling elements in a way my human brain still struggled to understand, the wretched evil that Dashelle had been, Opius...all of it. I wanted it all to fade away, and just be Rannoch and I.

But it was there, lurking. I couldn't push it away. No matter what, things were not simple. And that wasn't even considering the elephant in the room. Prince. He was a prince. What did that mean? Prearranged marriage? Duty to state? It indicated that the intricacies of the Fae realm were far greater than I had imagined.

Mmm, that's future Lily's problem.

It was all too much to process. I tightened my grip on him and nestled in further. I was so tired, the adrenaline that had pumped through my system had ceased, leaving me taxed and depleted.

"Let's leave this faexhole," Rannoch suggested, "this place is wretched."

"Yes, let's go," I responded, as I looked around at the horrible devastation. "We should check to see if there are any warriors we can help first. Maybe some of the fallen are just injured."

He smiled broadly and brushed a wisp of hair behind my softly pointed ear. "Even exhausted, you still think of others. That is a magna idea."

"Also the Umorfae," I stated resolutely, "there has been enough death here today. If some of them can be healed, I want to do it." I knew he would argue with me, so I leveled my gaze at him to indicate that I wouldn't take no for an answer.

He appraised me for a moment, the internal battle between what he would probably rather do and what I wanted to do clearly waged on his face.

"All right," he agreed finally.

I leaned in to take one more moment, closed my eyes and inhaled deeply. His skin held a warm spicy scent of cinnamon—or cardamom—reminiscent of something I had smelled before and yet wholly its own. I focused on it, on his strong presence, to center myself before we began the task of healing and the grisly work of sorting the dead.

I summoned the resolve to pull myself away. "Okay, let's get to work then. Felix, do you have healing powers too? That will make things go faster."

"Um, I don't think so, what do I do to find out?"

I thought, then said, "I feel a white light from the inside, and I focus it down my arms, then picture the light to be like a thread which I use to stitch up wounds."

He shrugged. "I guess I'll just try when we find someone that needs it."

We began the arduous process of combing through the fallen, the horrifying results of Dashelle's attempt at a Fae coup turned my stomach. Some that had been swallowed by the earth were completely encased below, while others only had a piece of a limb protruding from the ground. The various races lay scattered every-where, burned, eviscerated, or encapsulated.

Eventually we found a few survivors, several Ignisfae that had bones crushed by Dashelle. A younger male with a broken femur was the worst among the small group.

"Felix, try healing him. Picture the bone inside mending back together. Close your eyes and focus."

He bent down and scrunched his eyebrows, with his arms extended. The injured male cringed, wincing as he waited for the pain to ease in his shattered leg.

"I don't feel anything, I don't think I have that ability."

Not good at everything it seems. "Okay, let's triage the survivors. We'll set up a spot where I can heal the most gravely injured first." I motioned to Rannoch, who signaled a few Ignisfae nearby to help. A breath escaped me, as I realized how heartbreakingly low the remaining numbers were.

I murmured soothing words to the male Felix couldn't heal, while I helped move him. He was smaller than the others, perhaps young. He looked to be no more than seventeen human years old, lucky to be alive.

"Continue bringing the injured here, I'll get to work." I ordered. I knelt next to him, unwound my golden threads, and stitched. My first attempt at mending bone was slow and ineffective, the shards jutted in odd directions as I tried to wrangle them together. Once I pictured the fragments fitting back together like a puzzle, the process became more efficient. The healing light welded the pieces in place as I stitched down the length of his femur.

I took my time, moving from warrior to warrior, periodically resting between to let my well refill. I worked my way down the line, when at last I came to an Umorfae.

It was the same opponent Felix and I had bested earlier, with the deep slice in his side. He snarled as I knelt over him.

"May I heal you?" I asked evenly, trying to separate myself from the fighter I was the last time we faced each other.

"It will not change what you did to Opius," he seethed. "You will be hated by all Umorfae for killing him."

I sighed and rocked back on my feet as I balanced near him. *True, it won't change what I did.* "Well, perhaps not by the Empress, as Opius intended to kill her, and her children too. So maybe not *all* Umorfae." I raised an eyebrow as he glowered at me. "Now, may I continue?'

He turned his head away and set his jaw. "Fine."

I worked on sewing his gash back together, using the twinned threads to pull the two sides closed. I attempted to ignore the simmering hatred emanating from him. It was distracting, and slowed my progress. The flesh was as obstinate as he was, like a stubborn horse refusing to be pulled to the water trough.

I finally won out over the ornery wound and finished up. Woozy, and dangerously near a burn out, I sat back to regain my stability. My vision speckled with the threat of passing out.

"You are a foolish filia, wasting your energy healing an opponent," the now-healed jerk muttered. "I could cut you down right now if I wanted."

Rannoch was there in an instant, teeth bared and ready to shred the warrior to bits. His keen hearing had picked up the terse words even from a fair distance.

"Threaten her again and it is I who will cut you down, you ungrateful bastard," Rannoch spat as his chest heaved. He stood poised over the recovering Umorfae, the thin thread of promise he had made nearly snapped from the tension. I was sure that was all that held Rannoch back from unleashing his rage on him.

I stood and placed a hand on Rannoch's arm. "He didn't do it, just let him go. It sucks to be on the losing side." I implored him to stand down with my eyes, which he finally looked into after a good stare down with my former opponent.

Rannoch's gaze softened after a moment, and flicked his eyes to my lips. He quirked a side smile before responding, "You win, my love."

My heart fluttered. Even though we had essentially professed it, hearing the words out loud was startling.

I laughed nervously and batted my eyelashes reflexively. I remembered the Umorfae still sitting on the ground, watching the whole exchange.

I turned to him. "You should leave, if you can walk. No one will harm you, the battle is over."

He rolled his eyes, but did as I suggested and got up off the ground. He settled his shoulders and straightened his back as he addressed me, "I chose not to hurt you, after you healed the damage the two of *you* inflicted." He jerked his chin toward my brother, who stood a few feet away. "We are even there, but if ever we meet again, I will repay you for what you did to my Generalis."

"Got it, now take a hike," I snapped. *I am so done with threats.*

He narrowed his eyes to slits, then turned to leave.

"Are you sure it was a good idea to let him live?" Rannoch asked as we watched the Umorfae make his way toward the exit, the one that the Petrafae had torn open to enter the fight in the first place. A few other surviving Umorfae spotted him and hobbled over to leave as well.

"No, I'm not sure. But I am sure that I couldn't be okay with not trying to help, even if he is my enemy."

I scooted over to Rannoch's side and slung my arm around his waist. He pulled me in closer as the small group disappeared, presumably to limp back home to Lacausia Palace. Thinking of the mighty fortress reminded me that I had no idea where we were in Alternis.

"Lily," Felix said softly, "Mom is worried, and needs to know you're okay."

Mom. I had almost forgotten. My poor mom! I could only imagine how she must be feeling. Josie never came back, and never would. She must be sick with worry that I wouldn't come back either.

"Yes, of course," I answered, as I wrenched myself away. "Fortunately with the time difference I've probably only been gone for a day, right?"

"I've already been here for...like two weeks—Alternis time— while I searched for you. No, at this point I think you've been here for more than two days in the human world. Maybe more. Which means mom thinks we're both missing."

My mouth dropped as I scanned Felix's face. Two days? How

long had they drugged me for? "Is it night outside still? It was night when they took us."

He shook his head slowly. "No, it is dusk again, and night is falling."

I took a quick breath, and tried to sort out everything. The drugging cycle combined with the time difference left me disoriented.

"Well, we've healed all we can. We should be off then," I responded slowly as I glanced to Rannoch, when dread crept in. I had to go home, I knew it. But, I didn't want to leave him. I gave him half a fake smile, fake because it was driven by worry. Being in the human world for even a little bit would mean a lot of time would pass here.

Rannoch motioned to several Ignisfae who stood nearby, and gave a silent order to move out. They collected the remaining survivors, twenty in total.

So few, I thought sadly as I looked over the brave warriors. Some looked to me and gave a dip of the head in respect.

I took Rannoch's hand, gave it a tight squeeze, then headed toward freedom. Finally after the brutal fight, I could breathe a sigh of relief that we had made it. Exiting the enormous mountain felt like the world had lifted off my shoulders. As I stepped out of the doorway, the landscape below took my breath away.

Rannoch smiled at me, watching me take in the stunning view. The worry and fear I felt moments before melted away, the magic of what surrounded us removed the dark feelings entirely.

CHAPTER 43

We stood on a precipice, which erupted angrily out of the ground far below. Dashelle's mountain fortress left a scar in what was probably once just part of the forest edge. Mist drifted through the peak halfway up the spire. Dusk in Alternis was even more beautiful than in the human world. Lights flickered everywhere, and far off the glowing center nestled in the forest pulsed—where the Vale magic emanated, sending its drops of charmed lifeblood out into the atmosphere.

The rigid and barren terrain we stood upon was a stark contrast to the view below, teeming with lush life. The Praegra Forest spread in a wide expanse before us. The darkening, deep purple sky buzzed with cheerful twitters.

Rannoch marched over to the huddled Ignisfae, while I stared at the landscape, unblinking.

"What is that sound?" I asked, without looking away from the breathtaking sight.

"Those are the Faeries singing. They always sing at dusk, it is their favorite time," Kerenza answered.

"Faeries! How cute! I would love to see them." I grinned as I turned to her. "What are they like?"

"Well," she quirked a smile and looked into the air, "we call them sparkle ticks. They are cute, but they can be a bit bothersome."

"Sparkle ticks!" I unleashed a huge laugh. The name brought a completely different image to mind compared to what I had pictured the moment before.

Kerenza covered her mouth and giggled. "They do adore the Fae, so I feel a little bad saying that. They just get excited around us."

I smiled so big that my eyes squinted. I realized I had barely greeted her since she had swooped in, just in the nick of time. I threw my arms around her and hugged her tightly, my heart burst with joy. Part of me thought there was a chance I wouldn't ever see her again, the last time we had said goodbye.

She laughed as she returned the warm embrace.

"I'm so glad to see you! Where is Emblyn?"

Her smile fell. "I had to leave her at camp when we realized you had been captured. I could not risk her getting hurt. It was difficult to separate so soon after her rescue. But, it is what I had to do. She is safe, and so are you and Rannoch."

"Well, thanks for saving our asses!"

After a shared laugh, she flicked her eyes to her brother. "So, shall I call you sister now?"

My eyes went round and my jaw dropped, butterflies flurried in my stomach as I grasped for an answer. Instead I drooled out words. "Um, yea well, so the thing is, we were in the forest, and uh-"

"Relax," she chuckled and shook her head, "I am just having a bit of fun. For as old as Rannoch is, a female has never managed to get him to profess his love. And you can bet they have tried. You cannot blame me for wanting to savor it!"

I pulled back my head in surprise. "Wait, how old is he?" All of these things I never thought of. Did I even know this guy I had fallen head over heels for? My brain started to run further with questions of other things I didn't know. "And does that mean he has never, uh, like, done it before?"

I winced and regretted the question. *Way to go, Lily. Wow, this conversation has derailed.*

She raised an eyebrow and smirked at me. "Well, I will let him answer that question. But I will say that sex and mating are two different things. Sex is an act, mating is a promise." A sly smile danced on her face as she added, "A promise with some really great sex."

"What are we talking about?" Rannoch asked from directly behind me.

My blood went cold as I went utterly still. I stared at Kerenza like a paralyzed deer.

"Getting off of this wretched mountain, of course," Kerenza responded smoothly, looking over my shoulder with a sweet smile. She moved her head to the side, obstructing his line of sight of her, then opened her mouth in a silent laugh. I cringed, waiting for him to say something.

"Magna, let us depart," he stated.

I willed my features into a neutral expression as I turned to give him a nod, and prayed that my face would obey. Fortunately he appeared none the wiser, and pivoted to return to his companions.

"Your magical skills go beyond using fire," I said to Kerenza as I twisted back to her, "you have a wondrous way of nearly getting me into trouble with him."

"You said it, not me!" She choked out a laugh.

I giggled, *it's true*. "Good cover, by the way. That was flawless."

"I know, right? I have had practice," she chuffed as she looped her arm through mine and pulled me to the others.

We were still arm in arm and chuckling, when we approached the group.

"Let us get off this infernum hill," Kerenza announced. "I have supplies...and surprises, waiting at the bottom."

"Oh thank god, does that mean you have food? I'm so hungry," I said as I put my hand to my stomach. There was no telling how long it had been since Rannoch and I had eaten. I had only just realized how famished I was.

"You can thank all the gods, there is plenty of food, and more. But we have to get off this treacherous lump to get to it," she answered cooly as she gave me her haughty smirk.

I snorted and bobbed my head, *typical Kerenza*. But truly, I adored her. She was one of the few Fae that actually understood the nuance of humor.

"What's the surprise?" I asked.

"Nope, not telling," Kerenza answered as she wagged her finger, "you will have to get your rear off this rock to find out."

"You don't have to tell me twice!" I called out, as I jumped onto the steep slope.

"Lily, wait!"

But it was too late, I was already sliding out of control.

CHAPTER 44

Millions of tiny round pebbles gave way as soon as my weight was upon them. My legs flew out in front, arms flailing as the ground rushed in a formless current on the scree-covered slope. Every attempt to tread the debris had no effect, as I slid down the steep incline. A rock three times my height jutted up, right in the center of the path I was uncontrollably on. I panicked and desperately tried to scramble as I headed straight for it. I managed at last to pull my legs under until I got my body weight centered, lowered my hip over my back foot, then used my front foot to surf the wave of fine gravel. I nearly grazed the edge of the stone as my speed picked up, sledding with the fast moving rubble. My tangled hair flapped behind me, pulled straight back by the rushing wind. *Shit, that was close!*

When the path opened wide enough to sneak a glance, I looked over my shoulder to catch Felix—and all the Fae—skiing down as well. My jaw dropped as I saw the Petrafae coasting along the flowing mass, pushing the pebbles into solid platforms which they rode down on.

Finally near the bottom, the intensity of the inertia sent me toppling headlong as I hit solid ground, like a wave finally cresting. I pitched up and forward, sent into a mid air tumble. Time slowed as I rotated over the ground, my glance passing it as I flipped. I let my legs complete the spin and touched one foot down, then the other, landing like a cat righting itself during a fall.

My knees bent as I absorbed the impact, and I put my hands out to the side to help balance as I skidded a few paces, before coming to a halt.

I let go of a breath I didn't realize I was holding, and time sped back up to normal.

I was still gasping for air as the others arrived, each having to find their own creative way to deal with the sudden speed change. Felix blasted air to whirl himself around, then lowered himself slowly, graceful, like a weightless dancer. I rolled my eyes and at the same time stood in awe of him.

Kerenza's acrobatic, sideways double-barrel roll flung pebbles in an arc around her, as she touched down lightly in between, before springing off for the second one.

"Show off," I chided her as I dodged a few small stones. She grinned in return as she came to a rest.

The Ignisfae all did similar spinning moves, and the Petrafae simply pushed on the mass of moving rocks to slow their descent.

Rannoch tucked and tumbled forward toward me, using the contact point where his shoulder met ground to launch himself back up onto his feet. He barely slowed, and shot his arms under mine as he scooped me up above him. He spun me around, nestling his face into my bosom.

"I think you might be crazy!" He admonished me, but laughed

at the same time.

"I think so, too. You've got to admit though, that was fun."

"If you had waited just one more moment," Kerenza called out, "I could have warned you! Impulsive filia!"

I smiled as he lowered me back down. His eyes glowed with life and fervor. We stood, staring at each other. Everything else faded away into the background. His arms wrapped around me, encasing me in golden warmth. Alive, we were *alive.* I squeezed him tighter, not wanting the feeling to end, but I could feel Felix near me, waiting.

I sighed as the moment slipped away. I would much rather just lose myself in his arms, melding together as one. I gave him a smile before I released him, then turned to Felix.

Felix eyed us both, then gave Rannoch one long, hard look. He marched to us and thrust his hand out to Rannoch, holding it there until he eventually accepted it. It was Rannoch's second handshake, his first one with me—when we had made our bargain what seemed like an eternity ago.

"I'm Felix, nice to meet you, officially," he stated.

The words were pleasant, but the tone was harsh. Felix had always been protective of me. He had acted the same way when he met previous hopeful boyfriends, using his intensity as a silent threat and warning.

"It is nice to meet you also. I am Rannoch," he answered, as he maintained his ground. Though Rannoch was much taller than Felix, and quite a bit more muscled, Felix didn't waver. The two stood gripping each other's hands in a macho standoff for what felt like forever, as I squirmed uncomfortably.

"Well! Glad that's out of the way!" Felix announced as he

released Rannoch's hand, his expression lightened entirely. "Let's eat!"

I shook my head as they dismissed their pissing contest. Kerenza gave me a shrug before she began gathering bundles that had been left nearby.

"Let us move closer to the trees first, we are still too near this faexhole!" She exclaimed, as she motioned with her chin to the imposing crag that loomed over us. My thoughts darkened as I looked up at it, memories of all that had happened, all who were lost inside caused my breath to catch once more. So much destruction, the greed and lust for power which netted nothing but loss of life. Lives. Too many lives.

Rannoch touched my arm, pulling me out of the spiral that had yanked me down yet again. Everyone else moved toward the treeline, as he waited with me. He picked up my hand and searched my eyes, then cast his glance downward. "I need to explain myself," he said.

"Yes, you do. I understand some of what you hid from me—I think, but to hide your lineage for so long, as well as the rest of it. There were plenty of opportunities to tell me *something*, at least."

"You are right. In my defense, I did start to tell you before, when we…" his eyes flashed to my lips. "But I should have told you much sooner. The longer I waited, the bigger the task became. It started because my faeder could not be implicated in what I was doing, I had to keep who I was a secret for him. It could have started an all-out war. The cost was so high with the last war, the Caelifae and Petrafae were the worst hit when the Umorfae struck. They still have not recovered. Even the losses we Ignisfae had, I have not recovered personally from that. Nor has my faeder. I did it to protect him, even if he has made his own mistakes."

I blew out a breath. "Yea, I can see that, I guess. I have so many questions—all the questions. But right now, I'm too tired. We'll clear all this up later."

"Yes, I promise. I will not keep things from you again," Rannoch said, as he squeezed my hand.

I nodded as we turned to make our way over to the meadow that bordered the great trees. My skin tingled from a feeling in the air, alive with a jittering happiness as a sweet smell wafted through—like lemongrass in a dewy glade.

Little glimmers floated, wisps of light reflected from iridescent surfaces. The high-pitched singing a mixture of indistinct humming and tiny, tinkling bells. They flitted around, leaving speckles in their wake.

Several sparks of light ran up my arms in twining paths, then another across my cheekbones. I looked at my arms and realized they had left intricate, glittering designs where their miniature feet had touched, like beautiful patterned tattoos that could only be seen in certain glancing angles. I laughed as I beheld the evidence of their curious meandering. Some found the rips in my pants particularly interesting. They ran over and over the openings, leaving behind dozens of overlapping shapes, which left my knees frosted in shimmering dust.

"See what I mean?" Kerenza raised her eyebrows knowingly. "Sparkle ticks." She shook her head as she turned, then walked to the supplies that had been deposited.

I smiled as I watched them skitter around, feeling their flutters on my exposed skin. "I think they're beautiful." One flew up to my face and peered in close to my eyes. I strained to discern specific features, light bent around them, making them appear partially invisible. Only the transparent edges of their skin could be seen.

"Wait until you are covered in their dust, you may not think them so wonderful then," Rannoch said. I turned to him with a radiant smile, he laughed as he looked me over. "I do think you look particularly adorable with their footprints on your cheeks."

My face flushed and I rolled my eyes. Looking up at him from under my lashes, I wanted to slip my arms around him, and kiss him. He raised an eyebrow and looked at my lips, then back to my eyes. I held my breath, half ready to pounce on him. His ears twitched as he looked at me, honing in on my cues.

"Come over you two, quit drooling over each other and come eat!" Kerenza hollered.

I jumped, then let out a small giggle. "Let's go," I said with a sheepish grin.

We walked over hand in hand, to the spread that had been laid out. The bundles were blankets with food packed inside, Kerenza had set ours up a little further away from the others. When unrolled, they formed plenty of soft seating on the ground, with the meal ready to eat in the center. Everyone settled in, lounging and snacking, some quietly talking.

All I could focus on at first was stuffing my face. I gobbled down the plentiful rolls, dried meats, and dehydrated fruit so fast I barely took a breath.

"Slow down, it is not going anywhere," Rannoch said.

"Um, yes it is," I said around a torn off bite of crusty bread, "it's going in my stomach."

He laughed and shook his head, and began to tear at a large piece of jerky with his long canines.

"Wow, vicious," I chided. He raised his eyebrows while he continued to destroy the food.

"Here," Kerenza called out, then stood and walked the twenty paces over to us, offering a waterskin. I grabbed it, taking a huge swig, then nearly coughed up everything I had swallowed.

"Oh shit! Vinirubrum! Kerenza, why didn't you tell me! Sheesh." I wiped my mouth, as a little wine dribbled out.

She gave me a devilish grin. "It was more fun this way."

I took another draught and passed it to Rannoch. A flame ignited on the next blanket over, followed by a wafting tendril of smoke. The sweet, warm smell made me want to follow my nose to the source.

Rannoch snapped his head in the direction of the vapor. "Dhiren, bring that sativa here!"

Kerenza's eyebrows shot up. "You are going to partake Rannoch? You never do! I am always the only one who has any fun."

I swiveled my head to see who he was talking to. Felix had settled himself in with him and a female Ignisfae on a padded covering a ways off. He sat talking, laughing, and smoking with the two Ignisfae, their high cheekbones and silky black hair glinted in the soft light.

"We survived a dangerous event and ruthless foe. I think we deserve to celebrate," he said.

A small, rolled up tube of leaves circulated to us. I watched him intently as he squinted an eye and took a deep drag. He leaned over to me to kiss me, opened his mouth to let a little smoke out, then nodded to me in question. *What the heck.* I leaned forward to kiss him. He funneled the remaining vapor into me, the taste of him commingled with the smoke.

I felt as light as a feather floating on a softly drifting breeze as I let it out. He handed me the sativa, and I inhaled deeply. I looked around at the colors of the trees, the sky, the darting Faeries. I leaned forward and kissed him again, sending the smoke into him. The light and sounds surrounding me intensified as the herb took effect.

As he pulled back to let the breath out, a bunch of Faeries gathered around. Rannoch blew the smoke at them as they flurried into the path of the vapor. Their tinkling sounds erupted in a cheer, as they darted in and out of the plume.

Rannoch's deep laugh sent tingles down my spine and tickled my ears. His sounds, his touch, they made me want to rip off my tattered clothes. But we were surrounded by Fae, not to mention my brother. I smiled to myself and edged closer to Rannoch.

He twitched up the corner of his mouth in a cocky, lazy smile that warmed my core.

Heat rose off my chest and my breasts swelled.

He leaned in closer, and blew a breath along my cleavage in a mock attempt to cool me, which only served to make me flush more. After dragging his nose on my skin up toward my neck—taking in my scent—he whispered in my ear, "Let's not burn the blankets, my love. At least, not yet."

I closed my eyes and clenched my hands shut, so little was holding me back. I took a deep breath and opened my eyes. The look I gave him was unmistakable, *yes, later*.

We sat lounging, eating, drinking, and smoking. The Faeries continued their sparkling song as we unwound from the eventful battle. Each laugh, each joyous moment, pushed the atrocities further away.

A delicate Faerie with transparent, lavender hair hovered close to my face, peering at me with slowly blinking eyes. As she moved, her structure shifted, taking on a more male appearance.

"Are Faeries both male and female?" I asked as I looked at the lithe form in front of me.

"They are both," Kerenza answered. "They can be female, male, or anything in between. They have a gender spectrum rather than just two." She lounged on her back, watching the flits of light as they shifted through the air around us.

"I think they are lovely," I commented as I beamed at the little being, who wiggled their hips before bowing, then floated off to the next person of interest. My head cleared momentarily as I thought about the Faeries, and the nickname the Fae had given them. "You know, sparkle ticks is not a very...nice nickname. Unless a tick is something different here. In the human world it's a pest, and ugly. At first I thought the name was funny, but now that I've met them, well I think it's pretty mean spirited—it lacks sensitivity. You even said Kerenza, that you felt a little bad saying it. You must already sense that it's derogatory."

Rannoch raised his eyebrows and glanced at his sister. She chewed on her lip a moment before responding, "Yes, you are right, Lily. I think I knew it was unkind. It is a very old saying, and we do not change quickly."

Rannoch cleared his throat. "Yet another reason why you are good for Alternis, Lily. The Faeries deserve a champion like you. I think we have said it for so long, we did not hear the undertone it conveys."

I knew what he was saying without saying; he wanted me to stay. Maybe if I were to have another reason, I would not go back with Felix to Brennanfalk Ranch. I stood up and pointed a finger in the air as I announced, "Henceforth the Faeries shall be nick-named…" I stalled, what could suffice for something so precious and beautiful? "A name of their choosing!" I flourished a bow in the direction of the surging flock, a synchronized pulse rippled through the wondrous creatures.

Their song ramped up, and a beat thudded with an infectious rhythm. My body involuntarily moved with the music, I ached to dance. The Faeries swirled to their melody, swishing through the air like a flock of birds in a murmuration.

"I need to dance with them," I said dreamily to Rannoch, "they are calling me."

He laughed. "Then go, so I can watch."

I smirked at him, and let myself be carried away by the music. It flowed through me, inspiring me to extend my arms and spin. I elevated myself on one toe, pirouetting like an agile ballerina. I was never a great dancer, but their song flowed through me, directed me. I followed the melody as it pulsed. I could feel the music—sense it—as if it were an entity all its own, and I danced for its amusement and pleasure. The beat rewarded my maneuvers, increasing its intensity as it reverberated.

I was light on my feet and became more adventurous with my motions. Up on one toe again, I spun in place three times around, centered down through my middle. The Faeries swirled around me, their current carried me through the turn. As I completed the rotation, a gust of air whooshed up, taking me off the ground in an upward corkscrew.

Felix took my hands as I came back down, and spun me again. He lifted me high, with my hands held firmly down, his arms were outstretched above him. I felt like I had perfect balance, and could sense exactly how far I could go without drifting. As we rotated I raised my legs higher and allowed my upper body to dip lower.

The beat quickened as it reached a crescendo, the power of the rhythm channeled through me. He swung me down in an arcing motion. Felix let go as we spiraled away from each other in mirror moves, like twins dancing on a pinwheel, the paths of our arms and footsteps in perfect sync. Seeing my brother dance—free and uninhibited—gave a lightness to my heart.

The smile on his face was radiant. Fae hybrid or human, he was always beautiful; a rare person, with his heart of gold and will of iron.

The music slowed, and singing quieted in a measured diminuendo, the thudding base all but faded away. Felix and I swayed, the world had softened around the edges and glazed me into a dreamlike state. I curtsied to my brother, in thanks for the dance. He gave me a bow with a flourish, then padded off to return to the group he had been sitting with.

I drifted back over to Rannoch, who was watching and waiting, laying back propped up on his elbows.

"You dance so beautifully, I could watch you forever," he said with complete seriousness.

I lay down next to him, and stretched out. "Why don't you come dance with me next time?" I asked as he rolled over, his face inches away and his warm body against mine.

He traced my profile with his finger, starting from my forehead, down my face, my neck, my chest, and lower. I flashed my eyes to his, and quirked up one side of my mouth.

"I am not trying to start anything, I promise. I just could not help but admire you. Your form is so beautiful, everything about you is beautiful."

"Who says I don't want you to start something?" I giggled as I pulled him over me further in a settled hug. With his weight on top of me I smiled up at him. I loved how his eyes would burn for me, the warmth I would feel radiate when he shifted his gaze to mine.

He returned the smile, then lowered his face and kissed me gently. He hesitated, perhaps to temper the lust which could escalate from either of us at any moment. It was not the time, or the place. Surrounded by others, and each of our siblings. I sighed, he was right of course. *I will just enjoy his presence, and the fact that we don't currently have someone trying to kill us.*

My skin tingled from the herb, and the ethereal, glorious light around us. It truly was magical, just lying with him. It healed my soul, the emotional wounds that Dashelle had inflicted were starting to mend, though they would take longer than the physical ones.

I pushed the thought of her away as his hands roved lightly over me, gliding his fingertips over every surface in a soft caress. I closed my eyes, letting myself absorb the sensations.

CHAPTER 45

The Faeries had settled down to sleep, and the Fae had revelled themselves into a peaceful slumber. I drifted off in Rannoch's arms, the lush ground underneath our blanket comforted me in pillowy softness. The purple dusk sky deepened as the flits of magic streaked through the air. We slept nuzzled into each other, on our sides with legs tangled.

A faint tickle on my hand made me open an eye, the same Faerie that had investigated me earlier slept draped over it. Once again difficult to see, any plane of their body that faced me directly was transparent, with the sides being more visible as they glanced away. Their little mouth hung open and drooled onto my index finger, and their petite arm hung down toward my palm. They were so precious, as I watched them twitch and dream.

I looked at the sky, still darkening dusk. *The Fae must develop their own sort of circadian rhythm, to be able to sleep and wake in a logical cycle.* To my human brain, it was disorienting every time, to feel like I woke up at basically the same time of day as when I had gone to sleep.

I gazed at Rannoch. He looked so different in his sleep, no furrowed brows, no serious demeanor. His normally angled eyebrows arched softly in small crescent moons. His full lips puckered lightly with the most serene expression I had ever seen on him.

I glanced down and discovered at least a hundred Faeries, all in sweet repose in a line down his body. They had settled into any upward facing surface or nook. I smothered a laugh at the image. They had left their shimmering imprints all over him, and were now curled up in various positions everywhere. One stirred, opened a sleepy eye at me, stretched and readjusted to another position, clearly not ready to get up yet.

"Bonum mane," Rannoch's voice thrummed. I angled my face back up to him, and found his cognac eyes looking down into mine. He pulled my hips in closer to his, his current physical state was no different than when we had excited each other last.

"Quit taunting me with that! Unless you're going to take me into that forest, find another tree and continue what we started when we were so rudely interrupted."

He was suddenly fully alert. "Oh no, not here. I want to be able to shake the Vale with my howl when you return to me, and bury myself in you. I am going to unleash every bit of myself inside you."

My eyes widened, as he closed his eyes with a big grin. I pressed myself up against his impressive length, demanding that he do exactly as he promised. He slid a hand underneath my shirt, cupping my breast. The heat flared between my legs, my ache grew insistent as he touched me.

"You have to come back to me," he whispered dangerously close to my ear. "I will not rest until you do, and when you do, I will give you everything, more than you can imagine."

I gasped, then kissed him, wanting him to just ignore everyone around us and give in to the overwhelming desire. It was ridiculous, and not really what I would have wanted. But my need for him was so intense, so demanding, I could almost overlook the fact that we were surrounded by others. Almost.

I tried to slide my hand beneath his waistband, to feel him fully. He tightened the gap between us and hissed through his teeth, a pulse from the hardness pressing up against me told me he would like nothing better than for me to wrap my hand around his...*faehood?* I giggled silently and smiled to myself at the thought. His restraint was impressive.

I snuggled back in, trying to simmer from the picture in my mind.

"Don't move too much," I said. "You'll disturb all the customers."

He flashed his eyes open and blinked. "Customers? What does that mean?"

I motioned with my chin to all the Faeries napping on him. "All the customers who slept at Hotel Rannoch for the night."

He gave me a confused look and then glanced to where I had motioned. "Shoo!" He shook his legs and startled them awake. They let out little wails at being awoken, then fluttered their wings and took off.

Rannoch wiped at his arms and legs, trying to rub some of their sparkles away. He gave up and shrugged when he looked back at me. "It is hopeless to try, it has to be washed off," he said reluctantly.

"You look pretty cute with all that on you. I bet in the light you'd be absolutely radiant!"

He narrowed his eyes and scrunched up his lower lip, then released a laugh that fought its way out. I chuckled, I truly enjoyed it when I managed to get one out of him.

His eyes gleamed. "Get over here!" He pulled me in tighter, nuzzling his face into my neck.

The other Fae were beginning to stir, small murmurs rustled from nearby. I closed my eyes, *just a little longer.* I wanted to grab onto this moment and not let go, mantle it for the preciousness that it was to me.

"Who is interested in some food?" Kerenza announced.

Well, I guess that means it's time to get up officially.

I sighed as I went to sit up, but Rannoch held firm. "Not yet," he whispered against my neck. "Just let me savor it. I do not know when I will get to again."

I relaxed back down, and focused on him. With my eyes closed I listened to his breathing, and caressed my fingers through his wavy black hair, still pulled up into a messy braid. I ran my hand along his arm, feeling his warm skin with hardened muscles underneath. We lay together, holding each other, trying our best to stave off the inevitable.

Everyone was up and milling about around us. "I think it's time to get up, Rannoch," I said, sensing we were the last to rise.

"I know."

He pulled his face away from my neck, looked deep into my eyes, before relinquishing his grip on me.

As we stood, Kerenza strode over and held out some jerky to me. "Bonum mane! Here, replenish yourself before we depart."

I grabbed it and split it for myself and Rannoch. We devoured it as everyone else was readying to leave.

The blankets were rolled, the remaining supplies packed up inside of them. As I looked around, there was nothing to keep us in the glen any longer. I had hoped it would take more time to pack up camp, but the Ignisfae were adept travelers. Being partially nomadic had honed them into a swift and resourceful race when staying out in the wild.

"Ready?" Felix asked, eyeing me cautiously as he glided to me.

I sighed as I took in a deep breath and closed my eyes, smelling the lush sweetness of our magical little glade, where we found a slice of respite. "Ready."

CHAPTER 46

Rannoch took my hand, and nodded to me in reassurance. I knew it was time to go, the human realm was calling me back, my mother waited, my horse waited. My home of Black Oak Grove waited. But perhaps, it was not my home anymore, merely the place I was from. Born near the tear in the Vale, giving me an inhuman ability to cross the threshold and find my purpose, the ability to love again, and the strength to look forward in life.

I gulped at the thought of Josie, and the horrible reality that I would return without her. No happy ending for her, no reunion for her and her mother, like I would have soon. And no explanation that I could give her mom that would ever make sense. First Maris, then Josie. Why did I survive and they didn't? I shook my head at the thought. I needed to remind myself, always be brave. In whatever situation, hiding does not help. *Face my fears and move forward. I have to live for them, to respect the lives they had.*

Everyone milled around, ready to depart. Rannoch cleared his throat, all turned to him and quieted.

"We are heading to the Southwest Tear, so that Lily and Felix can return home. Asmik, Hiret, will you join us on our journey? Or do you plan to return to Adrilan," Rannoch asked the Petrafae.

"We will travel with you for some time, but we will need to go to Adrilan before long."

Rannoch rapped his fist across his chest.

I took in all their faces, beautiful, brave, and generous. The warriors who had risked so much to help myself and Rannoch.

We struck out together, a band of Ignisfae, Petrafae, and two Fae hybrids. The group moved swiftly, heading toward the center of the Praegra Forest. The light around us dimmed further, reminding me of my waiting, worrying mother. *I'm coming, Mom.* But in my heart, I had already left Black Oak Grove.

We pushed on for what might have been several rotations, until we reached the magic Well, glowing like a sparkling gem in the darkening night.

"We are going to replenish, then move on," Rannoch stated to all.

I stared at the luminous volume and remembered the last time I swam in the Well, the company I kept then and the things I had yet to learn. It felt like a lifetime ago, so much had happened and changed.

Rannoch pulled me close and kissed my cheek. "Not to worry, my love. He cannot hurt you again."

I gave him a small smile in return, as I recalled the last expression I had seen on Opius's face. Terror. I gulped and tried to shake the image from my mind. Rannoch was wrong, Opius could still hurt me. Memories can be powerful, I was well aware of that. *Maybe the Well will help.*

I squeezed his hand, then released it and dropped my selwaer and pack. I took one more breath, before I dove in head first.

The rush of the warm, watery substance down my body soothed my soul and uplifted my spirits, massaging negative thoughts out of my mind. The fluid slipped around me, encasing my whole being in a silky-smooth hug. It felt like being cradled by a goddess, tenderly holding my form as a mother holds her infant.

I marvelled at the liquid, like water and yet not. I glided further away from the group, toward the pulsing tree in the center. Its curving and swirling conduit-like tendrils emanated a soft glow from within. I swam close to the tree, and looked intently at its surface. I passed my hand over the fine, mottled pattern on the segmented trunk, short, threadlike hairs grew off the surface. They shifted in soft waves, giving it a velvety feel.

A soft voice hummed in my head, echoing in an inviting melody.

"Hommmme," it sang in a quiet, feminine tone.

I caught my breath and second guessed myself that I had heard anything.

"Hommmmme," it sang again.

Tentatively, I raised my hand and touched the tree. A bright glow surrounded my fingers, energy gathered at the perimeter of my imprint. Understanding dawned, washed over my consciousness in a moment of clarity. I was filled with relief, with the sense that I had returned to my origin. Somehow, this was where I had come from.

A tremor went through the tree, upward from the base then

out to the tips. A drop of bright light wriggled out, its harmonic song called out to me as it released into the air. I gasped, realizing it was just like the one I had seen when I arrived, just after stepping through the Vale. The reaction I had felt finally made sense. Kinship. It was like me, and I was like it. This magical tree had grown me within it, and sent my spirit off to germinate. It was my creator, my mother in a way, before my mother that carried me.

I closed my eyes and nearly cried at the emotional tidal wave, *this is why I felt I belonged here.* Beyond wanting to be with Rannoch, I was not really an outsider, but a wanderer. Only not the kind of wanderer I had thought I was. I had ventured out, to be born, grow, and to one day return. I looked up at the great tree, and could see her spirit. A beautiful maiden superimposed over—and within it—her flowing hair the soft curves of the branches. She smiled down upon me, greeting her child she had sent out through the tear in the Vale, when I was merely a speck of life.

Water lapped nearby. I looked to my side to see Felix, also looking up at the tree. He placed his hand next to mine, the glow surrounded it and intensified. His mouth dropped open, Felix closed his eyes as a tear slipped over his cheek.

Siblings in more ways than one, we looked at each other and held our gaze for a long time. He raised his palm to me, I pressed mine to it. With our hands clasped and touching the tree with the other, it created a circuit, the familial bond made solid. A slow surge tugged through me, the well of power within me lessened as a portion retreated down my arm, to my palm still planted on the trunk. I exhaled as the energy released from my fingertips, a last goodbye to an intangible presence.

My heart dropped as another face appeared next to the tree

goddess. Maris. She looked as beautiful as ever, radiant, and peaceful. She smiled at Felix and I.

I sobbed. I wished I could reach out and touch her. But she was spirit only, and she was returning to her birthplace. We had delivered her, brought her back to our tree mother. All this time, I had carried her within me. There was so much I wanted to tell her, my heart cracked as I thought about the life we had, and the things I never said.

Felix's lip wobbled at the sight of our sister, I held back more tears that threatened to spill out.

A caress washed in a gentle rhythm over my mind, like a mother patting her child's head in comfort.

"Saaaaaaafe," the goddess sang, as she continued to console me. "Hommmmme."

Felix and I wrapped our arms around each other in a shuddering hug. The wound from her loss healed, at least as much as it could.

I blinked my eyes open, my gaze fell on Rannoch at the far side of the Well, watching, waiting. Giving me respectful distance. I loved him even more for that—especially that. The space to figure myself out. As I thought about it, I realized that was the difference. Others had always demanded to be let in, when I wasn't ready. I had too much to process, too much to heal from, and no idea how to even start. So instead of starting, I had avoided. Rannoch had been there, waiting to be let in.

As I hugged my brother, my cheek resting on his shoulder while I watched Rannoch, I knew in my heart and deep in my soul what I wanted. I lifted my head, then looked at Felix, who squeezed me a little tighter. I glanced back at my sister's smiling face once more, before we released our embrace and turned back to the shore.

To my future. Our future. Whatever it may hold.

Acknowledgements

As the process of writing this book was years in the making, there are a lot of people who helped bring it to life. To all who were there for me, either as emotional support or as another pair of eyes, thank you for the bottom of my heart. I truly appreciate you all.

To my husband Kirt, thank you for your help with our three beautiful little gremlins so that I could find pockets of time to actually finish this book. Life is busy, life is crazy, and it feels like there is never time. But because we work together, we're both able to accomplish so much, and I am forever grateful for you. I love you and appreciate everything you do to support me.

To my bestie, Laura L. Hohman, the one who is always there to lift me up or bounce ideas off of, the one who has read for me time and time again. You've scraped me out of the gutter more times than I can count, and been there to high five the successes. Writing together has been one of the highlights of our friendship for me, and has just been the best experience. Thank you for your patience with me, for always listening, for reading through my cringeworthy first draft and always giving me helpful notes. You are, without a doubt, the most wonderful person I could hope to know and such an incredibly gifted writer. You never fail to support me, and I'll always gush about how good you are as a friend, fellow animation industry professional, and writer. I respect and admire you for all that you do. I cannot wait for the day when we get to celebrate the release of your book! I just know the world will love it as much as I do.

David Martin Lins, my talented editor and friend. Thank you for all you did to help me, for the suggested edits that made my work stronger, for the jokes to lighten the impact of notes, notes, notes! And for the praise, some of your comments are in the top five of "Nice Things People Have Said" list. Okay, top ten. You are such a talented writer, and I'm so excited that your book, Skull Valley, is finally going to be out in the world! I can't wait to put on my shelf and brag that I know the author.

My beta readers! You are all so generous to have given your time to read and give me notes:

Robyn the Bobbin, what can I say girl, I heart your forever and appreciate your careful eye for grammar errors. Also I loved fan-casting the book after you read it! Thank you for your life long friendship, I love your damn guts and think the world of you. EF sisters for life no matter how far apart we are!

Chris Sanchez, for reading my book not once, but twice! Thank you for your thoughts, advice, time, and laughs! Your insights helped bring the book to where it is now. You're a skilled writer and a thoughtful friend. And most definitely, not an asshole.

Melissa Clark-Campbell, thank you for your notes and feedback! They helped me write a better story.

Laura L. Hohman, you get another shout out, because you beta read for me multiple times! Thank you for all your suggestions and for helping me craft a story that I'm proud of.

To my Aunt Vicki, my self-appointed spiritual guide in all things mystical and esoteric. Madame Zelda has read your runes, you owe her $6.95 monthly for the subscription to her services. Thank you for all the inspiration and for teaching me how to be funny af, because you sure as hell are. I'm still working on being as funny as you, though.

Lastly I'd like to thank my parents. For always encouraging me and for supporting me in every creative endeavor that I've invested myself in since I was a child. Thank you for always giving me the space (including table space) to express myself.

Thank you for reading! If you enjoyed this book, I'd be very grateful if you posted a short review. Your support really does make a difference, I read all reviews personally and use them to keep bringing you great stories. Thanks again for your support!

Get updates on release information, exclusive giveaways, and insider info by signing up for my newsletter at www.lorinpetrazilka.com